STAR WARS

JEDI TRIAL

2005 Del Rey Books Mass Market Edition

Published in the United States by Del Rey Books, an imprint of The Random House Publishing Group, a division of Random House, Inc., New York.

Originally published in hardcover in the United States by Del Rey Books, an imprint of The Random House Publishing Group, a division of Random House, Inc., in 2004.

This book contains an excerpt from the forthcoming book *Star Wars: Outbound Flight* by Timothy Zahn. This excerpt has been set for this edition only and may not reflect the final content of the forthcoming edition.

David Sherman photo © Susan McAninley
Dan Cragg photo © Wendell Moore Studios

ISBN 0-345-46115-0

Printed in the United States of America

www.starwars.com
Del Rey Books website address: www.delreybooks.com

OPM   9   8   7   6   5   4   3   2   1

STAR WARS

JEDI TRIAL

—(A CLONE WARS NOVEL)—

DAVID SHERMAN and DAN CRAGG

LUCAS BOOKS

DEL REY

BALLANTINE BOOKS • NEW YORK

JEDI TRIAL

CLONE WARS
TIMELINE

With the Battle of Geonosis (EP II), the Republic is plunged into an emerging, galaxywide conflict. On one side is the Confederacy of Independent Systems (the Separatists), led by the charismatic Count Dooku, who is backed by a number of powerful trade organizations and their droid armies.

On the other side is the Republic loyalists and their newly created clone army, led by the Jedi. It is a war fought on a thousand fronts, with heroism and sacrifices on both sides. Below is a partial list of some of the important events of the Clone Wars and a guide to where these events are chronicled.

MONTHS
(after *Attack of the Clones*)

0	**THE BATTLE OF GEONOSIS**
	Star Wars: Episode II *Attack of the Clones* (LFL, May '02)
0	**REPUBLIC COMMANDO**
	Star Wars Republic Commando (LEC, Fall '04)
0	**THE SEARCH FOR COUNT DOOKU**
	Boba Fett #1: *The Fight to Survive* (SB, April '02)
+1	**THE DARK REAPER PROJECT**
	The Clone Wars (LEC, October '02)
+1	**THE BATTLE OF RAXUS PRIME**
	Boba Fett #2: *Crossfire* (SB, November '02)
+1.5	**CONSPIRACY ON AARGAU**
	Boba Fett #3: *Maze of Deception* (SB, April '03)
+2	**THE BATTLE OF KAMINO**
	Clone Wars I: *The Defense of Kamino* (DH, June '03)
+2	**DURGE VS. BOBA FETT**
	Boba Fett #4: *Hunted* (SB, October '03)
+2.5	**THE DEFENSE OF NABOO**
	Clone Wars II: *Victories and Sacrifices* (DH, September '03)
+3	**MISSION ON QIILURA**
	Republic Commando: Hard Contact (DR, November '04)
+6	**THE DEVARON RUSE**
	Clone Wars IV: *Target Jedi* (DH, May '04)
+6	**THE HARUUN KAL CRISIS**
	Shatterpoint (DR, June '03)

CLONE WARS
TIMELINE

MONTHS
(after *Attack of the Clones*)

+6   **ASSASSINATION ON NULL**
Legacy of the Jedi #1 (SB, August '03)

+12   **THE BIO-DROID THREAT**
The Cestus Deception (DR, June '04)

+15   **THE BATTLE OF JABIIM**
Clone Wars III: *Last Stand on Jabiim* (DH, February '04)

+16   **ESCAPE FROM RATTATAK**
Clone Wars V: *The Best Blades* (DH, November '04)

+24   **THE CASUALTIES OF DRONGAR**
MedStar Duology: *Battle Surgeons* (DR, July '04)
                            Jedi Healer (DR, October '04)

+29   **ATTACK ON AZURE**
Secrets of the Jedi (SB, March '05)

+30   **THE PRAESITLYN CONQUEST**
Jedi Trial (DR, November '04)

+30   **LURE AT VJUN**
Yoda: Dark Rendezvous (DR, December '04)

+30   **THE RENDILI FLEET CRISIS**
Clone Wars VI: *On the Fields of Battle* (DH, July '05)

+31   **BETRAYAL AT BOZ PITY**
Clone Wars VII: *Brothers in Arms* (DH, October '05)

+31   **THE XAGOBAH CITADEL**
Boba Fett #5: *A New Threat* (SB, April '04)
Boba Fett #6: *Pursuit* (SB, December '04)

+35   **THE HUNT FOR DARTH SIDIOUS**
Labyrinth of Evil (DR, February '05)

+36   **ANAKIN TURNS TO THE DARK SIDE**
Star Wars: Episode III *Revenge of the Sith* (LFL, May '05)

KEY:

DH = *Dark Horse Comics, graphic novels*
www.darkhorse.com
DR = *Del Rey, hardcover & paperback books*
www.delreydigital.com
LEC = *LucasArts Games, games for XBox, GameCube,*
PS2, & PC platforms www.lucasarts.com
LFL = *Lucasfilm Ltd., motion pictures* www.starwars.com
SB = *Scholastic Books, juvenile fiction* www.scholastic.com/starwars

PROLOGUE

"Obi-Wan!" Anakin Skywalker exclaimed when the hologrammic image of Jedi Knight Obi-Wan Kenobi appeared before him. Anakin had been pacing in his quarters, brooding over why was he consistently being passed by for his Jedi Trials, the chance to prove he was a full Jedi Knight. The welcome sight of his teacher lifted Anakin's mood.

"Anakin," Obi-Wan said, greeting his Padawan with a smile. "How are you settling in?"

Anakin shrugged. "All right, I guess."

Obi-Wan's smile turned wan. They had returned to Coruscant only two standard days earlier, but he was fully aware of how long two days without action could seem to Anakin. He knew his Padawan would not be pleased by the news he was about to break. "I just returned to my quarters from a meeting with the Jedi Council," he said.

Anakin's eyes brightened: a meeting with the Jedi Council must mean a new mission.

"I have an assignment—"

"Already?" Anakin interrupted, excited. "We haven't even been debriefed from the last one yet! Must be important." He turned away to begin reassembling his gear and clothing.

"Anakin—"

"I've barely begun to unpack—I can meet you at the spaceport in an hour."

"Anakin!" Obi-Wan tried again. "*Anakin!*"

Anakin didn't turn around. "Where should I meet you?"

"*ANAKIN!*"

Obi-Wan's shout finally caught Anakin's attention and he spun about, taken aback by the unusually harsh tone. "Master?"

"Sorry I shouted, but you weren't hearing me."

"Master? I'm listening." Anakin used all his self-control to stand still and wait.

"*I* have a mission, Anakin. Not us. The Jedi Council is sending me alone. It's an individual assignment, a quick in-and-out."

Anakin was clearly trying not to frown. "What am I supposed to do in the meantime?" he couldn't help asking.

"You'll be debriefed on our last mission, for one thing. I'm trusting that to you." Obi-Wan sighed. "When I get back, I'll suggest to the Council that you're ready to begin your trials."

"Don't you mean suggest *again*?"

Obi-Wan shook his head. "First there was no point, and then there was no time. But as soon as I return, I'll *make* the time—and the Council will listen."

"Why will they listen then, when up until now they haven't even wanted to hear?"

"Because while I'm gone, you're going to be the

model Jedi Knight. You'll allow them to debrief you, and then, if I'm not back yet, you'll hit the archives, looking for any strategies that can be deployed in planning our upcoming battles. You're going to show them that you are skilled in a Knight's most basic role, as well as in combat," Obi-Wan said confidently.

"Study." Anakin's voice was flat. "All right, I'll study."

"I've got confidence in you, Anakin—you know that."

"Yes." Anakin's expression softened. "I know you do, Obi-Wan. May the Force be with you."

Three days later, Anakin Skywalker flipped his datapad off. He'd spent the time since Obi-Wan had left in the library studying the campaigns and battles of the Clone Wars—and had discovered a few possibilities. He headed for the training area. Maybe he could find someone to spar with, to balance his inactivity.

The war was a severe drain on the Jedi resources, and nearly every physically able Jedi was away from Coruscant on a mission or campaign. Anakin found only one Jedi in the training area, Nejaa Halcyon, drilling with his lightsaber.

Anakin had met Halcyon once before and found him to be not only intelligent and witty, but also a tactically sound Jedi. Obi-Wan had assured him his impression was accurate. And yet Master Halcyon had been living in a state of semi-disgrace after losing his ship, *Plooriod Bodkin,* to a rogue ship's captain he'd been sent to apprehend. Anakin could only wonder how Halcyon had blundered so badly that his starship was stolen by the rogue he was supposed to arrest; he hadn't felt right about asking.

Moving with total focus and concentration, Halcyon was a pleasure to watch. Loath to interrupt him, Anakin remained on the side, waiting for him to pause.

At last Halcyon thumbed his lightsaber off and stood erect. He glanced over at Anakin and grinned. "Anakin Skywalker! Looking for a sparring partner?"

Anakin started briefly. "You honor me," he said with a slight bow.

Halcyon laughed. "Honor you? That means either you're surprised I remember your name, or you're surprised that a Jedi Master is so readily willing to spar with a Padawan he barely knows."

"Perhaps both?" Anakin grinned back at the older man.

"Of course I remember your name. There are so few Jedi here these days, it's easy to remember everyone. And of course I'm happy to spar with you. You're freshly out of combat, your reactions are sharp. I've been sitting idle for quite a while—I need the test." He gestured an invitation, and Anakin entered the sparring circle.

They faced each other and saluted, then took position and thumbed their lightsabers to life.

Anakin made the first move, a thrust that started high before plunging downward to dip under an anticipated high parry. The blades of the lightsabers sizzled as Halcyon easily deflected the thrust, laughing when he danced aside.

"You surprise me," Halcyon said mock-seriously.

"That's such a basic move. I'd have thought you'd have some new ones from being in combat." He launched a flurry of thrusts and slices of his own; Anakin easily parried or deflected all of them.

"Master Halcyon," Anakin said when they stepped back, "in a fight, one seldom has time to invent new maneuvers. The tried-and-true movements are usually the most effective." He reached out with his lightsaber to touch Halcyon's, then spun the tip of the blade in an unorthodox backhand that would have cut through Halcyon's left shoulder had he not stopped short—and had Halcyon failed to fall back out of the way in time.

"Very good, Padawan." Halcyon nodded with approval. "That was so close I'm not sure whether or not it counts as a touch."

Anakin grinned. "You don't have time to invent in a fight—but sometimes you have to improvise."

Then they settled into serious sparring.

The two Jedis' lightsabers flashed and sizzled when the blades struck in thrust and parry. When first one, then the other found his way through the other's defense, the shimmering light stopped just short of striking. The two Jedis' voices rang with pleasure at each skillful move.

After an hour of sparring, they stopped by unspoken mutual agreement. Both gleamed with sweat. Both were laughing.

"Ah, yes," Halcyon said happily, "a sparring partner makes the workouts much, much better." He eyed Anakin. "You're very skillful for someone so young."

Anakin's eyes sparkled. "Master Halcyon, I must

compliment you on *your* skill, which is remarkable for such an old man who has been sitting idle for so long."

"Ungrateful pup!" Halcyon snarled, and immediately laughed. "Shall we do it again tomorrow?"

"Sounds great."

"Same time, same place."

"With pleasure."

Jedi Master and Padawan saluted each other before heading their separate ways to bathe the sweat and salts from their tired bodies.

1

There was no word from General Khamar.

Ice-cold prickles of fear shot up the back of Reija Momen's arms to her scalp and then down her spine. She shivered, then shifted uncomfortably. *This is no time to panic,* she thought.

Everyone else was looking to her to remain calm. So she'd come out into the garden early, to relax, to gather her thoughts and compose herself before meeting with her staff. But it wasn't working. The carefully tended little garden nestled peacefully in a courtyard protected from the elements by the surrounding buildings and a solar dome that could be opened in good weather. Today the dome was open, letting in fresh air that should have been invigorating, but her nerves were strung too tight. Her staff were afraid; they thought no news from the south boded ill.

Eyes closed, Reija tried thinking of home. In five more years, her contract would be up, and she would head back to Alderaan. Maybe. A breeze wafted in through the dome. It carried with it the aroma of the native grasses that grew in such profusion on the mesa where the Intergalactic Communications Center was located. During the first months of her contract she had thought she was allergic to the sagebrush, coughing and sneezing profusely whenever she emerged from the control complex to inspect the outlying facilities, but gradually she had become accustomed to the pervasive scent. Now she found it pleasant. Physically, at least, she'd never felt better. It had become a pet theory of hers, not yet verified by medical science, that prolonged exposure to the grasses of Praesitlyn was good for human physiology.

Reija Momen had accepted the job as chief administrator of the Intergalactic Communications Center on Praesitlyn because she liked the work—the handsome salary counted only as a nice bonus. Someone else in her position would likely have been thinking of the end of her contract, comfortable retirement back on Alderaan, perhaps even starting a family. Though middle-aged, she was still young enough to think about settling down someday, and she was attractive enough in a handsome, matronly way. But she was content in her job. With her warm heart, good sense, and solid managerial skills, she had quickly established a fine rapport with her mixed staff of human and Sluissi technicians. She was the type of administrator, rare in any gender or species, who exercised her authority as a matter of responsibility, not out of any sense of pleasure. She worked hard and well because she enjoyed work as an end in itself, and she treated the people under her more as partners in a joint enterprise than as subordinates. And unlike so many busy bureaucrats, consumed by their sense of self-importance, she knew when and how to relax.

Start a family? Well, for all practical purposes, her staff on Praesitlyn had been her family for the past seven years; they loved her and they called her "Momma Momen."

Go home? She was already home! *I'll renew my contract,* she thought. *If I live that long.*

A labor droid, modified to tend the trees and shrubs in the garden, rooted among rumsy bushes nestled under the stunted kaha trees imported from Talasea years earlier by a previous chief administrator. Ordinarily the sound of the droid's rustling about in the foliage would have been comforting, but not today. Reija shifted her position again. She opened her eyes and sighed. Relaxation was out of the question. Members of her staff were already filtering into the garden and finding places to sit—not to enjoy the informal midday luncheon that had become a tradition in the years she had been chief administrator, but to get the news, to get their orders. Reija felt a brief flash of anger that their routine was being interrupted. Not that their luncheons were anything special—just friends and colleagues enjoying each other's company and engaging in easy conversation over their food—but they were as enjoyable to the staff as their regular off-duty trips to Sluis Van.

Today everyone spoke in worried whispers, all ears for any news from the south. What could she tell them? Not knowing what was going on there was worse than bad news. Several standard hours earlier an invasion fleet had landed approximately 150 kilometers to the southwest of the center.

"Mistress," General Khamar had said in his last report, "two of our starfighters on a routine patrol over the ocean just off the coast have engaged a large number of hostile craft. The airborne control ship that was monitoring the patrol has been shot down, but before we lost contact with it, the crew reported a large droid army landing. The invaders don't appear to be as numerous as my own command, but they may be just an advance party preparing a foothold for a larger force. Either way, we have to destroy them without delay. I'm taking my main force overland to attack them."

"How big is their fleet?" she had asked.

"Several transports and capital ships, nothing we can't handle. Should we need reinforcements, which I doubt, Sluis Van will supply them."

"Wouldn't it be prudent to call for them now, just in case?"

Khamar grunted. "We shall if we need to, but it wouldn't be good tactics to call for reinforcements before we know the extent of the enemy threat. I'll leave a detachment here under Commander Llanmore to provide security for the center." A gruff Corellian, Khamar was a professional soldier, and Reija trusted his judgment. The young Commander Llanmore she especially liked; she couldn't help smiling at the air of military punctiliousness he adopted when in her presence. She saw right through him, of course. To her he was one of the many sons she had never had.

But for the past hour she had received no word from General Khamar. If this was an all-out attempt by the Separatists to seize the communications center, her comfortable little world on Praesitlyn was coming to an end.

The solar dome that roofed the garden slammed shut without warning. There was a bright flash and a deafening roar. Heart in her throat, Reija jumped to her feet and ran back inside the main control room. Slith Skael, the Sluissi chief of the communications staff, sidled up beside her. She had never seen the methodical creature move so quickly or look so worried.

"Is Khamar returning?" Reija asked hesitantly. She glanced about the control room. Normally it was a place of quiet confidence, technicians working intently at their stations, droids quietly going about their tasks. But not now.

"No, Mistress," Slith answered. "It is strangers." He swayed nervously. "I believe it is another invasion force. I ordered the dome closed when the first ship landed. I beg your forgiveness if you were startled. What are your orders?"

Reija had grown very fond of Slith over the years they'd been together on Praesitlyn. Under his calm, unruffled exterior lived a devoted and compassionate being. And she knew she could count on him now. The control room was in chaos. Technicians babbled among themselves, working their instruments frantically. A deep-throated roar rumbled through the facility. She could feel the vibrations in the floor panels.

"A large number of ships are landing below the mesa," a technician said with an edge to his voice that told Reija he was on the verge of panic.

"Quiet, everybody! Listen to me," she called loudly and firmly. It was time to make order out of this confusion. "Everyone take your places and listen." Her calm, controlled demeanor had the desired effect. People stopped babbling and took their seats. "Now," she said, turning to Slith, "send an alert to Coruscant and—"

"I already have," the Sluissi answered. "The transmission was blocked."

"That's not possible!" she said, startled.

"Evidently it is," Slith answered matter-of-factly. He was just reporting the fact, not debating it. "What are your orders, please?" he repeated.

Reija was silent for a moment. "Commander Llanmore?"

"I am here, Mistress." Llanmore, wearing his body armor and fully armed, stepped up and drew himself to attention beside her.

"What is happening out there?" The control room had gone completely silent, all eyes staring intently at the two.

"A large droid force has landed below the mesa," Llanmore answered in precise, clipped tones. "We cannot hope to hold out against them without immediate reinforcement, and—" He hesitated. "—that will not happen."

"Any word from General Khamar?"

"No, Mistress, and—" Llanmore's voice caught. "We must assume that he is—he has been defeated."

Reija considered for a moment. "Very well then. Somehow the invaders are blocking our transmissions. General Khamar cannot help us. We cannot resist. Listen to me, everyone! We cannot let this complex fall into the invaders' hands." She paused for a moment to gather herself before announcing an order she'd never dreamed she'd have to give. "Destroy your equipment."

Quickly she began instructing individual technicians, directing them to disable specific pieces of equipment first. But it would take time; they had never prepared for such an emergency, nor did they have the means to ensure the rapid and total destruction the situation now dictated. "Commander."

"Yes, Mistress?"

The only sign that Reija was at all nervous was a small rill of perspiration slowly escaping from under her hair by the side of her right eyebrow. "Can you delay the invaders? All we need is a few minutes."

"I can try." Llanmore was also perspiring faintly, but he turned sharply on his heel and left the control room. The last she saw of him was his ramrod-straight back as he marched steadfastly back to his command. She was afraid she'd just sent the young man off to his death.

"Get busy!" she ordered the technicians, many of whom had stopped to listen to her conversation with Llanmore. Why, she thought, had no one ever made any emergency destruction plans for a contingency like this? The Intergalactic Communications Center was vital to the Republic, and its facilities could not be allowed to fall into enemy hands.

From outside on the mesa came the crashing roar of weaponry. Llanmore was engaging the invaders. Reija felt a rising sense of despair. Her comfortable world was at an end.

2

ount Dooku wishes a status report, Tonith."

"Count Dooku wishes a status report, Tonith."

The Muun commander of the invasion force, Admiral Pors Tonith, quietly sipped his dianogan tea and smiled, ostensibly ignoring the disrespect clear in the way Commander Asajj Ventress addressed him. "He has the complete battle plan, Ventress," he replied easily, showing her the exact same level of disrespect. He set his cup on a nearby sideboard. "I gave it to him before I left. He knows that once I have developed a plan I carry it out. That is why he chose me to lead this campaign." He smiled amiably, purple-stained lips parting to reveal matching purple teeth and black gums—an effect of the tea. The temporary stain was an indignity Tonith was willing to suffer in order to savor the exquisite aroma, flavor, and mildly narcotic effect of the tea brewed from a chemical substance found in the spleens of the dianoga. Besides, he was commander of a vast invasion fleet: no sentient being would dare laugh at him, and droids had no sense of the ridiculous.

Ventress's expression didn't change, but her dark eyes flashed through the HoloNet transceiver like two burning coals. "A plan is not a status report," she replied, her voice even. She was not used to being talked down to, especially not by this bloodless financier suddenly turned military commander.

Tonith sighed dramatically. He considered the assassin an interloper in strategic affairs that were beyond her primitive grasp of the real art of military command and planning. But she was Dooku's protégée, and he had to tread carefully. "Really, I cannot command this expedition if I am to be interfered with by—by . . ." He shrugged and reached for his teacup.

"The report?" she insisted.

"I am extremely busy just now."

"Make your report. To me. Now." Her voice cut through the vast distances like the lightsabers she was reputed to wield so expertly.

Tonith sat up straight and folded his hands in his lap. Actually, he found this Ventress woman rather attractive. He felt they had something in common: she, a ruthless warrior; he, a ruthless planner and schemer. When Tonith thought of women, which was not often, he preferred them with a head of hair, but Ventress's baldness was not totally unattractive. She radiated power and confidence, even via the transceiver. He respected that. "We would make a good team," he said. "I could use your help."

She sneered. "Little one, if I were to come out there it wouldn't be to help you, it would be to replace you as commander. But the Count has more important business for me just now. Stop wasting my time and make that report."

Tonith shrugged languidly and bowed to the inevitable. "As we speak, a fleet of one hundred twenty-six ships," he said, "seventy-five of them capital ships, is investing Sluis Van to block any reinforcements from that sector. I am at this very moment landing a force of fifty thousand battle droids on Praesitlyn in a feint to divert the garrison from the Intergalactic Communications Center. When that operation is fully under way, I will land the main force, composed of, give or take, a million battle droids, crush the defenders in a containment maneuver, and capture the center intact. I have two hundred ships in my invasion fleet. This operation cannot possibly fail. I guarantee you that within twenty-four standard hours of the commencement of Operation Case White, Praesitlyn will be ours. We will sit firmly astride the communications link that connects the worlds of the Republic. Our forces will be poised at this strategic crossroads to strike without warning at any of the Republic's allies. Most important, our control of Praesitlyn will be a vibroblade thrust directly at Coruscant itself." He stabbed his arm forward as he spoke. "This is the move that will win the war for us," he concluded, a confident smirk on his purple-stained lips. "They'll never know what hit them, those technicians down there and their security forces. They'll soon all be dead—or be assets belonging to us." He sat back and sipped at his tea.

Ventress did not seem impressed. "The electronic countermeasures suite?"

"Fully operational. The center tried to dispatch a pan-galactic distress signal a brief while ago, but it was successfully blocked." He smiled, showing his purple teeth and black gums.

"The stealth suite? Your fleet is undetected? You have achieved tactical surprise?"

"Yes. Not just tactical surprise, but strategic surprise, not to put too fine a point on it."

"Very well. Count Dooku will require regular updates as your campaign progresses. You will make them to me, so get used to it now."

"Yes," Tonith answered, his voice tinged with false resignation, making clear that he thought he was succumbing to a nuisance he could do without. He had never met Ventress in person, but he had heard she was a deadly opponent in individual combat. That didn't worry him in the least. Only stupid people lost fights. He was not stupid. Where a warrior like Ventress could cut down an opponent with lightning speed, Tonith cut down his enemies by outsmarting them. That was why Count Dooku had given him this command. He wouldn't waste his time in individual combat or expose himself to possible harm—that was what droids were for. He would command and he would win.

"By the way, I'm impressed by your interesting dental work," Ventress said.

Caught completely off guard, Tonith didn't immediately know how to reply. Was she fooling with him or was she serious? He might have to reevaluate his estimation of her level of intelligence. "I thank you," he said at last, bowing at the hologram. "And I compliment you on your unusual choice of hairstyle."

Ventress nodded, and her image vanished.

*   *   *

Pors Tonith was one of the most successful products of one of the InterGalactic Banking Clan's most ruthless families. For him, life was constant struggle and competition. He approached business as if it were war. For generations it had been his family's practice to consummate hostile takeovers of companies, whole worlds if need be, by the use of force. Tonith had reduced these unpleasant maneuvers to an art—a military art.

Tonith did not present a very warlike figure. His height—he was over two meters tall—and his painfully thin physique and sallow complexion gave him a corpselike appearance; his long, equine face and blazing black eyes set in a skull-like head heightened this cadaverous aspect so that meeting him suddenly in a darkened companionway aboard the *Corpulentus,* his flagship, often gave his crew quite a start.

Count Dooku had picked Tonith to lead the force against Praesitlyn because of his proven ability as a planner. Commanding an army of droids was more like playing a game than engaging in actual combat. Living soldiers bled and died, had to be fed, experienced morale problems, knew fear and all the other emotions common to beings who could think. And though some might feel that using a droid army to inflict pain and death on a force composed of sentient beings was another matter, Tonith not only looked upon a battlefield dry-eyed, but found sustenance, meaning, and sublime purpose in the destruction of his enemies.

Pors Tonith not only looked like a corpse, but deep down inside him, where other beings had consciences, he was dead.

3

Nejaa Halcyon was doing stretching exercises when Anakin Skywalker walked into the training area.

"I hope you're ready for a workout," Halcyon said in greeting.

"After the workout I've been giving my brain, I'm more than ready for a physical workout, Master Halcyon," Anakin replied. "I feel the need to take it out on somebody."

Halcyon laughed and gave a last stretch before drawing his lightsaber from his belt. "Before you try to take anything out on anybody, you'd better loosen up, or you're going to be in too much pain to defend yourself." He grinned. "Or maybe that's what you want, to be too uncomfortable tomorrow to go back to the library."

"I did my stretching on the way here," Anakin said as he put his cloak aside and drew his lightsaber.

Halcyon sparred better than he had the first day, but so did Anakin. In the end, the Jedi Master bowed to the Padawan.

"You do very well. I need a sparring partner even more than I'd realized." He shook his head sadly.

"Who would have believed that a mere Padawan could best me with a lightsaber?" Then he smiled. "Shall we do it again tomorrow?"

"I look forward to it even more than I looked forward to today," Anakin answered with a broad grin.

They sparred again the next day, and the next, and the day after that. Each day, each improved, and each surprised the other with new moves and tricks.

After the first few days they didn't immediately part company when their sparring was over, but sat and talked. The next day they talked for a longer time. And the day after that, they dined together.

"Obi-Wan speaks highly of you, you know," Halcyon commented as they were relaxing over dessert.

"You know Obi-Wan?" Anakin asked, surprised.

"We're old friends," Halcyon said, nodding. "He's a great one, Obi-Wan is. And very powerful in the Force. I believe he'll become a member of the Jedi Council one day. You're fortunate to have him as your Master."

Anakin's chest swelled with pride, then deflated just as quickly. "Maybe he's too great."

Halcyon cocked his head. "What do you mean?"

"He thinks my progress sometimes seems to be slow. Perhaps he's too great, too busy to properly train me."

Halcyon barked out a laugh that made nearby diners turn to look—but when they saw that he was a Jedi, their expressions of disapproval vanished and they returned to their own meals and conversations.

"Maybe you're too impatient. But mostly, your progress isn't as fast as it might be because you're too busy fighting in a war. What you need is for this war to end. Then you'll be surprised at how rapidly your progress is recognized."

"Do you really think so?"

"As sure as I know that nobody has ever impressed Obi-Wan with their potential as much as you have."

Anakin shook his head. "Then why am I still a Padawan? We're fighting a major war, and I could do more to help win it! I'm good enough to go on small missions, I'm good enough to fight under someone else's command, but they think I'm not good enough to handle my own command!"

"Oh, you're good enough," Halcyon said. "I've watched you and listened to you these past few days, and I definitely think you're good enough."

Anakin reached out with his prosthetic hand and clamped onto Halcyon's forearm. "Would you speak to the Council for me, Master Halcyon?" he asked earnestly.

Halcyon's shoulders slumped. "Anakin, right now, the only way the Council would listen to me is to decide against whatever I recommend." He shook his head again. "No, having me speak to them for you would be counterproductive." He cleared his throat. "I'm sure the Council is aware of your abilities. You'll begin your Trials when you are ready, Anakin."

"We'll see," Anakin Skywalker replied, unconvinced.

4

Luck, good or bad, is the great unknown factor in war. Often the outcome of battles, the fate of entire worlds, is determined by luck.

It was luck of one sort or the other that placed Lieutenant Erk H'Arman of the Praesitlyn defense force and his Torpil T-19 starfighter on patrol along the southern coast of the continent on which the Intergalactic Communications Center was located, about 150 kilometers from the center itself, when the invasion began. He and his wingmate were cruising at a leisurely 650 kilometers per hour at twenty thousand meters. For the Torpil T-19, 650 kph was almost standing still.

"Looks like a big sandstorm down there," Erk's wingmate, Ensign Pleth Strom, commented. Neither pilot bothered to scan the terrain beneath the raging storm with his onboard surveillance suite. A storm is a storm is a storm—nothing they hadn't seen many times before. "Hate to have to do a forced landing in that stuff."

Starfighter pilots considered atmospheric flying the worst possible waste of their skills, and both men claimed at every possible opportunity that their tour with the Praesitlyn defense force was a form of punishment for some unspecified transgression. It wasn't, of course, but rather the luck of the assignment system: their numbers had come up, that was all, as they knew perfectly well. But if hotshots like Erk and Pleth weren't showing what they could do by taking on the entire Separatist fleet, they complained about being misused by their commanders.

Flying a high-performance fighter in an atmospheric environment was a lot different from piloting the same machine in the vacuum of space and, in truth, required a range of skills no less impressive. In an atmosphere, a pilot was subjected to g forces, air drag on his or her machine, and fatal malfunctions caused by high-flying creatures that got sucked into a fighter's power system and gummed it up, not to mention what would happen if a flock of the things penetrated a cockpit while the craft was traveling at a thousand kph.

The worst aspect of combat in an atmospheric environment was that the great speed and maneuverability of their craft often could not be used, because most of their combat missions would be in a close air-support role for ground forces. Even the gaudy paint jobs that aces tended to affect on their craft had to be abandoned for ground-support missions. While all kinds of stealth measures were available for use in space, in an atmosphere the fighters had to be invisible to the naked eye; they were coated with a self-camouflaging substance so that to ground observers or fliers at higher altitudes they blended in with the sky above or the ground below.

Erk and Pleth were more than just good pilots who could fly in all conditions. Others might also be good pilots, able to master the *science* of flight, make the same number of landings as takeoffs, exercise good reflexes, and remain in touch with their ships while in flight, attuned to every nuance of their onboard systems. But pilots like Erk and Pleth were great pilots who "wore" their ships like comfortable old boots, or a second skin, using their machines as an extension of their own bodies and wills. In short, they had mastered the *art* of flight.

"I hate to land anywhere on this blasted rock," Erk said with a laugh. He consulted his planetary navigational chart. "Nothing here even has a name! That's 'Area Sixty-two, South Continent.' You'd think someone would have taken the trouble to give the places names. Now down there could be 'Desert Delite,' and back at base it could be—"

"Jenth Grek Five One, cut the chatter. This is a combat patrol. And please, get off the guard channel! Go to eight-point-six-four." A thousand kilometers away, high over the ocean—another geographic feature that had no name—"Waterboy," the petite ensign on board JG51's airborne control ship, smiled. She knew both Erk and Pleth well and knew they were talking over the open channel just so she would butt in. Channel 8.64 was the discreet encrypted frequency, a scrambled freq that hopefully no potential enemy could intercept. Regulations strictly forbade pilots to go to an open channel when on a combat mission, except in an emergency, but there never were any emergencies, because nothing ever happened on Praesitlyn. And because duty there was so boring, commanders turned a deaf ear to the shenanigans of hotshots like Erk and his wingmate when they violated military protocol.

"Copy, switching to eight-point-six-four," Erk said laconically, "and begging you to have a beer with us tonight, Waterboy."

"She said, cut the chatter, JG Five One," a strong male voice interrupted.

"Copy that, sir," Erk replied, trying—and failing—to inject the appropriate inflection of contrition into his voice.

". . . approaching!" the female voice shouted in the next instant.

"Waterboy, repeat that transmission," Erk requested, frowning. In switching channels he had missed the first part of her message, but he thought he'd heard a note of panic in the controller's voice.

"Marks, lots of them!" Pleth shouted at the same instant Erk's warning system buzzed.

Now Erk saw them, a swarm of tri-droids emerging at great speed from that cloud of "dust" on the surface. Instantly Erk became a functioning component of his fighter. "Arming," he reported casually. "Break to starboard," he ordered Pleth. He put his machine into a half roll and commenced a steep dive to port. The T-19 could reach a top velocity of twenty thousand kph, but he knew he would not need that much speed to perform the maneuver that instantly came to mind.

Erk's fighter flashed through the approaching formation of enemy ships. Several fired at him as he roared groundward. At two thousand meters, with the enemy ships now far above him and no targets in his sights,

Erk threw his ship into a steep climb. His anti-g couch successfully protected him from losing consciousness. As soon as his target acquisition system ranged in on the enemy fighters, his blaster cannons began pumping lethal bolts into their underbellies as he approached from astern. He had less than a second to acquire and fire at a target, and still enemy ships exploded all around him as he flew through their formation and soared far above it. He rolled his ship to starboard and plummeted through the fighters again, blossoming several into bright balls of flame. He had lost sight of Pleth.

Confused by Erk's lightning attack, the tri-droids quickly formed a protective circle at fifteen thousand meters. Erk laughed out loud. He came up under them again, firing at very close range as the first target vanished beneath the nose of his fighter. He continued his climb, rolled inverted, and came down behind another target, which also disappeared in a ball of flame.

"Your six!" Pleth warned suddenly. High-energy bolts lanced past Erk's cockpit from astern. Either some fighters had broken away from the defensive circle, or another flight had come up to join the first. Erk instantly went into an inverted roll, pulled hard into a vertical dive, and pulled out in the opposite direction from his attackers. He climbed back up and took them from astern. Both exploded.

"Too many of them!" Pleth shouted.

"Copy that," Erk replied calmly.

". . . break . . . Waterboy . . ."

"Say again, Waterboy," Erk said in response to the garbled call from the controller aircraft. He switched to the guard channel. "Waterboy, say again your last transmission on guard." He knew someone on the ship would be monitoring the guard channel.

". . . going in," a female voice replied calmly, and then there was nothing but static.

Erk switched back to the scrambled frequency. "Head for home, Pleth. Waterboy is down, repeat, Waterboy is down."

Since they were only 150 kilometers from base, Erk descended to within meters of the surface, where the enemy craft would have difficulty tracking them against the ground clutter, and gave his engines power. They would be back at base in less than sixty seconds, muster the rest of the squadron, and return to do permanent damage to the invaders' fighter screen and the landing party. At last, something was happening on Praesitlyn!

Erk had accounted for ten of the enemy fighters in a dogfight that lasted only one minute from beginning to end, an impressive score for any pilot. But Lieutenant H'Arman was bold when he had to be and cautious when caution was called for, and now caution was being called for loud and clear. It was time to head back to the farm, rearm, and return in force. He had been so involved in the dogfight, however, that he'd had no time to gather useful intelligence on the strength of the enemy force or its intentions.

"Bad luck about Waterboy," Pleth said. They were both thinking of that young ensign.

Yeah, Erk thought, *very bad luck.*

*   *   *

Skill, not luck, had brought Odie Subu and her speeder bike undetected to a spot just behind the crest of a ridge where she could observe the enemy landing force deploying on the plain below. She was a member of a reconnaissance platoon General Khamar had spread out before his army to develop intelligence about the enemy landing force. The orbital surveillance system had been destroyed or was being electronically jammed, and the recon drones the defense force had sent out earlier had failed to report. Even communications with the army's main force were being successfully jammed—only short-range, line-of-sight transmissions via tactical communications nets were possible. So General Khamar was forced to rely exclusively on his living recon detachments.

Odie lay prone beside her speeder, just below the military crest of the ridge. She lifted her faceplate to wipe perspiration from her forehead. Her face was burned a dark red from constant exposure to wind, sun, and sand, but the area around her eyes, protected from the elements by the faceplate, had remained perfectly white. She ran the tip of her tongue over her parched lips. Water? No, no time for that now.

Inside her helmet a tiny voice whispered, "Droids." It was another soldier from her squad, deployed somewhere farther down the ridge from her position. The recon trooper was too excited by what he saw to use proper comm procedure and, because of the distortion caused by all the jamming equipment in use, she didn't recognize his voice. Probably Tami, she thought. But they were all excited. Except for Sergeant Makx Maganinny, the recon squad leader, this would be their first taste of combat. Evidently Tami had already been able to bring his electrobinoculars to bear and was directly observing the assembling army below the ridge. From her position, Odie could clearly hear the roar of landing ships and the rumble of heavy equipment rolling into position.

Cautiously she crawled to the top of the ridge and deployed her electrobinoculars, making delicate adjustments. Suddenly a sharp image of thousands and thousands of battle droids leapt into view. The screen readout indicated a range of 1,250 meters. Odie's TT-4 binocs, the only pair in the squad, began recording images that would be invaluable to General Khamar when she got back—*if* she got back—to the main body. Given the cost of the data cards that recorded the hologram images, only one set of TT-4s had been issued to each squad. Sergeant Maganinny had given her this pair because she was the best rider he had.

"It'll probably never happen," he had told her, "but if the comm breaks down or gets jammed in a tactical situation, we'll need someone who can ride like the wind to get the word back to battalion, and that's you, young soldier." The old noncom had smiled and rested his hand on her shoulder. "Remember this. In real war the best plan evaporates soon as the first shot's fired. Could be you on that speeder of yours could save the whole army one day."

"Lots of them!" Tami whispered.

Odie's heart began to beat faster. She had never seen real fighting machines up this close. Rills of nervous perspiration rolled down from her forehead and dripped off the tip of her nose. She felt nauseated, but she kept the electrobinoculars steadily focused on the scene below, slowly sweeping back and forth as she'd been trained to do.

"Use proper procedure and keep the comm open!" Sergeant Maganinny grunted.

Every second any portion of Odie's head remained exposed above the ridgeline upped the chance that an enemy surveillance device would spot her and she'd be fired at. Her heart was racing like a beamdrill. Another ship landed on a vast plume of fire and smoke. Huge clouds of dust rose into the air to obscure the craft. She increased magnification to reveal any markings on the landing ship.

Ker-whump! A concussion wave like the side of a Wookiee's hand slapped up against the left side of Odie's helmet from a hit a hundred meters down the ridge from her position. Momentarily the image in her electrobinoculars blurred. A huge cloud of dust rose up from the impact area, and even this far away she was pelted with falling dirt and stones. Other hits began impacting all around her and then she was being buffeted left and right. Her body shook like a rag; the concussions were so powerful, the breath whooshed out of her lungs. The entire ridgeline exploded in huge gouts of fire and dirt. The tactical channel inside her helmet erupted with screams and shouts. Someone began to wail in a high-pitched wavering screech, and suddenly Odie realized it was her! But she never took the electrobinoculars from her eyes. Even if she couldn't see anything, they could still record valuable data. She could feel moisture gathering inside her suit. Was it blood or—?

Someone cursed foully over the comm. Only Sergeant Maganinny talked like that. "Get out!" he yelled. The transmission ended in a painful grunt. That was all Odie needed to get going. She slithered back down the ridge, carefully put the precious electrobinoculars with their invaluable recordings inside their case, and righted her speeder. It had been knocked over by the explosions but was otherwise undamaged.

The speeders used by the recon squad were not made for military purposes, but were a civilian version that the military techs on the Praesitlyn defense force had modified—yet another economy measure that the force had been required to adopt. If the enemy had speeder scouts riding 74-Zs and they came after her she would be in trouble—her speeder was no match for the 74-Z with its high maneuverability, speed, armor plate, and onboard weapons. All she had with which to defend herself was a hand blaster. But Odie knew the ground between here and General Khamar's army, and she could use that to advantage if she were pursued by ground troops, or even by aircraft.

She also had another advantage: she could outride almost anyone in the galaxy. When Odie mounted a speeder she turned into someone else. Often, traveling at top speed in training exercises, she could not even remember making course corrections, they came so naturally to her. Her comrades marveled at her skill as a rider. In the many long months she had been assigned to the defense force on Praesitlyn she had honed her natural skills to a fine point. Armies train and train some more to keep their fighting skills sharp. Soldiers complain about their training bitterly, even as they go through the sequences they know will save their lives in combat. But Odie loved every moment of it.

The run she was about to attempt was what she lived for.

Using the ridge behind her as cover, she roared off at top speed, 250 kph, hugging the ground contour, less than a meter above it. At that speed, so close to the ground, even the slightest mistake could spell disaster. About a kilometer from the ridgeline she drove into a deep arroyo and reduced her speed. Suddenly her heart froze: just above her but out of sight over the lip of the canyon she heard the roar of another speeder bike. Her practiced ear told her the bad news: it was not one of hers. She pulled to a stop in the deep shadows beside the canyon wall and took off her helmet to hear better. The only sound was the pulsing of the blood in her own veins: the other speeder had stopped.

Carefully, she eased her blaster out of its holster. Because of her very small hands, Odie had asked army ordnance technicians to modify the weapon for her grip. They'd removed the scope and emitter nozzle to permit a quicker draw and reduced the length of the barrel, which lightened the weapon considerably. They'd narrowed the grip and installed a smaller power pack so her fingers could get a better hold on the weapon. A three-dot iron sight system replaced the cumbersome scope.

All this made the blaster much lighter and easier to draw, but its effective range in the hands of an ordinary shooter was reduced from twenty-five meters to only ten—but Odie was no ordinary shooter. The other members of her platoon had good-naturedly ribbed

Odie about her "popgun" because the smaller power pack reduced the number of shots it could fire, and they delightedly pointed this fact out to her. But an old ordnance sergeant had told her, "If the first shot counts, you don't need all that firepower the bigger models have. Let those guys blast away with their hand cannons."

The techs had proudly described their reworked blaster as a "belly gun," to be used only at very close range. Even firing it one-handed, however, Odie had learned to hit targets out to sixty meters with impressive accuracy and after that display her comrades' jibes had turned to respect. Accurate shooting with a hand weapon requires good hand–eye coordination, and that was a talent Odie had plenty of. But reconnaissance troops weren't intended to engage the enemy in firefights anyway, and the modified pistol was just what she needed to travel light and fast.

Odie slung her helmet behind her. She shook out her short brunette hair. It was damp with perspiration and gritty with sand. From here on she'd need 360 degrees of visibility, and since she was now probably completely on her own, communications didn't matter. Safety off her blaster and her finger off the trigger, she drove her speeder with one hand, easing it forward cautiously. Ahead, the ground rose steeply. She paused, looking up the slope, over a jumble of fallen rock, to where the canyon rose to the surface.

She came out of the canyon at two hundred kph. A trooper sat on a speeder bike right in front of her. She snapped one shot at his center of mass but didn't wait to see the bolt slam into him and knock him completely off his speeder. Instantly she wondered if she should return and take his vehicle, but her training took over, and that saved her life. She zigged sharply to the left and then back to the right just as a high-energy bolt zapped over her shoulder, fired by a second trooper she hadn't seen off to one side. He roared after her. With its superior speed his machine shot past in a blur of speed. He made a tight turn and came charging straight back at her. She stopped abruptly and fired, but missed as he flashed by. The trooper's shot went far wide. She could have sworn he grinned as he passed her.

A hundred meters ahead rose a jagged rock formation weathered into a jumble of bantha-sized boulders that extended several kilometers in the direction Odie wanted to travel. She had noted the formation on the way out from the main body of the army. She drove her speeder into it and hid behind a huge boulder, waiting to ambush the trooper if he was stupid enough to come in after her. He wasn't. Something flashed overhead. It was the military speeder, traveling at top speed about twenty-five meters above the rocks—too fast for her to get off a shot.

The shadows had begun to lengthen. She glanced at her wrist chrono. Not too long until sunset. If she could stay concealed among the rocks until full dark, her chances of getting out would be somewhat improved. But that was not an option. The intelligence she had gathered had to get back to headquarters quickly. She had to operate on the assumption that she was the only rider to have survived the attack. She'd have to chance making another break for it. It would already be dark by the time she made it back.

She moved farther forward into the rock formation, cautiously edging her speeder ahead at slow speed. A series of huge boulders blocked her path. She could see no way around them and dared not take a chance of going over even if her speeder could make the height. The only way through was via a gap about fifteen meters wide. It was very dark inside the passageway. She hesitated. *Ambush alley,* she thought. The hairs on the backs of her arms bristled and a cold chill worked its way down her backbone. She took a deep breath and entered the narrow declivity.

The shadows deepened into twilight between the rocks, plunging some areas into near-total darkness. Odie considered putting her helmet back on so she could take advantage of its night-vision function, but rejected that idea. She just felt encumbered wearing it. Slowly, she moved farther into the darkness, carefully skirting or riding over obstructions.

Her heart suddenly skipped a beat. Was that a noise off to the left in that patch of darkness? She froze and reached for her blaster.

"Freeze!" a voice commanded. The trooper stepped out of the shadows, holding a blaster aimed directly at her chest. "Don't move," he ordered.

Odie leaned forward, preparatory to making a break for it, and the trooper fired a warning blast in front of her. In the brief flash of light she was surprised to see another figure lurking in some shadows just a little way behind the trooper, heading toward him. Two of them? The trooper's head turned slightly in the direction of the approaching figure. At the same instant the figure fired his blaster, Odie gunned her speeder forward. Amazingly, the blaster bolt was aimed not at her but at the other trooper, who staggered back into the shadows, a jagged, steaming hole in his chest.

"Odie!" a man's harsh voice called out. She applied the brakes instantly. She'd know that voice anywhere—it was Sergeant Maganinny! He staggered toward her, his blaster hanging loosely in one hand. Even in the dim light she could see that he was hurt. The flesh on the left side of his face hung in loose strands and his left ear was gone, the hair on that side of his head burned away. And by the way he was limping, she could tell that he'd sustained other wounds, as well.

He swayed in front of her, a twisted smile on his face. "Good to see you again," he rasped.

"Sergeant Maganinny!" Odie dismounted from her speeder and helped him into a sitting position on the ground.

"I thought—I think they got everyone else. My speeder—" He paused to catch his breath and gestured behind him. "I thought it was all over for us, kid," he said.

"Sarge—"

He shook his head. "My face isn't as bad as it looks. It's mostly superficial. Leave me here. You can send help. Get back to HQ."

"No." Odie shook her head firmly. "You can ride with me. I won't leave you here."

"Look, trooper," he said, a note of the old noncom command presence creeping back into his voice, "you do what—"

"No." She put a hand under his armpit and helped him to his feet. "We can ride tandem. It'll be dark soon and we can use the terrain to cover us."

Maganinny groaned, partly from the pain of his wounds, but partly because he was too weak to argue. "One thing, though, trooper," he said. "I'm not riding with any soldier who's out of uniform."

"What?"

"Get your helmet on," he said.

Odie stared at him in disbelief for an instant, and then they both burst into hysterical laughter.

General Khamar turned to his chief of staff. "Let's move. We can take these droids. Get our armored infantry and artillery onto this high ground here—" He jabbed a finger at a three-dimensional terrain map. "Dig in. Get them to come to us. Hit them with every fighter we've got right now to cover our advance." He turned to his staff officers. "If we get to that high ground first, we can hold them." The officers dispersed to their various commands to issue the necessary orders and get the army on the move.

Odie had stood quietly at attention while the general and his staff used the information she had gathered to plan their attack. She wondered about the fate of her comrades, none of whom had been heard from. She struggled to control the lump in her throat when she realized they were probably dead. Occasionally someone would nod at her, or give her a thumbs-up gesture, and these silent acknowledgments helped soften the sorrow she felt—and the physical exhaustion that was now taking over—by causing her chest to swell with pride.

At last Khamar turned to her. "At ease, trooper. You are one brave soldier, and pretty lucky to boot."

She had never been this close to high-ranking officers before and was impressed at the quiet efficiency with which they laid their plans. Now the general himself was talking directly to her! She had not been able to clean up; her face was stained with dirt and sweat, and her hair hung in dirty strands about her face. Her voice sounded too high-pitched when she spoke, but she did not hesitate in her reply. "I was scared all the time, sir, and I didn't need any luck: Sergeant Maganinny backed me up when I needed him."

The general looked at her for a moment, then nodded. "Well," he said, "now you know what really makes an army work."

5

General Khamar and several of his principal staff officers were observing the invaders from the same ridge where Odie had watched them barely hours before. Khamar had succeeded in reaching the ridge before the enemy deployed and quickly established a strong defensive position. So far, the invaders had been content to direct only harassing fires against Khamar's force, but had made no attempt to attack him.

"We're too well entrenched," one of the officers remarked.

"They're mostly droids anyway, no match for our troops," another observed.

General Khamar glanced at him. *No match for our troops?* Obviously, that was an officer who had no idea how deadly the droids were. He briefly considered replacing him with someone more in touch with the realities of their situation, but realized there was no time to call up a replacement. He returned his thoughts to the situation before him. There was something odd about all of this. An army of an estimated fifty thousand droids was sitting down there without making a move against him. What could they be waiting for?

"Sir, they can't flank us—we have strong forces to both sides," an officer observed. "If they're going to attack, they have to come at us straight up this slope. We'll cut them to pieces if they do. They must be waiting for reinforcements."

General Khamar frowned thoughtfully as he rubbed the stubble on his chin. He had not slept in the past forty-eight hours. That was a big problem about going to war: one never got enough sleep. Many times Khamar had requested more troops from Coruscant— as well as capital ships to protect the planet from orbit—but his requests had been refused. The Republic, he knew very well, was engaged on a vast scale, and the forces he felt he required to defend Praesitlyn had been denied because they were needed in other theaters. When he pointed out how strategically important the Intergalactic Communications Center was, he'd been told merely that he'd have to make do and to prepare his defensive plan with the forces at his disposal. Not even the Sluissi, who had the ships, would help him; they needed all their spacecraft to protect their shipyards.

It was almost as if the Republic wanted the Separatists to attack Praesitlyn. The general had kept this thought to himself, of course. It was ridiculous anyway. Everyone knew how important Praesitlyn was. Everyone knew how dangerously thin the Republic's forces were spread.

But . . .

Suddenly the general knew with absolute clarity what was about to happen. He turned to the hologram map of his positions and the surrounding terrain and put his finger on a vast, jumbled rock formation about ten kilometers behind his line.

"I want a redoubt established here," he said, speaking rapidly. "Start moving our troops on the double. Move fast but in small increments, infantry and support troops first. If the enemy gets wind of a retrograde movement and attacks, I don't want the bulk of our troops caught in the open. Have the combat engineers go in with the first group, to fortify the area. Armor and mobile artillery will lay down a barrage on the enemy to keep his head down. They'll move last, to hold on to this ridge until the last possible moment until we can secure that area, then withdraw into it. How many fighter craft do we have?"

"A full wing is operational, sir, but—"

"Good! We can use the air assets to cover our withdrawal."

"But, sir," another officer protested, "we have a classic defensive position where we are. They can't possibly break through here." Other members of his staff murmured their assent, glancing nervously one from the other and casting questioning looks at their commander.

"They aren't going to break through here, and that is not the main force," the general announced quietly. "We've been duped. The main force hasn't landed yet. When it does, it'll land behind us, between this position and the center. This force"—he nodded down the ridge—"is the anvil. The hammer is about to strike—from behind us."

Absolute silence enveloped General Khamar's command post for a full five seconds as the meaning of his words sank in. "Oh no," someone whispered.

General Khamar sighed. "Listen carefully. There's no easy way to put this except we're retreating. Call it what you want, but it's vital that morale not be affected."

"General," an officer said, "let's not say we're retreating, then. Let's just say we're moving our position to attack from a different direction!"

General Khamar smiled and clapped the officer on his shoulder. "Brilliant! All right, hop to it. I intend to save what I can of this army, and if the Separatists succeed in capturing this planet, which they will if I'm right about this, at least I'm going to make them pay for it. Just hope we aren't too late to make it to those rocks."

Pors Tonith didn't bother even to glance up at Karaksk Vet'lya, his chief of staff, when the Bothan brought him the news. "So he's not as stupid as we thought," Tonith commented, a tight smile on his purple-stained lips. "How long has this retrograde movement been going on?" His tone was deceptively mild.

Karaksk's fur rippled softly as he searched for the proper words to make what he had to say appear in the best possible light. "About an hour, sir, but we—"

"Ah!" Tonith finally looked at Karaksk, holding up his forefinger for silence. "We, you say? We? Have you by any chance a dianoga stuffed in your pocket? Who is this we who are making decisions in my command?"

Karaksk swallowed nervously. "I meant, sir, that our staff observed this retrograde movement on the part of the defending forces and we, the staff and I, that is, we decided to observe it for a time to, ah, determine the enemy's plan." His fur rippled less gently as his fear moved closer to the surface.

"You did?" Tonith carefully set his teacup on a saucer and stood. "The plan seems to be to withdraw, wouldn't you say?" He smiled. Then: "You idiot!" he screamed. Spittle flew from his lips, and a damp spot appeared on Karaksk's fur. "They've figured out what our plan is. They're moving to a more defensible position! A droid could have figured that out!" Tonith managed to calm himself. "How much of their force remains in the original position? How far is the main body from the communications center?"

Feeling more confident now, Karaksk replied, "Their mobile artillery and armor remain in place, sir. Some of the infantry and support troops have reached the redoubt, a natural barrier some ten kilometers behind their original main battle line. The rest seem to be en route. They are about one hundred fifty kilometers from the center."

Tonith was beginning to sense a challenge here. "Interesting. We shall proceed to the bridge. I'm ordering the main force landed immediately. I have two choices, it seems: I can let this garrison fort up, and isolate them while I move with the rest of my army to take the center; or I can first destroy the garrison and then move on the center. Which course would you advise, my dear fellow?"

"Well, sir, if I may. Isolate them and move on the Intergalactic Communications Center. We do not need the entire army to take the place. Your plan, sir, is working perfectly!"

"And leave an enemy force in my rear? Really?"

"Well . . ."

"Dead enemies cannot fight back. We will destroy this army in detail and then take the communications center. We have the strength, we have the time. Now leave," he finished with a glare.

Tonith smiled at Karaksk's rapidly retreating back. Bothans were duplicitous, opportunistic, and greedy—characteristics he well understood and could manipulate. And the rippling of their fur allowed the astute person to read them so easily.

"I have a mission for you."

Odie stood at attention before the reconnaissance platoon commander and another officer whom she recognized by his collar tabs as an engineer. "This is Lieutenant Colonel Kreen, the commander of our engineer battalion. That rock formation where you met Sergeant Maganinny, I want you to take Colonel Kreen back there. Right now."

"Yessir," Odie responded.

"Let's go, trooper," Colonel Kreen said. He stepped off with a short nod at the lieutenant. As he and Odie briskly headed for the engineer battalion's bivouac, he briefed her on the mission.

"I have a convoy of cargo skiffs all loaded and ready to go. I want you to lead it back to that rock formation, where they'll unload and prepare another defensive position." He smiled down at her, but her heart skipped a beat as she instantly interpreted the nature of this move for what it really was. "It's not a withdrawal," he cautioned her. "We're just establishing a rear supply base." He smiled reassuringly, seeing her expression. "Are you ready to leave right now?" He grinned. His confidence was reassuring, but that slight pause spoke volumes.

"Yessir!" Odie replied enthusiastically. Since she wasn't needed for any reconnaissance missions at the moment, she'd been put into the army's field communications center to work in her secondary specialty—and she was bored to death.

Reconnaissance trooper Odie Subu straddled her speeder as she closely watched the three hundred vehicles of the engineering battalion finish forming up for the rearward movement to the redoubt. There were dirt movers, bridgers, graders, ground clearers, diggers, and more exotic machines whose uses she couldn't guess. The most numerous, though, were cargo carriers, many of which were marked with symbols she recognized as indicating their cargoes were explosive ordnance.

She estimated there were enough explosives in the convoy to obliterate the army's entire position. She briefly wondered why General Khamar didn't order the engineers to use the explosives to destroy the droid army. Then she realized the army had no way to get the explosives into the midst of the droid army without whoever was doing the job getting killed before they could accomplish their mission. Still, she thought, it seemed a waste to not set some of them in the droids'

path, to destroy as many as possible when they followed the retreating army.

Well, she decided, *General Khamar must know what
he's doing.* Besides, how did she know the engineers
hadn't already emplaced explosives to kill the droids
when they passed over this ground?

"Recon scout," Lieutenant Colonel Kreen's voice
came through her helmet comm.

"Recon here, sir," she said into her mike.

"We're ready. Move out."

Odie took a last look at the convoy. Whatever route
she chose had to accommodate the largest of the engineering vehicles. The shake of her head went unseen
inside her helmet. The biggest of those machines was
so big, she was going to have to lead them in a round-
about manner.

"Moving out, sir," she said, and eased her speeder
into gear.

She wasn't able to lead the convoy at speed, not even
the paltry 250 kilometers per hour that was all her
speeder was capable of. Over this rugged terrain, she
had to keep her speed down to under fifty kph, which
was the fastest the slower vehicles in the convoy could
manage—at times she had to slow to little more than a
trot for them to keep up, and sometimes she had to
slow because Colonel Kreen said they were raising too
much of a dust cloud. The distance they had to cover
was only ten kilometers, line of sight. But the route she
had to follow, this way and that, and sometimes dou-
bling back, made it nearly four times that distance—
and more than four times the length of time to cover.

But at last they made it. She stopped and pulled aside, while the engineering vehicles trundled past.

Colonel Kreen had his command vehicle pull off the trail next to her.

"Well done, trooper," he said. "I'll see to it General Khamar and your platoon commander both get a report on how well you did. Now you'd better get back."

"Thank you, sir." Odie saluted and waited until the engineering commander was back in his vehicle before she turned her speeder around and gunned it. She headed back at top speed.

Lieutenant Erk H'Arman knew he was going down, but even as he plummeted toward the ground he remained cool, calling upon every fiber in his body and all the skill he could muster to save his starfighter. The hit from the enemy fighter had slammed into him like a hammer and sent him into an uncontrolled spin downward. He had only just been able to pull out and stabilize his machine at a mere thousand meters above the ground. His hydraulic system was failing fast, and he knew he had but two choices: eject or ride his fighter in. So far there was no fire inside the cockpit. A pilot's worst fear was to burn alive in his or her cockpit; crashing was no problem—that would be over quickly.

This was the most target-rich environment Erk and his fellow pilots had ever encountered. Not even in the many simulated practice sessions had anyone thought to program this many marks. Already, three pilots in Erk's wing had been killed crashing into enemy fighters—not on purpose, but simply because there were too many of them to fly through without hitting one. The fight continued far, far above Erk. The enemy was winning, but now Erk H'Arman was intent on saving his life and, if possible, his ship.

A dust storm had developed below, obscuring the terrain. Erk's suit was filled with perspiration, and he knew he must have lost two liters of fluid during the dogfight. Already that loss of fluid was making him thirsty. But he had no choice: he'd have to go down in that storm. He made his decision. "Well, old girl," he muttered as he struggled to keep his starfighter level, "I'm not going to leave you." He would go in with his fighter.

Odie was only halfway back to the main army after guiding the engineers to the rock formation where they were to dig the new defensive positions when the storm hit with a suddenness and ferocity typical of such events on Praesitlyn. The wind quickly rose to fifty or sixty kilometers an hour, buffeting her from all sides and making controlling her speeder difficult. She stopped and zipped up. Millions of granules of sand blasted at her. When at last the storm was over, which could be in ten minutes or ten days, she knew her helmet would be scoured white by the sand. Right now, though, she couldn't see two meters in front of her. She dismounted and, turning off the repulsors, she tipped her speeder over and curled up beside it to wait out the storm.

A ground-shaking roar, momentarily louder than even the howling wind, washed over her as an enormous object passed no more than ten meters above where she lay. The ground trembled beneath her, and the huge tail of flame that came out of the dust cloud was so hot she could feel it even through her protective clothing. She heard a screeching, smashing noise as if some metallic object had impacted. Some distance off to her right, there was a brief reddish glow that was immediately obscured by the rolling clouds of dust. A fighter had just crashed only a short distance from where she lay. She didn't hear an explosion, so she presumed the fighter had come down mostly intact. *Would the pilot have survived?* she wondered. Then she wondered whose ship it was. She lay beside her speeder, undecided whether to investigate.

The wind suddenly abated somewhat, and raising her head above the frame of her speeder, Odie saw a faint glow from the downed fighter's engines. She was familiar with the design of all types of Separatist craft— that was one of her jobs as a reconnaissance trooper— but at this distance in the bad visibility she couldn't tell which side the crashed machine might belong to. All she could see was that it hadn't broken up on impact.

She righted her speeder, mounted, and started out toward the downed machine. As she eased her way along, she unsnapped her holster and withdrew her hand blaster.

When she got close enough to see the fighter's markings, she identified it as a Praesitlyn defense force fighter. The canopy was closed and she couldn't see the pilot. The fighter ticked and creaked and groaned like a living thing in pain as its overheated components began to cool. She wondered if it would explode. No time to lose. She jumped off her speeder and clambered onto the fighter's airfoil. She couldn't see through the canopy. She banged on it with her fist, and suddenly it popped open. The pilot sat there in his harness, a blaster pointed directly at her face.

"Don't shoot!" she screamed, instinctively leveling her own blaster at the man.

They froze there for a very long moment, weapons leveled at each other. "Well," the pilot said at last, lowering his blaster, "am I ever glad to see you!"

Odie helped him out of his harness and they crouched on the ground in the lee of the fighter. "Do you have any water?" he asked. "I came off in such a hurry my ground crew didn't have time to load my hydration system."

She unfastened the two-liter canteen strapped to her speeder and passed it to him. He drank sparingly and passed it back with thanks. As he did so, he studied his new companion. She was small, and he judged she might be pretty by what he could see of her chin and lips beneath her helmet. Likewise, Odie scrutinized him. A fighter jock! Fighter pilots were the only other people in the army with whom reconnaissance troopers felt any bond. Like the recon troopers, fighter pilots operated on their own, out in front of everyone else, surviving on their guts and skill.

At the same instant each realized what the other was thinking, and they both laughed.

"Well," the pilot said, "I guess whatever we're going to do, we'll be doing it together. I'm Erk H'Arman. Who're you?" He reached out with one hand.

Odie was surprised that an officer would speak to her so casually—he hadn't even identified himself as an officer—but quickly recovered. "Trooper Odie Subu, reconnaissance platoon, sir." She took his hand and shook it.

"Reconnaissance? That's good, very good. You can get me back to base, and I can get back into the fight."

Odie liked the sound of his voice. He had sustained a gash on his forehead in the crash, but the blood that had trickled down one side of his face had dried. His short black hair and striking blue eyes offset by a ruddy complexion made him look like an athletic outdoorsman just come in from a long hike.

The wind had diminished significantly by now. Odie stood. "Sir, follow me!" she said, extending her hand to help him up.

At that instant the world around them exploded.

6

The fight for the Intergalactic Communications Center was fierce but short-lived, and the outcome was never in doubt. The valiant Commander Llanmore and the mixed human and Sluissi soldiers in his battalion knew that the rest of their army, even if it was still fighting and hadn't already been destroyed, wasn't able to come to their aid. They knew that now their mission was to delay the capture of the center long enough for Reija Momen and her technicians to destroy the communications equipment. They were only partially successful.

"Stop!" Reija ordered her technicians as the first battle droids burst into the control room. "Don't resist them. I don't want any of you killed." But she couldn't save them all. Three technicians didn't hear her command and continued destroying equipment. They died when droids blasted them.

"I think, Mistress, that we are about to become prisoners," Slith Skael muttered. He stepped in front of Reija to protect her from the advancing droids, while everyone else was raising his or her hands in surrender. With blows and shoving, the droids forced the techni-

cians into the center of the control room and surrounded them, weapons leveled.

Cleaning droids scurried about the bodies of the three
technicians, scrubbing at the mess on the floor. One
of them, programmed to haul away small amounts of
trash, vainly tried to move one of the bodies. Frustrated, it emitted a whirring noise but wouldn't give
up trying. If the situation hadn't been so desperate,
Reija would have found the droid's attempts highly
amusing.

"What next?" someone asked.

"Si-lence!" one of the droids commanded.

"I demand to speak with your commander!" Reija
said in a voice of authority. A droid darted around
Slith and jabbed the muzzle of its blaster into Reija's
midsection, knocking the wind out of her. Slith spun
about and grabbed her in time to keep her from falling.
He raised his caudal appendage protectively between
Reija and the droid as he cradled her in his arms.

"Si-lence!" the droid repeated.

"Ah, most touching." A tall, cadaverous figure
stepped into the control room. He bowed slightly toward
Reija, who stood bent over, gasping in Slith's arms.
"May I introduce myself? I am Admiral Pors Tonith of
the InterGalactic Banking Clan, and I am now in charge
of this miserable rock." He bowed again. Pretending dif-
fidence, he brushed some dirt off his cloak. He grinned at
Reija, revealing his horribly stained teeth. "I presume,
madam, that you are the chief administrator of this facility?" He did not wait for an answer, but signaled the
droids to stand back. The room's quiet was broken by a
whirrr, whirrr, whirrr.

"What is that infernal noise?" Tonith looked about the space until he saw the cleaning droid that was making the noise. "Blasted things are always underfoot. Destroy it," he snapped at one of the battle droids. In a moment, the cleaner was crushed. Components clattered to the floor, and other droids scuttled over to sweep up the debris.

Tonith smiled, shrugged as if settling his cape more comfortably, and reached out for Reija, but Slith hissed and raised his appendage defensively.

"How gallant!" Tonith smirked, but he stepped back quickly. "Oppose me again, you Sluissi garbage, and I will have you killed. Come here, woman!" He pointed to the floor in front of himself.

"General—Khamar—" Reija struggled to get her breath. "G-general Khamar and his forces are not that far away, and he's coming to—"

Tonith shook his head, pretending sadness. "Alas, no. Your tiny and ineffectual army has been destroyed. Now, come here."

"Mistress?" Slith asked, reluctant to let her go.

"I'm all right, my friend," Reija gasped. Slith released her, and she walked unsteadily to stand in front of Tonith. He smiled broadly. She was close enough to smell his breath, which was exceedingly foul. Grinning even wider, Tonith deliberately exhaled in her face.

"I've always hated your kind," Reija gritted. Years before, one of the clan families had helped her father with the mortgage on his farm during a period of bad harvests, but when he couldn't make the loan repayments on time, they seized his property. All very legal and very unfortunate, but the old man lost his farm.

The Momens had had to move to the city, and the loss of his beloved farm had caused Reija's father to fall into a state of depression that eventually led to his death.

"Oh?" Tonith leaned very close to Reija now. "Love? Hate? Those emotions mean nothing to me. Neither does your life, woman. I am here to do a job and you are assets to me, nothing more than assets."

Reija had had enough. Her hand shot out reflexively to slap the face of this *creature* who had come to ruin her life and kill her people. The *smack* of her hand startled everyone, but no one as much as Pors Tonith, who staggered backward into one of his droids, a hand clasped to his cheek and a look of total surprise on his face so ludicrous that Reija, knowing she had nothing to lose, started to laugh.

With unexpected strength and agility, Tonith lurched forward, grabbed Reija by the hair, and threw her to the floor. Slith leapt up to protect his boss, and Tonith whirled on him. "Kill this reptile!" he shouted. The nearest droid shifted its blaster in Slith's direction while the technicians, some screaming in fear, crouched out of the line of fire.

"No! No!" Reija screamed from where she lay on the floor. "No more! Please, no more!"

Tonith gestured to the droid to lower its weapon. "Listen to me, all of you," he said, addressing the small group. "You are totally abandoned by the Republic, and *I* own Praesitlyn now. You are my prisoners. You will be treated well if you follow my orders."

Reija had managed to get back on her feet. "I dispatched a distress message to Coruscant," she began, knowing it was a bluff but determined to say something defiant.

Tonith waved her into silence. "You mean, you *tried* to send such a message. But you know it was never received. We blocked all transmissions to and from Praesitlyn. No message from here will ever reach Coruscant unless I will it." He grinned again. "No one even knows what's going on here, and by the time they find out, it will be too late. Well . . ." He nodded at the frightened technicians and bowed again at Reija. "It has been a rather touching experience, this brief interview, but now I must be getting back to my army."

He turned and walked toward the door, but just as he was about to exit the control room, he stopped as if he'd remembered something and turned back toward Reija. "Madam, one more little thing. Keep that big mouth of yours shut from now on, or I'll turn you over to the droids." With that, swirling his cloak, he stepped through the door.

The dust storm had started up again, and worse, the temperature had plummeted. Odie and Lieutenant Erk H'Arman found shelter in a clump of rocks and huddled shivering under the scant protection offered by the ground sheet she had unfolded from her equipment pack.

"What do we do now, sir?"

"Hey, let's get one thing straight: none of this military protocol stuff, okay? I'm Erk and you're Odie. I'm a fighter jock, remember? Not a staff officer. Besides, if we ever get out of this I think it's going to be you who gets us through. Now, if we were in a fighter—" He laughed and punched Odie lightly on the shoulder. A strong gust of wind threatened to blow off the ground sheet, but they grabbed handfuls of the light fabric and managed to hold on.

The massive attack by Tonith's ships in orbit against General Khamar's army had caught the pair in the open, between the main lines and the fortified position. Both positions had been blasted and then assaulted by ground troops. Unable to do anything to help, they had taken cover and waited for the battle's outcome, which was neither long in coming nor ever in doubt. Using her electrobinoculars, Odie had seen no sign of resistance in either place once the fighting subsided.

"Battle droids," she had said, her voice wavering. "Thousands of them."

Battle droids were on the ridge where General Khamar's army had been camped. And then, as if even the weather were allied with the invaders, the dust storm had started up again, and Odie and Erk had been forced to find precarious shelter.

"How much water do we have?" Erk asked now.

Odie checked her canteen. "Little less than a liter."

"Well, surrender's no option."

"No."

"Is there any place we can hide out for a while?"

"Yes, but shouldn't we go back to the center? Maybe they're still holding out."

Erk shook his head. "Maybe, but the center has to be the Separatists' objective, and I think we ought to stay out here until we're sure who's holding the place. Besides, you saw yourself how powerful this landing force is." He shook his head. "No, nobody's holding out back there."

"Oh, no!" Odie's shoulders began to quake as the impact of what had happened sank in. "All my friends! Everyone . . ."

Erk laid a hand on her shoulder. "Mine too, Odie, mine too. That's what happens in war. Ah, we were a heck of a crew," he muttered. He took a deep breath. "Look. We're still alive and we're going to stay that way," he said, as much to reassure himself as her. "Hey, I'm no pebblepusher. I won't last long down here if you give out on me."

"Y-yes. Yes. I mean, no, I won't give out on you. Let me think. There are some caves about seventy-five kilometers to the southeast of here," she began. "I've seen them on patrols. We can hide out there. I don't know what's in them, maybe there's water. I have a small supply of rations on my speeder. They'll last us awhile if we take it easy."

"Can you get us there in—this?" Erk nodded at the storm all around them.

"Hey! Can you fly a fighter? Sure I can get us there!" She laughed without humor.

"You know, once we get out of this, why don't you volunteer for flight training?" Erk said.

She snorted. "Are you serious?"

"Sure I am. You've got the right attitude. Come on. We may be on our own, but two hotshots like us? Sheesh, with your skill and my brains—"

"My brains and your skill—"

"Now you're really talking like a fighter pilot!" They shook on it.

*   *   *

It took them two agonizing days to find the caves. The small amount of water they had was exhausted by the time they reached the shelter, and they were on the verge of dehydration. But at least crawling into the shadowy coolness of the caverns spared them the devastating effects of the broiling sun.

"We've got to find water," Odie gasped.

"You're telling me?" Erk croaked. "Let's rest here awhile in the cool, then we can look for a way down into the caverns. There should be water here somewhere. Do you know how extensive these caves are?"

She shook her head. "No. We stopped here once on a routine recon mission, but nobody was interested in doing any exploring."

They lay resting for a time before regaining enough strength to start the search. Odie produced a brilliant white signal flare from a pouch on her equipment belt to light their way. "This'll burn for twenty minutes," she told Erk over her shoulder as they walked carefully over the rock-strewn floor. "Then we'll have to switch to some other color."

"Make sure you save some so we can find our way back."

The piercing flarelight cast their shadows huge on the walls around them, like grotesque cave creatures picking their way along.

"Hold it!" Erk shouted suddenly. "Move your light over here." He indicated a patch of rock that appeared darker than its surroundings. He ran a hand over it. "Moisture! Water's seeping through this rock. We're in business." A little farther on, the narrow passage widened abruptly into a huge cavern.

"Hey!" Odie shouted. Her voice echoed off the chamber walls. She held the flare high over her head. "I can't even see the ceiling. This place is huge."

"Listen!" Erk held up a hand. "Listen. I hear running water! Can you hear it, Odie? There's an underground stream down there."

The cavern floor sloped gradually downward, and as they worked their way toward the bottom, the wonderful sound of running water came distinctly to them from somewhere ahead, where a cool stream of fresh water fed into a deep pond before rushing off to disappear deeper into the cavern. Odie jammed the flare between two rocks and flung herself bodily into the pool; Erk followed her immediately. They drank themselves dizzy on the glorious, life-giving liquid.

They lingered in the caves for two days, recuperating. "We have to move on," Odie said on the evening of the second day, "if for no other reason than we're out of food."

"What say we start out at first light tomorrow?" Erk suggested. "We'll ride until it gets too hot and then rest until late evening. We can cover some ground during the night if there's enough starlight to see by. How long do you think it'll take us to get to the communications center?"

"Two, maybe three days? The terrain's mighty rough out there, and we had to detour a bit to get here. Can we survive on two liters of water for three days? All we have to carry it in is this canteen."

"We'll have to. We've got your speeder—that'll save

us expending all our energy on walking. We'll take it easy, conserve body fluid as much as possible. Odie, there's nothing you and I together can't do!"

He put his arm around her shoulders and kissed her lightly on the cheek. Her face turned even redder than usual, then she turned and kissed him full on the lips. They held the embrace for a long moment.

"Ah," Erk said at last, "what'd I tell you? You're the best wingmate a fighter jock ever had!"

After a moment, Odie said, "I wonder if any of our people survived . . ."

"I'm sure some did. Come on, let's get some sleep."

They lay close together for a long while, not speaking, thinking instead about what might lie ahead of them. Just before he dropped off to sleep Erk turned to Odie. "Maybe we're the only two left alive on this blasted rock, but we're going to stay that way, right?"

"Absolutely," Odie answered. She snuggled closer to Erk's warmth.

7

But they weren't alone—not quite.

"Just like those parsimonious fools," Zozridor Slayke remarked to one of his officers. "The Republic Senate has always been foolish about defense spending. They leave a strategic place like this to be defended by only a small garrison. What do you expect the Separatists to do, eh? Sit on their hands?"

"The Republic forces are spread thin, sir," the officer replied, shrugging. "Do we go in now?" He grinned at his commander and leaned forward expectantly. This was the moment he had been waiting for.

Zozridor Slayke grinned back. "And give them the surprise of their short lives? You bet. Assemble my commanders."

The atmosphere was tense in the wardroom of *Plooriod Bodkin*, as it always was before going into battle—but there was no nervousness. The officers gathered around the battle charts were charged with the anticipation of action, like a group of Cyborrean battle dogs waiting to be released by their handlers.

Zozridor Slayke himself, however, was relaxed, as he always was. Standing a full head above his officers, a mixed group of humans and nonhuman sentients, he would never be mistaken for anything but the leader. It wasn't just his unadorned, long-sleeved, military-style tunic with the high collar, the standard officer's uniform in his army, it was also the body language of his officers—each leaning expectantly toward him, eagerly anticipating his words. Slayke projected the confidence of a man who knew he was in charge and knew what he was doing, and his officers—and every soldier in his fleet down to the lowest ratings—knew it, too.

"Mighty crowded out there—" Slayke gestured at the holographic chart of the space lanes around Praesitlyn and Sluis Van. This comment generated some laughs among his officers. "They outnumber us at least four to one." He made the comment as if he were merely remarking on the brightness of the stars flickering on the chart. "Well, now that we're here, does anyone have a plan?" He looked around expectantly.

"B-but, sir! We thought *you* did!" a man standing next to him blurted out, feigning horror. At this everyone burst into loud laughter. They all knew that Zozridor Slayke definitely had a plan. And they all knew him well enough that they did not need to be told the essence of that plan: attack, attack, attack.

Slayke let them enjoy the moment, then held up a hand for quiet. "Let's see, at last report they had one hundred and twenty-six ships in a cordon around Sluis Van, am I right?" He nodded toward his intelligence chief, who confirmed the figure. "That's bad," he continued, "because the Sluissi will be occupied defending their own world. But the Separatist fleet will also be busy with its cordon. That's good, because those ships

won't be able to interfere with us. The enemy commander has divided his forces. That's good, too. And the
Separatists don't know we're here . . . yet—that's even
better." The way Slayke emphasized the word *yet*, re-
sulted in more good-natured laughter among his officers.

He pointed a finger at the display of the Sluis sector.
"He has about two hundred ships in orbit around
Praesitlyn, many of them capital ships. Now, that's
bad." He stroked his short black beard thoughtfully,
then rubbed a forefinger beneath his nose and pulled
on his earlobe, as if not sure what to say next. He nodded again at his intelligence chief. "Your reconnaissance drone reports a big droid army down there."

"Yessir. They seem to have defeated the defense force
and have taken the Intergalactic Communications Center, as well. I estimate, from the number of transports
on the ground and the quantity of equipment deployed,
that the army tops a million battle droids. They mean
to stay there awhile, sir."

"Well, then. They outnumber us. That's very bad,"
Slayke said. "But they're only droids! That's good."
More laughter.

"Sir, they have managed to block all communications to and from Praesitlyn," Slayke's chief communications officer said. Slayke only nodded. "We have to
assume," the communications officer continued, "the
Republic doesn't know what's happened. I don't know
how they managed that—it must be new technology.
The blasted Trade Federation's got billions of credits
sunk into research, so it's not unlikely. At least our

communications are unaffected, until we get down on Praesitlyn, anyway."

"Those idiots in the Senate," Slayke murmured as though to himself, "will lose this war yet." He leaned with both hands on the edge of the display and focused on the enemy ships around Praesitlyn, bright little blips so numerous that they resembled an asteroid belt around the planet. "We are the only force within striking distance," he said. "You all know the importance of Praesitlyn to the Republic, to our homeworlds, our friends, our families." He paused, then said quietly, "Here's how we're going to do it."

Slayke's fleet was small in comparison to the one he was about to attack, consisting of CloakShape fighters, gun tugs, and *Phoenix Hawk*–class light pinnaces. His capital ships consisted of several *Carrack*-class light cruisers, Corellian corvettes, gunships, and Dreadnaughts. While his ground forces were only fifty thousand strong, they were highly trained, highly motivated, and equipped with armored vehicles, Bespin Motors Storm IV twin-pod military cloud cars, and a full array of supporting arms. The great advantage of this small force was that it was an integrated combined-arms force of infantry, air, armor, and artillery, operating under a carefully thought-out but flexible battle plan. Moreover, Slayke's commanders were officers whom he trusted completely to take tactical initiatives in fluid battlefield conditions.

A reasonable person might think it utter insanity to use a force as small as Slayke's to attack Tonith's army. But Zozridor Slayke was not always a reasonable man.

He turned to his officers and held up his fist. "We go

in like this—" He rammed his fist toward the chart. "A huge armored fist. We'll concentrate all our forces on one sector in their cordon, hit them with everything we've got, and blast open a hole to land the army. It's going to be real hot for our ships in orbit," he added, nodding at his captains, "but we'll be counting on you to keep their orbital fleet off balance. Once we're on the ground we'll close with the enemy and grab him by the belt, hold him tight. That way his fleet won't be able to attack us without fear of hitting his own forces. Our initial attack will be a total surprise to him, and it'll take some time for him to recover. We'll exploit that surprise and cut right through." He paused. "We're about to cross a bridge, and once over, we're burning it behind us. It's do or die."

They all knew that. Once on the ground, Slayke's army could not be reinforced if things went badly. Failure was just not an option. But Slayke was no overconfident fool.

"I have dispatched a message to Coruscant," he continued, "requesting reinforcements." He shrugged. "Perhaps they can spare a Jedi or two." This also caused laughter: everyone knew how much Slayke despised the Jedi.

"Well, look at it this way, sir," an officer in the back of the compartment said. "We won't have to share the glory with them!"

"Well said! Before they can get here to mess things up, we'll have some fun with those metal soldiers down there. Now, what do you think?"

"*Ooooorah!*" the officers shouted, stamping their boots in unison on the deckplates.

"You will have your operations orders before you get back to your ships," Slayke announced. But they were not yet dismissed.

This was Zozridor Slayke's great moment. He had risked everything, even became an outlaw with a price on his head, to get to this place with this army at this crucial instant in time. He saw himself now as the fulcrum of history.

Slayke drew himself up to his full height. He addressed his officers—many, he knew, for the last time. These soldiers had been recruited from all over the galaxy, and they had risen to positions of trust and authority in this small army through courage, devotion, and demonstrated ability. "Remember who you are!" he shouted. The last word echoed through the compartment. "What you are about to undertake is not done for fame or reward or ambition; you are not compelled into this fight by necessity like slaves! We go into battle now out of simple duty to our people."

Slayke paused. The wardroom had fallen completely silent. There were tears in some eyes—all of which were focused on their commander. Slayke took a deep breath. When he spoke again he raised his voice to its full timbre, and it rang from the bulkheads: "Freedom's Sons and Daughters expect every person to do his duty!"

Odie and Erk didn't get far from the caves before once again the ground beneath and the air about them heaved and reverberated to the sounds of battle, this time somewhat farther away.

"General Khamar must be counterattacking," Odie said, removing her helmet.

Erk pulled aside the ground sheet that he was using to protect his face from windblown sand particles and searched the sky. "I don't think so. Look!" He pointed to the north where, just above the horizon, bright fingers of flame lanced down from the heavens. The sky there suddenly exploded in brilliant flashes followed seconds later by a deep rumbling; one of the flame pillars descending toward the ground blossomed into a brilliant chrysanthemum of fire. "Ships are landing!" he shouted. "One was just hit. It's a relief force—Coruscant's sent a relief force!" He threw his arms around Odie and impulsively kissed her on the cheek.

Odie was so surprised—and pleased—she didn't know how to react, so she blurted out quickly, "Sergeant Maganinny said recon troopers always ride to the sound of the guns. Shall we?"

"Turn this thing around and let's go!"

But when Odie depressed the foot pedal, the speeder's motor only whined feebly.

"Out of power?" Erk hoped he didn't sound as worried as he felt. He hopped off the speeder so that Odie could access the power-cell compartment housed in the rear.

"No," she answered, a concerned expression on her face. "And these things are usually maintenance-free."

"Here, look at this." Erk pointed to a small hole in the housing cover. He felt the hole with a finger. "You've been shot. Feel the edges around this hole: it was burned through."

"I—I did have a run-in with some enemy troopers,"

she said, popping the cover. She grimaced and looked away. The compartment was full of grit, and the power cell was coated with sand heat-fused into glass. As they stood looking down into the compartment, the cell gave a little *pop!* and a thin tendril of smoke rose upward. "That's it," she said. "We're foot-mobile now." She stepped back and looked down at her speeder for a moment, then began to cry.

"Hey!" Erk laid a hand on her shoulder. "We're okay. We'll make it."

"It's not that." Odie shook her head. "It's—it's my speeder!"

"Oh," Erk said, mentally kicking himself. "I should've known," he muttered. "A recon trooper and her speeder, a pilot and his fighter." He shrugged. "Come on, trooper, we're both widows now."

Odie smiled through her tears. "It's stupid but, well, you know, that speeder and me . . ." She threw up her hands.

"How far do you think we are from the center?"

"Maybe seventy-five or one hundred kilometers?"

"Can we make it on foot?"

Odie shook her canteen. "If we can conserve our water." They had both drunk as much water as they could hold before starting out from the caves in an attempt to tank up for the long journey ahead of them, but they had been figuring on riding Odie's speeder, not walking.

"Do you know where there's any water along the way?"

Odie shook her head. "We'll look as we go." She popped open the storage compartment beneath her seat and began to withdraw items they'd need on the trek.

"We just have everything going for us, don't we?" Erk said wryly.

"Well, I hope those bug stompers you're wearing will hold up." Odie gestured at her own heavy boots, standard issue for reconnaissance troopers, who needed such footwear to protect their feet and legs from brush, stones, and debris. Erk's boots were much lighter and didn't look very sturdy.

"With me as your copilot, we've got it made," Erk replied as, bowing, he bade her lead the way.

"We are *what*?" Tonith shrieked, jumping to his feet and spilling some tea down the front of his white robe when his chief of staff told him they were being attacked. "By whom? Full details," he demanded, recovering some of his composure.

"Apparently, sir, we were being shadowed by another force. They couldn't have come from Coruscant or Sluis Van, and they had to be small to avoid our detection—"

Tonith impatiently waved a hand at Karaksk. "Get on with it." Already his mind was working. He didn't like surprises, but one had to deal with them. By the time the Bothan finished with his report, his fur was continually rippling, but the worse the news became, the calmer Tonith grew.

"Sir," Karaksk ventured, "I believe you should have stayed with the fleet. The ships are being thrown into confusion." As soon as he uttered those words he regretted them and almost cringed at the angry outburst that he was sure would follow.

Tonith held up a hand. "No, the issue shall be decided here, not in orbit." He paused, and Karaksk sighed with relief that the admiral had let his remark pass. "Very well," Tonith went on, as though talking to himself. "They are much smaller than our force; they are behind us. Here is what they'll do: they will attempt to close with us as soon as possible, get close enough so our ships in orbit won't be able to fire on them for fear of hitting us. We should expect a flexible battle plan and plenty of individual initiative—they'd have to have that, and boldness, to attack us like this." He raised a bony forefinger and waggled it at the Bothan. "There is a fine line between boldness and foolhardiness. Let's see how we can turn that against them. Begin fortifying our positions immediately. We'll let them attack us all they want. When their strength is depleted, that's when we'll counterattack."

Carefully, Tonith recovered his teacup. He shook out the few remaining drops and methodically, in a well-practiced gesture, poured more of the steaming liquid. From close by came the rumble of fighting. He grinned, revealing his purple-stained teeth. "Ah, a challenge," he said, sipping the tea. "Very interesting, very interesting indeed."

The one factor Zozridor Slayke hadn't counted on was Pors Tonith.

8

Supreme Chancellor Palpatine made a series of calls, one of them to Senator Paige-Tarkin.

Senator Paige-Tarkin had never seen the Chancellor looking this worried, HoloNet transceiver image or not. His hair appeared even grayer than it did in person, and his face was more lined by worry. She felt a genuine surge of pity for the great man. She had watched him carefully since his assumption of emergency powers to deal with the Separatist threat, and she believed the cares of public service in this crisis were wearing the poor man down.

"This is a matter of the utmost urgency," he said. "I need to see you at once."

"We can't discuss it now?" she asked. "I'm expecting dinner guests."

"No, I am afraid this venue is not secure for what we have to talk over." The Chancellor's image smiled sadly. "I do apologize for interrupting your plans like this, Senator."

"No, no, not at all, sir, I am at your disposal. How long do you think we'll be?"

"It could take some time, Senator. I do apologize again."

She hesitated. A member of the powerful Tarkin family, Paige-Tarkin was an unabashed admirer of the Supreme Chancellor, and in her public and private life she described him as the one person who could lead the Republic to victory in this crisis. Now he, who had devoted his entire life to public service, was apologizing for asking her to interrupt an evening at home with friends to deal with important galactic business? "No bother," she responded, her voice catching with emotion, "but can you give me any idea what it involves?"

"All I can tell you is that a situation has arisen that might have the most serious consequences for the inhabitants of the Seswenna sector, Senator."

Paige-Tarkin's heart skipped a beat—Seswenna was the sector she represented in the Senate. "Where shall we meet?"

"My apartment, as quickly as you can get here. I must—"

"Your apartment, Supreme Chancellor?" she blurted. "Not your office?"

Palpatine shook his head. "This is a matter of the utmost sensitivity—it's best if nobody knows about the meeting yet. My security droids are sweeping my apartment even as we speak; it would take longer to assure the security of my office. Now I must invite some others, so please excuse me." The image vanished before she could ask who the others might be.

Quickly, Paige-Tarkin canceled her engagements, changed, and called for transportation.

Mas Amedda received the next call. As Speaker of

the Senate and a loyal follower of the Supreme Chancellor, Amedda was best known for keeping his mouth shut and maintaining order during Senate debates. He had also supported granting Palpatine the emergency powers he believed the Supreme Chancellor needed to deal with the Separatists. Palpatine knew he could count on Amedda in this crisis, and his help would be invaluable when the inevitable debate broke out in the Senate.

Then Palpatine summoned Jannie Ha'Nook of Glithnos, a senior member of the Security and Intelligence Council. Ha'Nook saw everything in terms of profit and loss to herself. Although of a somewhat independent mind, she had also voted to grant Palpatine his emergency powers.

Next on the list was Armand Isard, director of Republic Intelligence, a man who knew much but said little.

Finally, Palpatine called Sate Pestage, controller of the Senate's executive agenda. Pestage was a master of persuasion. Many times since Palpatine's assumption of emergency powers Pestage had convinced recalcitrant Senators to get behind the Supreme Chancellor.

Thus Supreme Chancellor Palpatine gathered his staunchest allies to deal with his enemies.

Palpatine's apartment was comfortable but not ostentatious, as befit an abstemious public servant in the service of the people. Since not everyone arrived at the same time, he engaged his guests in small talk until they were all present. As soon as everyone was seated, he nodded to Sly Moore, his administrative aide. At his signal she engaged the security system that provided additional asssurance that no one eavesdropped on their deliberations.

"We may begin, sir," she announced.

"I apologize again for getting you all here on such short notice," Palpatine opened as his guests settled in. "I will come straight to the point. A very powerful Separatist force has captured Praesitlyn. A much smaller force—a rogue force, in fact—is opposing the invasion, but the outcome of this opposition is very much in doubt. Armand, give us the facts as we know them."

"A Trade Federation invasion force—we don't know its size or composition but must assume it is very large and very potent—has taken Praesitlyn. We must assume, because all contact has broken off, that they are now holding the Intergalactic Communications Center. We must also assume that they are preparing to use the planet as a springboard for further incursions into the Core Worlds. We received this information in a message sent by the commander of the force the Supreme Chancellor mentioned, which had been shadowing the invasion fleet for some time."

Paige-Tarkin gasped. "So that's what you meant!" she exclaimed, looking at the Chancellor. "Have they made any move against the Seswenna sector?"

"Not that we know of," Palpatine answered. "But they have some means of blocking transmissions, so anything is possible. We do know that they have invested Sluis Van with another fleet of about one hundred twenty-five ships of different classes, evidently a holding operation, not an outright invasion. We must assume that once they've consolidated their hold on Praesitlyn, yes, they will move against Seswenna, Senator, either by force or by argument."

"We're making a lot of assumptions here. How do we know all this?" Jannie Ha'Nook asked, looking first at Palpatine and then at Isard.

The Chancellor nodded at Isard to continue. "We received intelligence of this event from Captain Zozridor Slayke."

"The pirate?" Ha'Nook interjected. She twisted a lock of hair around a forefinger and pursed her lips as she thought.

Palpatine smiled. "Not anymore. I pardoned him."

"And a good thing you did," Isard added, "because right now he and his army—the Sons and Daughters of Freedom, as they call themselves—are all that is opposing the Separatist force on Praesitlyn."

"Who is commanding the invaders?" Ha'Nook asked.

"Through other sources," Isard replied, smiling cryptically, "we think it might be Pors Tonith of the InterGalactic Banking Clan." He glanced over at Palpatine, who nodded that he should proceed. "We don't know much about Tonith, but he is no pushover. As a financier he is known for his ruthlessness, applying almost military precision and determination against his rivals. Apparently he's had some success leading military operations, too. Anyway, the last message we had from Slayke was that he was about to attack."

"How big is his force?" Mas Amedda asked.

"I'm not sure how many capital ships, but it's estimated he has an army of fifty thousand beings."

"Great balls of fire!" Paige-Tarkin exclaimed. "And he's going up against a whole Separatist army with a force that size? Unbelievable!" The guests all looked at one another in astonishment.

Palpatine steepled his fingers, carefully placing the tips beneath his nose. "So," he began, "the situation is desperate. As you all know, our deployable forces are all engaged throughout the galaxy. I do not believe that Captain Slayke, despite his obvious qualities of bravery and resourcefulness, will be able to expel the invaders. He can only upset them, delay them, and even if he does succeed in this, no doubt the Trade Federation is planning on sending an overwhelming follow-on force to secure Praesitlyn."

"Why would this Slayke and his army ever undertake such a desperate measure?" Ha'Nook asked.

Palpatine shrugged and smiled before he answered. "Slayke is an idealist, a rare commodity in these times." He smiled again and gestured vaguely, as though saying such people were incomprehensible. He cleared his throat and shifted his position. "Now you see why I called this meeting," he continued. "I do not want to give our citizens the impression of hasty decision making, but we must act swiftly this evening. Also, it's very important our people understand the gravity of what has happened and support us totally in our effort to retake the planet and support Captain Slayke—or rescue him, if that's what is required. I need your help because you are all respected and influential members of the Republic who can convince others to put their support behind me in this. I know, I know, I can dispatch forces at will, I have the power to do that, but we are still a democracy and I don't want later to be accused of exercising dictatorial powers or to have my decisions subjected to the sniping of armchair critics after the fact. I'm relying on you to convince your supporters and constituents that I have acted in the best interests of the Republic and that we cannot give up our struggle for freedom because of temporary reverses."

"And I would add this," Isard put in. "Slayke's is not a droid or a clone army. His soldiers are all volunteers and highly motivated individuals. He will give Tonith a run for his credits, no pun intended."

"What forces do we have that we can spare?" Ha'Nook asked.

Palpatine shifted in his chair and stretched his legs. "The garrison force on Centax One, some twenty thousand clones." He shrugged. "We shall have to commit them; they're all we have that are immediately available." Centax 1, Coruscant's second moon, had been transformed during the early stages of the present emergency to provide a staging base for military operations.

"So that means, Chancellor, that we shall have no reserve left to deal with any other contingency?" Ha'Nook exclaimed. "What if we need troops here on Coruscant? Chancellor," she said, shaking her head gravely, "I think this is a serious strategic mistake."

The Chancellor steepled his fingers again and made no reply for a long moment. The others remained silent. At last, Isard leaned forward to speak, but Palpatine silenced him with a glance. "Senator, consider: once the Separatists have consolidated their foothold on Praesitlyn and reinforced its garrison there, we shall never be able to retake the planet. Instead of it being our eyes on that vital sector, it will be a dagger pointed directly at the heart of our Republic. We have no choice. We must act and we must do it now."

"Chancellor . . ." Ha'Nook leaned forward, a forefinger raised to make her point. "If that is the case, then why wasn't Praesitlyn reinforced earlier?"

Palpatine shrugged. "My mistake. I take full responsibility for not foreseeing this event."

"Tipoca City has promised us a large batch of reinforcements," Isard began.

"When will they be ready?" Ha'Nook snapped.

"Two or three months."

Ha'Nook snorted and sat back in her chair. "I will have to think this over, Chancellor. It may require a full vote of the Senate. After all, we cannot endanger the security of—"

"I was hoping to avoid that, Senator," Palpatine interrupted. "Of course I understand what you are saying. But in times of emergency, decisions have to be made; leaders have to take on the responsibility of their offices and commit themselves boldly—"

"And suffer the consequences of failure?" Ha'Nook shot back.

"And accept the consequences, yes, Senator," Palpatine replied. He had expected this from Ha'Nook. He nodded almost imperceptibly at Sly Moore, who had remained hovering silently in the background during this conversation. Only the Supreme Chancellor saw her smile. He rose. "Shall we sleep on it? Let us talk again in the morning."

"And who shall command this expedition?" Paige-Tarkin asked.

Palpatine straightened, smoothed his robes, turned toward her, and smiled. "A Jedi Master," he said.

Jannie Ha'Nook was half expecting the call that came less than an hour after the meeting at Palpatine's residence broke up. The fact that the caller was using a holoshroud to disguise his image did not surprise her, either. That technique was frequently used on Coruscant when politicians, lobbyists, or informants desired to keep their true identities unknown.

"Is that you, Isard?" Ha'Nook asked, laughing.

"I am not Isard, Senator," the caller replied in a deep, gravelly voice as unrecognizable as the image dancing before Ha'Nook's eyes.

"Well, come straight to the point then. I haven't eaten in hours."

"I am your ally, Senator," the image said, "and I wish to help you."

"How?" This could be interesting.

"You have been recognized as a person who is capable of being far more than a practitioner of base political intrigue. I can use my considerable influence to further your career in ways you cannot even begin to imagine."

There was a compelling, even hypnotic quality to the voice. "Go on." Jannie twisted a lock of her hair around a forefinger and pursed her lips in thought. The more the mysterious caller talked, the more hair she wrapped around the finger.

"There are great events about to take place in the

galaxy. You have just come from a meeting where they were under discussion."

"How did—" But Ha'Nook caught herself immediately. Of course someone had been eavesdropping—despite all of Supreme Chancellor Palpatine's measures to prevent spying. It was done all the time on Coruscant, and no one could completely avoid it; total security was never truly possible.

"The invasion of Praesitlyn is but a ripple in a vast wave of history, Senator, and I am about to offer you a ride on that wave."

"Pray continue." Ha'Nook was beginning to enjoy this conversation.

"The events now taking place in the Sluis sector shall be resolved. When they are, someone will be needed to oversee the Republic's interests there. Let me be frank: an appointment as ambassador plenipotentiary can be highly profitable."

"Ah," Ha'Nook gasped.

"Yes," the voice rumbled.

"You can arrange that?"

"Yes."

"How?"

"I can. But I need something from you first."

"I thought we'd come to that." Ha'Nook smiled, but she was more than intrigued with the conversation at this point. Her mind was whirring. Ambassador plenipotentiary? That sounded about right to her. The work of a mere Senator, no matter how influential, could be immensely boring, dealing day in and day out with inanities such as bills for the improvement of the sewer system on Coruscant, or endless discussion of

some silly resolution guaranteeing the religious freedom of some primitive species on some far-flung chunk
of rock. After enough exposure to the routine business
of the Senate in session, even important business failed
to challenge or excite anymore. Here was a chance to
really be in charge of something big!

"Supreme Chancellor Palpatine asked for your support to dispatch a relief force to Praesitlyn. Can he
count on you, Senator?"

"Yes," she answered without hesitation. *What possible difference could it mean to me,* she thought, *if the
relief expedition fails and the Separatists defeat the Republic? If I can't be an ambassador, I can be an ally.*
Whichever way this war came out, Jannie Ha'Nook
planned to be on the winning side.

"Excellent! Stand fast in your support of the Chancellor, Senator, and I shall stand fast in my promise to
reward you." The transceiver went dead.

On the other end Sly Moore sat back and smiled.
Time now to send that message to the Jedi Council.

9

Jedi Nejaa Halcyon had no idea why he had been summoned so suddenly to appear before the Jedi Council. He had already been reprimanded for his failure. Perhaps, after the long period of idleness imposed on him because of the *Scarlet Thranta* affair, the Jedi Council was ready to reinstate him? He desperately wanted a chance to redeem himself. Perhaps this summons was it.

Nervously, he stood before the entrance to the Council Chamber, smoothing his hair and beard, composing himself. The palms of his hands were sweaty. *I'm reacting like a Padawan.* The thought made him smile. He straightened his cloak and entered the chamber.

Eleven of the twelve members of the Jedi Council sat in a semicircle just as he remembered from the last time he had stood before them. The huge windows framed a vast panorama reaching all the way to the city, its skyline reduced to miniature size by the Council Tower's soaring height and the distance. Myriad black specks, aircraft of all sorts engaged in the affairs of the vast metropolitan complex that was Coruscant, flitted over the horizon. It was a clear day, and the sun washed brilliantly over the scene. To Halcyon this vista alone was worth a visit to the Council, no matter what message he was about to receive. He relaxed.

"Welcome, Nejaa," Mace Windu said.

Halcyon bowed.

Yoda smiled. "Since we last saw you, a long time it has been," he said.

"Yes, Master, too long."

"You have been well, Nejaa? You are rested?" Adi Gallia asked.

Halcyon bowed again. "I am well."

"We have an assignment for you," Mace Windu said. He gave Halcyon a searching look. "Supreme Chancellor Palpatine himself recommended you for this mission."

Halcyon tried not to show his surprise. "I—I do not know the Chancellor personally, but I am honored he should have such confidence in me, Master. Why did he recommend me?" he stammered.

"You don't know why the Supreme Chancellor recommended you?" Master Windu asked.

"No, I don't."

Windu nodded as though Halcyon's negative answer explained everything. "Are you familiar with Praesitlyn in the Sluis sector?" he asked abruptly.

"Only that we have an important communications relay there, but I've never been there."

Briefly, Windu explained what had happened. Halcyon listened with growing wonder; this was indeed a major assignment, and it was an honor to be entrusted with it.

"You will be interested in knowing who it is that is

in command of the opposing force," Windu said when he finished describing the situation and the mission.

"Yes, indeed. Nobody but a Jedi Master would dare attempt a counterattack like that, not unless he had a severe death wish." He racked his brain, trying to figure out which Jedi might be in a location from which he could launch such a mission.

"A Jedi he is not," Yoda said, chuckling lightly.

"Not a Jedi?" Halcyon asked, taken aback.

The Council members exchanged quick glances.

"That man is Zozridor Slayke," Master Windu stated.

There was a moment of silence in the Jedi Council Chamber.

Then Halcyon cleared his throat and nodded briskly. "Captain Slayke is a good soldier," he said.

Yoda smiled, and the other members of the Council visibly relaxed. "To hear you say that is good," Yoda said. He nodded at Mace.

Mace Windu spoke in rapid, clipped tones, as if reading a set of orders. "Nejaa Halcyon, you will take a relief force of twenty thousand clones to Praesitlyn. Once there you will effect a landing of your army, assume overall command of the combined force, and destroy the Techno Union army there. You are authorized to dispose your ground and naval forces according to the battle plan you and your staff will devise en route to accomplish this mission in the most expeditious and effective way possible." He paused. "You may select your own staff and designate whomever you wish to be your second in command. Time is short. When you leave here you will repair to Centax One, where your fleet is preparing for departure. You will effect that departure with all possible haste."

"I am honored to accept this mission," Halcyon said formally.

"This Slayke, work with him you can? Toward him no animosity you feel still over his stealing of your ship?" Yoda asked.

Halcyon bowed deeply. "No, Master Yoda. Slayke is an intelligent and resourceful soldier. I was overconfident and foolish, and he exploited my weakness. I am glad," he finished with a smile, "to have him as my ally, and I know together we shall smash the Techno Union forces."

Yoda nodded. "Of our Order, Nejaa Halcyon, a true Master you are."

"Do you have anyone in mind who might be your deputy on this expedition?" Windu asked.

"Yes, Master. Anakin Skywalker."

Was that a hint of surprise in Windu's eyes? The formidable Jedi Master was, as always, hard to read. But all he said was, "Why?"

"He is brave, resourceful, and ready for a real challenge. And he is here, right now, in the Room of a Thousand Fountains."

"But this mission requires Jedi commanders, and Anakin has limited experience leading troops," Adi Gallia said.

"I've been watching," Halcyon replied, "and talking with him. He's been studying battlefield tactics and past battles. I believe he's ready."

"Obi-Wan Kenobi's advice have you sought?" Yoda asked.

"I know Obi-Wan—we've talked about Anakin. He told me Anakin hasn't had command yet simply because the opportunity hasn't arisen, not because he's not ready."

"Is no one else available?" Adi Gallia asked.

"I am sure others are available," Halcyon answered. He took a steadying breath before continuing. "Perhaps one or two other than you yourselves. But what if another emergency arises, one that requires a Jedi experienced in diplomacy, or some other solo mission? Whom will you send if I take someone more experienced, and Anakin Skywalker is the only Jedi left available?"

Windu studied Halcyon for a moment, then nodded. "We leave the selection of your subordinates in your capable hands. But remember this, Nejaa Halcyon: this assignment is as much a trial for you as it is for young Anakin. More important, it is a trial for the Republic. On its outcome may rest the fate of the entire galaxy. May the Force be with you."

Anakin flexed the fingers of his prosthetic hand and regarded the fist it made. The prosthesis that had replaced his right arm and hand was even better than the original. The fingers were electrostatically sensitive to touch. The interface module linking the hand to his nervous system permitted the device to operate as would a normal human hand. The unit was activated by a power cell that didn't require recharging. *If I'd known the thing was going to work this well, I might've had the other arm replaced, too,* he thought wryly. Now, if only it were covered in synthflesh . . .

The phantom pains from the nonexistent nerves in the vanished hand bothered him occasionally, but they were the lesser of several other kinds of phantoms that were troubling Anakin just now.

He rose to his feet. The grotto where Nejaa Halcyon had asked to meet with him was one of many situated at various levels throughout the Jedi Temple. The bench he'd been sitting on was shaded by the overhanging branches from the trees that grew around the pool into which a waterfall splashed; a light mist hung over the pool, condensing on the path where he stood. Altogether this was a very pleasant spot, but Anakin Skywalker was in no mood for pleasant spots this day.

He walked down the path a short distance, did an abrupt about-face, and stalked back to the bench. He drove his right fist hard into the palm of his left hand. The sound of the satisfyingly sharp *smack* it would have made otherwise was deadened by the surrounding foliage. Anakin flicked moisture off his cloak. Voices? He whirled. Two Padawans, a boy and a girl, engaged in conversation, approached down the path behind where he was standing, oblivious to his presence. They suddenly burst into a peal of laughter. They saw him then, standing under the tree in front of the bench that was obviously their destination, and stopped suddenly.

"Oh, I'm sorry, sir," the boy blurted. "We didn't know anyone was here." The girl smiled nervously. They both knew who Anakin was.

Looking at the girl close up, Anakin was reminded—painfully—of Padmé. "I'm here on business of the Jedi Council. I hope you'll excuse me." Not exactly a lie:

Halcyon was before the Jedi Council, so whatever news he had for Anakin would come from there—sort of. But his frustration at the unexpected reminder of his wife must have been too obvious in his tone of voice, because the young man's face reddened.

"Sorry, sir, very sorry," the lad stammered. The pair hastily turned and left.

Anakin suppressed a flash of guilt for having spoken to the young man so sharply, but then he shook his head. No. They'd have to learn their place, just as he had. And what *was* his place? He, too, was still a Padawan, even with all his combat experience and acknowledged talents—and the sacrifice of his arm in personal combat—and still he hadn't heard a word about Jedi Knighthood. He'd been weeks on Coruscant, studying, practicing his skills. Under the circumstances he'd rather be spending his time with Padmé—*No, no, don't think of that,* he told himself. *Think of the future.* Master Halcyon was going to offer him something—that had to be why he'd asked for this meeting. Coruscant was rife with rumors these days. Everyone was talking vaguely about new threats from the Separatist forces. Big things were afoot, and Anakin itched to be a part of it all.

Jedi Nejaa Halcyon. Anakin had gotten to know him rather well during the time of his enforced idleness. Anakin respected Master Halcyon, but could not understand what had gone wrong on the mission to Bpfassh, which had ended in such great embarrassment to him and the Jedi Order. Specific details about the mission had been kept quiet, but still there was talk. Anakin assumed Halcyon had been recalled to

Coruscant because the Jedi Council was trying to decide on his future employments, but he was too polite to ask. What really mattered to Anakin, though, was that Halcyon seemed to like and have confidence in him, and now that might be about to pay off.

He sensed Halcyon's approach and turned to greet him at the same moment that Halcyon said, "A credit for your thoughts." Both men smiled.

Halcyon draped an arm across Anakin's shoulders. "My young friend," he announced, "I have come with news."

"Yes?" Outwardly Anakin maintained an icy-cool demeanor, but inwardly his heart raced.

Halcyon, though, could sense the surge of anticipation in the young Jedi and he smiled more broadly. "The Jedi Council is sending us on a mission. I've been given a chance to prove myself—no, don't deny it, Anakin, that's what this assignment is, a trial—and I've asked for you to be my second in command. The Council agreed."

Anakin felt a very slight twinge of disappointment. Halcyon, not the Jedi Council itself, had asked for his services. But . . . the Council had agreed, so . . . "What is the mission, Master?"

"Are you familiar with the Intergalactic Communications Center on Praesitlyn, in the Sluis sector?"

"Not really. I know it's a vital communications hub, but I don't know much more than that."

"It's been seized by a Separatist force. We're assuming the garrison has been defeated, but the enemy force is being opposed by a friendly armada that was tracking the invasion fleet and has broken through the cordon around Praesitlyn. They are now heavily engaged with the Separatist ground force. We are going to relieve that army, if it can be done." He paused. "We're not sure how big the Separatist force is, but it's very powerful; taking it on will not be an easy job."

"Who's in command of the intervening force on Praesitlyn?"

Halcyon smiled weakly. "Zozridor Slayke."

Anakin looked up sharply. "You mean—?"

"Yes, the same—my nemesis." Halcyon's lips twisted in a wry smile. "But we are going there to retake Praesitlyn, Anakin. If Slayke's still alive and able to fight by the time we get there, well, he'll be so glad to see us I don't think I'll have any problem working with him."

Neither said anything for a long moment. The water splashed merrily into the pool; Anakin didn't notice the occasional droplets of moisture that fell from an overhanging branch down the back of his neck. "Master, what, precisely, will be my role as your second?"

"We'll have an army of twenty thousand clones. We'll form it into two divisions. I'll hold overall command, as well as command of one division, and you'll command the other. If anything happens to me, you will then command the entire fleet. You can do it, Anakin—that's why I picked you." He paused and nudged a glob of mud with the toe of his boot. "Our force includes supporting arms and combat-support units, so besides the clone infantry force, we'll have small contingents from all over the Republic as integral parts of our army. We'll have to do most of our planning on the way."

"When do we leave?"

"Soon, very soon."

"So, what's our first step?" Anakin asked.

"Our first step? Well, first you and I are going to meet someone very special."

No society is without its underworld. With more than a trillion inhabitants, Coruscant, the gem of the galaxy, the hub of the Republic, had its bottom feeders deep beneath its soaring spires. Coruscant was like a vast ocean: while luxurious liners full of happy party-ers plowed the waves on the surface, hideous denizens, strangers to light, lurked in the murky depths far below. It was into this world that Jedi Master Nejaa Halcyon took Anakin.

The Golden Slug, a run-down flophouse with a sleazy bar in the lobby, was the only spot of activity on a dead-end side street just off a main underground thoroughfare. Piles of garbage littered the gutter; one flickering sign—the other lights weren't working—provided dim and intermittent illumination. The farther end of the street beyond the Golden Slug was enveloped in pitch darkness.

"What are we doing here?" Anakin whispered as he carefully threaded his way through the garbage. A sudden barrage of guttural shouting and the noise of something being smashed came dully from inside the Golden Slug, and a tall, reptilian creature burst from the hotel lobby and skittered past. Wondering what in the galaxy could scare a Barabel, Anakin reached for his lightsaber.

"Easy does it, Anakin," Halcyon murmured, putting a restraining hand on the Padawan's forearm.

The sign above the Golden Slug's doorway sputtered. GOL EN S UG it announced, two of the letters long since broken in some drunken melee.

"I don't think we'll have any trouble," Halcyon went on, "there's no need to have a weapon in hand. But be ready—just in case."

Anakin glanced toward the end of the street where he sensed something lurking. Then he reached out into the Force to scan the hotel lobby. "Well," he whispered, "there aren't any Force-sensitives in there, so lead on."

The lobby was a shambles. Most of the furniture that was still intact was unoccupied, except for something snoring loudly on one of the couches. An overhead fan stirred the stale air lazily. A bored clerk, a character with a huge set of ears and a long proboscis, glanced up at the two Jedi, squeaked an exclamation, and disappeared underneath the counter. Several patrons sat at the bar on one side of the lobby. The floor there was littered with debris, the remains of a destroyed table and chairs—and something that looked suspiciously like an arm or a leg freshly separated from its owner.

An unprepossessing figure hunched alone at one end of the bar. Three other barflies sat at the opposite end, as far from the figure as they could get, studiously ignoring its presence.

"Grudo!" Halcyon shouted.

The lobby went deadly silent. Even the fan slowly whirring above them seemed to stop its lazy perambulations. The bartender dropped the glass he was pretending to clean and ducked behind the bar.

The hunched figure turned slowly, stepped to its feet, and moved toward them. Anakin blinked. It had bumpy green skin and bulging, multifaceted eyes; a stubby pair of antennae protruded from its head. Numerous sheathed knives hung from two bandoliers crossing its chest, and more knives rested uneasily in scabbards on its belt. A pair of blasters sat in holsters on its belt. Anakin thought he could make out other tools of the bounty hunter's trade poking out here and there. The dim light glinted wetly off the knives where their metal was visible, as if they had recently been used. This being was the meanest-looking Rodian Anakin had ever seen—and he headed straight toward them. Anakin reached again for his lightsaber, but Halcyon held him back with a steadying arm; the Rodian's hands were empty.

As soon as he got within reach, the bounty hunter lurched forward and grabbed Halcyon around the waist and danced him around in a macabre circle.

"Halcyon!" he hooted. "It's good to see you, old friend!" He stopped dancing, and the two embraced warmly.

"This is Grudo," Halcyon told Anakin as soon as he was able to disentangle himself. "Grudo, this young Jedi is Anakin Skywalker. Say hello, Anakin."

Anakin smiled crookedly and said, "Hello."

The Rodian released Halcyon and stood at attention. "Jedi Anakin Skywalker, Sergeant Grudo reporting," he said in an impeccable Basic that contrasted sharply with his appearance. "I'm pleased to make your acquaintance, sir."

"Sergeant?" Anakin asked, bemused by the Rodian's clipped tones. "I didn't know bounty hunters had ranks."

The barflies, who had been studiously ignoring the trio, turned their heads for a quick glance, then returned their attention to their drinks. Even the bartender peeked out from hiding when Grudo hooted in raucous laughter.

"Come," Grudo commanded, and led them to the bar; the barflies huddled inconspicuously over their drinks. "Barkeep! Come out from wherever you're hiding—I want to buy a drink for my friends!"

The bartender, a nervous, sallow-faced human, edged up from his hiding place. Looking like he was ready to drop back down to safety at any moment, he poured a dirty yellow fluid out of a bottle containing some kind of root into glasses that looked none too clean. Grudo raised his glass in a toast. Halcyon and Anakin followed suit.

"Aaarrggh! Whew!" Halcyon gasped. Grudo patted him hard between the shoulder blades. "Strong stuff!" the Jedi Master wheezed, thumping his chest with a fist.

Anakin sipped cautiously at his drink. The liquid burned its way past his lips, over his tongue, down his throat, and into the depths of his stomach, where it exploded in a ball of blazing fire. He choked. "Good!" he rasped. "Very good! Thank you—Grudo."

Grudo laughed at Anakin's feeble attempt to hide his discomfort. "There's nothing *good* about the taste of that drink," he said. "It's supposed to incapacitate Gamorreans, Trandoshans, Wookiees, and other large species, so Rodian bounty hunters can take them into custody without getting hurt."

The Rodian was smaller than a normal human male, but Anakin remembered the Barabel who had run screaming out to the street and looked pointedly toward the shambles in the lobby. "I don't feel in the least incapacitated, Grudo. Are you sure you need to tranquilize a large person to capture him?"

Grudo laughed and slapped him on the back. "Maybe. *If* I was a bounty hunter."

"If you're not a bounty hunter, what are you doing on Coruscant? I thought the only people your world allowed to leave home were bounty hunters."

Grudo raised a suction-cup-tipped finger in front of his pendulous snout, so much like a human raising a shushing finger to pursed lips that Anakin had to laugh. "If *I* don't tell, *you* can't tell," the Rodian whispered conspiratorily. Then he turned to Halcyon. "I'm glad to see you again, Halcyon. And happy enough to meet Jedi Skywalker, as well."

"And I was very glad when I heard you were still here, Grudo. Though I'm surprised that you haven't found another job."

Grudo shrugged. "Unfortunately true. Which is hard to imagine in time of war. But . . . you know the bounty hunter reputation." He shook his head. "Makes it hard for an honest Rodian to find work as a soldier. Do you have a job for me, Nejaa?"

"Possibly."

"There's trouble on Praesitlyn, I hear."

The two Jedi glanced at each other in surprise.

"How do you know that?" Anakin demanded.

Grudo shrugged noncommitally. "Word gets around."

Halcyon sighed. "Well, if they know about our mission here, the Separatists know, too, or they will soon." He gave his drink a suspicious look and pushed the dirty glass aside, then said to Anakin, "Grudo isn't a bounty hunter, he's an old soldier. He's been in more battles and on more campaigns than most regular soldiers. He's led troops in battle his whole life. I want him to come with us. He'll be a good addition to our team, especially when it comes to directing small-unit operations." He turned to Grudo. "Will you come with us?"

"So you two are going to be generals on this mission," Grudo said.

Halcyon flinched and muttered, "Nobody's supposed to know that."

Grudo smiled. "You're going to need a good sergeant major. Especially the whelp here." He flung a surprisingly strong arm across Anakin's shoulders, forcing the young Jedi's nose almost into his glass. "Let's have one last drink—for old times, and for the future!" He leaned over the bar to peer at the cowering bartender. "Give us a round of the good stuff this time!"

10

Both Lieutenant Erk H'Arman and recon trooper Odie Subu had received survival training and were well aware of the dangers of dehydration. But neither had been prepared for this long walk through the high-desert region, and it proved much more difficult than either had anticipated. It was one thing to fly over it at ten thousand meters or zoom along on speeder patrols with communications and comrades left and right, but walking, without any prior preparation, was another thing entirely. Although they tried to conserve their small supply of water, the heat, the lack of humidity, and the physical exertion that confronted them every step of the way caused them to lose more fluid than they could replace. Also, the burning sun was so intense they almost wished another sandstorm would strike just to provide them some cover. They began to blister, even under their clothes. And that first night, as the daytime heat radiated off into space, they almost froze to death.

By noon on the second day they were in serious trouble. They found a rock outcropping and flopped down in its shade.

"Let's rest here awhile," Erk croaked. Odie didn't bother to reply, but dropped down, raising a cloud of dust. They lay there in the intense heat and panted. Odie's canteen was long since empty, but neither could remember when or who had sucked the last drops out of it. It was getting hard for them to focus their thoughts on anything.

Dimly, Erk became aware that Odie was saying something. "What?" he rasped, but she didn't answer immediately. She said something else, several words, but he couldn't make them out. With effort he rolled over and faced her. "What did you say?"

"Let's head back home, Tami," she answered. "It's time for chow."

Tami? Oh, yes, wasn't he one of Odie's buddies? Erk had difficulty remembering exactly—anyway, he thought it was someone she had mentioned. "Odie . . . ," Erk gasped, but, too exhausted to point out that she was hallucinating, he just rolled over on his back. Odie continued talking to her imaginary comrade.

The heat enveloped them like a scorching blanket despite the shade provided by the rock overhang—and as the minutes dragged by and the sun moved gradually, even that slight protection began to disappear. Once it did, they would fry. But there was nothing they could do about it now. Soon the sun blazed down on them like a raging furnace. The air was so hot it hurt to breathe.

Gradually—everything was happening in slow motion now—Erk became aware that something was blocking the sunlight. He squinted up at it. It was huge. It spread its enormous wings and made a terrible squawking noise. A giant beak filled with razor-sharp teeth fastened onto one of Odie's legs and bit it off. Dimly, Erk was aware that there was no such creature native to Praesitlyn, but here it was anyway. As it threw back its head to swallow the limb, Erk drew his sidearm with his last remaining strength and fired.

Watching an army preparing to embark on a campaign is one of the most exciting experiences in life, second only to being shot at and missed. Grudo the Rodian had been shot at and missed many times, but even he caught the tempo of the moment as the fleet based on Centax 1 prepared for war.

While the Republic's available ground forces were limited to the twenty thousand clones now embarking on the waiting ships, fortunately its naval forces were of considerable potency, consisting of many capital ships—enough, Halcyon reasoned, to break through the Separatist fleet he would encounter blockading Praesitlyn. The situation on the planet's surface would be a different matter, but getting there, he hoped, should at least prove easy.

Halcyon had chosen as his flagship the *Centax*-class heavy frigate *Ranger*. Built by the expert shipwrights of Sluis Van and outfitted in the shipyard on Centax 1, the *Ranger* was a fast and powerful vessel equipped with the latest weaponry and auxiliary systems. It was on this ship that Halcyon held his first council of war as the fleet readied to depart.

"We have deployable ground forces of twenty thousand clones. I will form them into two divisions. I'll command one, and Anakin the other. As I see it, each division should consist of four brigades of four battalions, each with four infantry companies. This will give us great maneuverability in the attack and—"

Grudo snorted. "I thought you knew better than that, Halcyon. No wonder I beat you so handily that—" He caught Anakin looking at him with intense interest and dropped that line of thought. "Divide your divisions by threes: three brigades, each with three battalions of three companies."

"What?" Halcyon asked.

"I think what he means," Anakin interjected, "is that two up, one back, is not only the standard military formation, but also a more powerful structure. With larger formations you have more combat power. You attack with two brigades or battalions or companies and keep one in reserve. At least, that's what it looks like in everything I've studied."

Grudo's laughing hoot warbled with the swinging of his snout as he shook his head side to side. "Age must be getting to you, Halcyon—you're forgetting things even the youngster knows!"

Halcyon nodded ruefully. "I stand corrected, then. We'll organize our troops into a triangular formation.

"On to logistics," he went on quickly. Anakin listened intently.

The next days passed in a whirlwind of activity. The two Jedi and their Rodian comrade soon began to work as a well-oiled team. Grudo followed Anakin everywhere, interjecting advice whenever appropriate, but otherwise not saying much. The clone infantry had been divided among several transports, in order to minimize their losses if a ship was hit, so the trio were kept busy moving among the ships. At night they met in Halcyon's stateroom to go over the details of the day.

One evening, Halcyon asked Anakin, "Are you familiar with the capabilities of the specialized troopers?" He was referring to the fifty clone commandos aboard the battle cruiser *Teyr.*

Anakin nodded. Clone commandos were trained to be used for only the most dangerous missions, and as such were bred to possess a larger degree of independent thought and action than ordinary troopers. Equipped with highly advanced armor and weapons, they were capable of fighting successfully on their own, but with a Jedi commander their potential as an attack force was virtually unlimited.

"They're yours, then," Halcyon told him. "Take Grudo, go over to the *Teyr,* and get to know them."

Surprised and pleased, Anakin wasted no time getting a shuttle to the cruiser.

Earlier, he had taken charge of his division, met with his brigade, battalion, and company commanders, introduced himself to the troopers, inspected them in ranks, and asked probing questions about their armor, equipment, and weapons. Grudo had had him bone up on these things and read the readiness reports the division's commanders had submitted.

"You're their leader," he had said. "Soldiers don't respect a commander who doesn't know their weapons, equipment, and tactics better than they do. But remember this: all the clones are like brothers—twin brothers—and all clones think they're the best. They work best under their own officers; they wouldn't fight under me. Under you, yes, of course—you're a Jedi. But although they respect you as a Jedi, now you must show them they can respect you as a soldier like them. You have to show them *before* we go into battle that you know what you're doing."

Anakin had done his best, and Grudo had been impressed with his handling of the troops. Now, as he headed for the *Teyr*, he was feeling more confident, eager to meet the clone commandos who were to be his to command.

The captain in charge of the commandos called them to attention when Anakin entered their bay.

Anakin traded salutes with the captain. "At ease!" he commanded. He spread his legs slightly and clasped his hands behind his back as he scanned the soldiers before him. There were two sergeants in the group, judging by the green markings on their armor.

"I am Commander Anakin Skywalker," he began. "You have been assigned to the Second Division, which I command. You will serve as part of my headquarters battalion, under my personal direction. Captain, you will not report to or receive orders from any other officer during this campaign. I will assign you missions as required by the tactical situation on Praesitlyn. I will not ask you to do anything that I wouldn't do myself. Is that clear?"

"*Arrrrruuuhh!*" the troopers shouted in unison, coming to attention with a loud slamming of boots on the deck. The compartment echoed with their shouts.

The captain permitted himself a slight smile. "My troopers are ready, sir!" he reported.

Anakin glanced at Grudo, whose face was pulled

down in the Rodian smile. "Captain, have the troopers fall out and fall in by their assigned bunks. I wish to inspect their armor, weapons, and equipment."

Anakin spent the rest of the night inspecting the troopers. He found no dust, grease, or dirty weapons. Throughout the inspection, the captain followed Anakin with a datapad at the ready, but he was never told to enter anything.

On the way back to the *Ranger*, Grudo leaned over and told Anakin, "You did a good job with that inspection. You looked at everything you should, and weren't petty, like some might have been. The troopers appreciate that. They'll fight well for you, I can tell."

Feeling his chest swell with pride and excitement, Anakin swiftly ran through the Jedi Code in his mind: *There is no emotion; there is peace . . . A Jedi does not act for personal power . . .* He was here to do a job—and what was more, a job that would cost soldiers their lives. He would do well to remember his training, he told himself. He was a Jedi, and he would do the Order proud. Taking a deep breath, he reached out to the Force, seeking serenity . . .

11

Someone was pouring water over Odie's face. The water was warmer than normal human body temperature, but to her it was as sweet and cool as any mountain freshet, heavenly balm to her blistered face and cracked lips, and she gulped it down for what it was: life. She luxuriated in the cooling wetness and tried to laugh, but her voice wouldn't work. She opened her eyes and saw a shadowy figure bending over her.

She tried to speak, and managed to croak, "Erk."

"Yes," the shadowy figure standing over her said.

"Erk?" she said again, mustering what she could of her returning strength to get the name out. But the voice that responded was strange. "Who are . . ." was all she could get out.

"Sergeant Omin L'Loxx at your service," the shadow replied. "Who did you expect?"

"Pilot," she gasped.

"The flyboy? We're pumping him up, too. We put him under another shelter, give you room to breathe under here. My partner is Corporal Jamur Nath. Come on, can you get up? We're taking a big chance hanging around out here like this. There are droid patrols all over the place." He poured more liquid into Odie's mouth.

She felt less groggy and managed, with a little bit of help, to sit up. She looked around, but didn't see anybody other than Erk and the two recon troopers. "What are you doing here?" she asked.

"Scouting. The Separatists have patrols out all over the place, looking for weak spots to hit. It's our job to find them and disrupt their plans—and report any maneuver units we find trying to circle our positions." He changed the subject. "I see by what's left of your gear that you're a recon trooper. Where's your speeder?" He lifted her head gently and gave her more to drink, then shook the canteen. It was almost empty. "You sucked up a full two liters. It'll bring you around in no time. Good thing you two aren't one of the other species. This stuff is brewed up special for humans— restores fluids, electrolytes, minerals, all sorts of stuff you lose through dehydration. What happened to you two? If you hadn't fired that shot, we'd never have known you were here, and you'd both be dead by now."

Brokenly, Odie explained what had happened. "I—I don't remember firing a shot," she stammered.

"Well, must've been your boyfriend over there. Or you just don't remember doing it. When you get into the last stages of death by dehydration you hallucinate all over the place. But I suppose you know that. We saw the flash and came to investigate. Whoever it was fired straight up into the air. We figured it was a signal."

Odie wanted to deny that Erk was her "boyfriend" but didn't have enough energy, so she let the man's observation pass. Instead, she asked, "Wh-who are you?"

"I'm a recon trooper, just like you. Were you part of the garrison here? Poor devils. Come on, let's get you on your feet and moving. You can ride on the back of my speeder. That sidearm of yours. Can you use it?"

"Y-yes. But where'd you come from? You weren't part of General Khamar's army."

"No, we weren't. We'll explain everything later. Right now my first priority is to get out of this desert and back into our positions before one of their patrols spots us. While you were coming to, I reported in and got orders to bring you in immediately. Come on, take my hand, let's get going."

Odie staggered slightly as she stepped out from under the shelter half, involuntarily raising a hand to shield her eyes from the brilliant sunlight.

"Here," L'Loxx said, handing her a helmet, "put it on. It's a spare." Gratefully, Odie donned the helmet, a standard recon trooper's multipurpose field operating unit. She was feeling much better now. Expertly, she adjusted the helmet's features. There stood Erk with the other trooper beside his speeder. It was like seeing two old friends again, Erk and the speeder. The latter was almost the image of her own machine.

"You ride with me, trooper," L'Loxx said. "Come on!" he called to Corporal Nath. "Let's get out of here!" Rapidly, L'Loxx repacked some of the gear on his speeder to make room for Odie. "Hold tight," he cautioned, "we're not going to waste any time getting back to base." Odie knew from the instant the sergeant put his machine into motion that he was an expert.

Cautiously, L'Loxx guided them over some extremely rough terrain. He stopped below the crest of a long ridge. "Just below us is a dried-up riverbed. We'll follow that almost all the way back. Do you know it?"

"Yes. Your base is near the Intergalactic Communications Center?"

"Right. We occupy the center and the foreground below the plateau. We're dug in in front of them—our rear is in this direction. Their fleet can't intervene because ours is holding them too close. The first day we fought off waves of battle droids, but we held our lines. Now we've settled down into positional warfare, sniping at each other and sending out patrols to find weak places in the lines. It's a standoff. Whoever gets reinforcements first wins."

"Are reinforcements coming?"

"Ours? I don't know. Our commander sent a message to Coruscant before we attacked, before we entered the zone where the enemy managed to block all other transmissions. Theirs? Yeah, they probably planned big reinforcements before they attacked. All right. Draw your weapon. I'll drive, you shoot."

Odie drew her blaster and took it off safe. "I'm ready," she said, more strongly than she felt.

"Listen up," L'Loxx said over the tactical net. "We have a long ride ahead of us. If we meet up with enemy patrols we have one advantage. We have an extra person on each speeder who can shoot while the other maneuvers. You can shoot, right, flyboy?"

"Sure can, dirt-eater," Erk snapped back. "So can my copilot there."

L'Loxx grinned. "Well, I guess you rescued us then, huh? The enemy is riding seventy-four-Zs. Your 'copilot' knows what that means if it comes to a running fight."

Odie groaned. She certainly did know what that would mean.

"But we aren't getting into any fights," L'Loxx continued. "We're taking it easy and we're playing it very cool. So follow me."

They descended rapidly into the riverbed. The bottom was strewn with boulders and debris. In some places water had cut deep, narrow gorges that temporarily blocked out the sunlight; in others it had meandered over the flat country, fully exposed to the surrounding terrain. Still, the banks were high enough that if they moved carefully they could find a degree of cover. They traveled that way for half an hour.

They were attacked at a point where the river rose to the surface in a floodplain. The first bolt sizzled between Odie and L'Loxx so close it singed the cloth on his shirt and burned the tip of her nose as it passed. For the briefest instant Odie wondered what had happened; then instinct honed by training took over. She swiveled and fired in the direction the shot had come from—and then she saw them: three 74-Z speeders coming like the wind across the floodplain. L'Loxx jumped his speeder over the low bank and gunned it directly at the attackers. Badly aimed blaster bolts sizzled past them. Odie leaned around his right side and snapped off two more blasts. She could clearly see one hit a speeder, but its armor absorbed the energy and bled it out onto the sand as an electrical discharge. The other hit the rider she had aimed at, and he flipped backward over the tail of his machine.

"Whooie!" someone—it sounded like Erk—yelled over the comm. Odie glanced to her left. A few meters behind them and a bit off to the side she could see Erk leaning forward around Corporal Nath's side, firing methodically at the two remaining enemy speeders. The four racing speeders threw up tails of dust that hung suspended in the still air behind them.

"Break! Break!" L'Loxx shouted. He swerved to the right so sharply that Odie's knee scraped the ground as he roared around the oncoming troopers. The maneuver confused the attackers. Behind them, instantly and at two hundred kph, L'Loxx aimed his speeder at the closest enemy rider, who broke to his left sharply. L'Loxx followed him around, keeping close on his tail. Odie kept firing, but her bolts disappeared harmlessly into the enemy speeder's armor. Still, it forced the enemy trooper to keep his head down and concentrate on maneuvering his machine, so he couldn't return the fire.

A huge cloud of dust rose up to cover the melee as the speeders pirouetted desperately around each other, seeking to ram their opponents or gain an opening for a shot that would count. Flashes from blaster bolts ripped through the curtains of dust so that anyone observing from a distance might have thought the cloud was pulsating with an energy and life of its own. The dust, thick and choking in the windless air, clung to them like a second skin and blinded them. Suddenly, L'Loxx stopped his speeder and took off his helmet. Odie was taken aback by the utter silence.

"Where are they?" she whispered, swiveling her head, listening carefully for the sound of the other speeders. There was none. No firing, either; the only sound was the air rasping in their lungs.

"Good shot," L'Loxx whispered, meaning the one with which Odie had hit the first enemy trooper. "I can't raise my partner," he added. "He must be down."

Odie pushed her helmet back behind her ears so she could hear better. It was then she felt the gentlest of breezes passing by her face. She looked up. The sun penetrated the dust like a small golden ball, but gradually it grew brighter. The cloud was dissipating. The two tensed like threatened feral beasts, not sure if they'd have to attack or run.

The wind grew stronger and the dust began clearing rapidly. Like a curtain being rolled back from a stage whereon a tragedy was about to unfold, the dust cloud trailed away on the wind to reveal, not ten meters from where they were standing, an enemy trooper sitting on his speeder. He was looking away from them.

Before Odie could swing around and fire, L'Loxx leapt off the speeder, sprinted across the space between them, and smashed into the enemy trooper. Odie could clearly hear the crash as the two slammed into the dirt. The enemy trooper was big, and he wasn't human. The two grunted and cursed in different languages as they rolled in the dust, but the advantage was with the enemy trooper, who wasn't as stunned as L'Loxx had thought.

Odie ran up and leveled her blaster at them. "Surrender or I'll shoot!" she shouted. No good. She risked hitting L'Loxx if she fired. She holstered her piece and jumped into the fray.

The enemy trooper grunted as Odie's weight came down on his back, but he didn't loosen his grip on L'Loxx's throat. He stood up slowly, holding L'Loxx by the neck with one arm and shaking him. With the other hand, he reached over his shoulder, grabbed Odie by the head, and wrenched her off his back. He flung her away like a doll; she crashed and rolled in the dust, stunned. He dropped L'Loxx to the ground, put a massive foot on his chest, and drew a macelike weapon from his belt. L'Loxx lay half stunned, gasping for breath. The enemy trooper, a Gamorrean, whirled the mace around his head several times, grunting victoriously in his own language. L'Loxx groped for his blaster, but he'd lost it in the struggle. He grabbed the foot pinning him to the ground and tried to wrench it to the side, but the Gamorrean was too strong for him to budge.

A blaster bolt hit the Gamorrean in the right pectoral. He grunted in pain and dropped the mace. With his left hand he drew his own sidearm and fired. Odie was finally able to get off a shot and hit him squarely between the shoulders. A parasitical morrt fastened behind the Gamorrean's left shoulder detached itself and burrowed into the sand as its host staggered, whirled, and fired back, but his shot went wild and hit L'Loxx's speeder instead. Another bolt hit the Gamorrean in the lower spine, forcing him to his knees. Unable to turn around and shoot back, he fired again in the direction where Odie lay. But now L'Loxx found his blaster and he put three quick bolts into the Gamorrean, who finally crumpled to the ground and lay still.

Erk walked up, his blaster covering the downed Gamorrean. "You picked the wrong guy to tangle with," he said. With one arm he helped L'Loxx to his feet, keeping his blaster trained on the still form of the Gamorrean. "How many bolts did that guy absorb before he went down?" he asked in awe.

Odie limped up. "Five, at least. I think he's still breathing. Are you all right?" She broke into a great grin as if she'd only just now recognized the pilot standing there.

"Where's my trooper?" L'Loxx asked before Erk could say anything.

"I'm sorry, Sarge, the bad guy shot him. I dropped him with one shot. I'm sorry about your man, I really am."

L'Loxx nodded. "My speeder is trash, but we now have two serviceable seventy-four-Zs. I'm going to collect my partner's body. You come with me, Odie, and bring back the other seventy-four-Z. Flyboy, you stay here. I don't know if they reported us or not before they attacked." He nodded at the prostrate Gamorrean. "Our long-distance transmissions are blocked, so maybe theirs are, too. But we'd better move out smartly, just in case. Where'd you leave Jamur?"

Erk pointed. "That way, about half a kilometer."

"All right. You wait for us here."

*   *   *

"I need those reinforcements, my lord," Pors Tonith said to the image of Count Dooku floating in front of him.

The Count's somber features twitched in annoyance. "I thought I told you to deal with Commander Ventress on all operational matters."

"This operation will fail without those reinforcements," Tonith continued, ignoring Dooku's displeasure.

"You will learn to follow my orders." At Dooku's meaningful look, Tonith blanched. He remembered another time Dooku had taught him a lesson. At that time, he'd experienced a sudden shortness of breath as if a great weight had been placed on his chest. He'd struggled to draw in air. As quickly as the seizure had come over him, it had passed. Dooku wasn't near enough to use the Force against him now, but Tonith knew he'd suffer in the future if he persisted.

"I am following your orders, my lord," he said hastily. "They are to capture and secure this planet. The plan you devised for this campaign, which I've followed to the letter, called for immediate reinforcement once that was done. I repeat, lord, where are they? This rogue force is causing me problems, and if it is reinforced before I am, we will lose Praesitlyn."

Dooku's image floated silently before Tonith for a long interval before he replied. "They are on the way. Why did you not foresee this intervention?"

Tonith caught his breath. Now he was being blamed for not anticipating what had happened? Monstrous! Blast the Count. But he replied calmly, "It was one of the great imponderables of war, my lord, but we still hold the Intergalactic Communications Center intact. But I have lost many droids, and can replace only a few of those losses from my repair shops. For every one of them we kill, they destroy five or six of my droids."

"You started out with a million battle droids; throw them all in at once and overwhelm this rogue force."

"My lord," Tonith responded patiently, "I have far fewer than a million droids now. Wave attacks are wasteful and bad tactics. If I were to do that I'd be left with a severely reduced army and no reserve. The opposing commander is very shrewd. He keeps his lines close enough to my own that I can't bring my heavy weapons to bear effectively without sacrificing my own forces and weakening my own defenses."

"We all must make sacrifices," Dooku said dryly.

Tonith paused, mustering his dwindling patience. "Lord, his ships are keeping mine at bay in orbit so I can't rely on reinforcements from their crews, and they cannot engage the ground forces with their onboard weapons systems. I repeat, if the Republic sends reinforcements before—"

"He cannot replace his losses at all, can he?" Dooku smiled.

"No, my lord," Tonith replied sharply, "but if the Republic has been alerted and dispatched a force against us—"

"—so your enemy is being worn down by attrition."

"—and they get here before my reinforcements—"

"They will not. Keep your foe engaged. Hold your positions. Help is on the way. I have confidence in you." The transmission went dead.

Far, far away Count Dooku smiled. That Pors Tonith was a feisty one, but a bit too cautious—just like a banker, he reflected. But he was the right officer for the job. Things were going precisely according to plan. It just wasn't the plan Tonith thought he was following.

12

"An army travels on its stomach, I'm here to tell you," old Quartermaster Mess Boulanger stated, his bright blue eyes sparkling. No one before now had ever asked him the details of his duty as a quartermaster officer, and since this young commander—Skywalker was his name—had inquired, old Mess was not about to let him go without a thorough lecture on what he called "the sinews of war."

Carefully, Mess caressed his long, drooping brown mustaches and regarded Anakin balefully. He held up a bony forefinger. "Many think it's valor, planning, the offensive spirit that wins battles, sir, but I say, 'Pish!' I'll tell you what wins battles, sir. It's logistics! The sinews of war, I call it, sir. Logistics! That's the thing, I'm here to tell you. That's what makes armies function. Well—" He made a deprecating gesture with one hand. "—that is if they're not *droid* armies." He spat out "droid." "With them, all you need is lubricants and spare parts, but!" He held up his forefinger again. "That's logistics, too! Yessir, even with an army of machines, you've got to know how much lubricants, spare parts, electronic components to stow in your ships! But with living beings, it's far more complicated, far more, I'm here to tell you. We're lucky this time, sir. Clones all eat the same foods. But when you have other creatures along, well, you've got to figure in their special diets. Very complicated, sir. But it's been done, I know the formulas . . ." His voice trailed off as if he were contemplating those very formulas.

"Remember this—" Boulanger perked up again, although he looked askance at Grudo, not sure whether he should be talking about sensitive matters in front of someone he wasn't convinced wasn't really on a bounty hunting mission. "COMETS-Q! Yessir, it's COMETS-Q that gets you to the battlefield, sustains you once you're there, and gets you home again. That's the combat-support branches of modern warfare, sir: Chemical, Ordnance, Medical, Engineer, Transportation, Signal, and Quartermaster."

Anakin was about to ask a question when Mess suddenly added, "And that's not all. Not at all! Do you know, sir, what an army consumes in just one day of heavy combat? Do you know how many calories an infantry soldier burns up in just one day's fighting? Eh? Well, I do, I'm here to tell you, sir! You have to know this if you're going to supply your army in the field. You have to estimate casualties, too, yessir, very important. You may think that's impossible, the nature of combat being unpredictable in the extreme, but it's not, it's not." He nodded his head firmly so his mustaches waggled. "Before we even left Coruscant, I conferred with your operations staff, and we estimated that by the third day of battle you'll have lost ten percent of your fighting force. So we stocked enough medical and hospital supplies to accommodate such losses. Remember, for every one soldier killed in battle, three others are wounded!" He held up his forefinger again as if this were an immutable law of nature that permitted no argument.

"Ask him." Boulanger gestured at Grudo, who'd sat silently throughout the lecture. "If he's been around as much as he claims, he'll tell you."

Grudo nodded and said, "It's all true."

Boulanger bowed his head in satisfaction.

"Quartermaster, we may have to supply Captain Slayke's forces when we arrive on Praesitlyn. Have you planned for that?" Anakin asked.

"Yessir, I have, I have! You know, of course, that Praesitlyn is an uninhabited world—no forage there for an army, none, unless you want to poison yourself on the horrid plant and insect life. It's a quartermaster's nightmare, I'm here to tell you! And yes, Captain Slayke's command is a mixed bag, I've been told, humans and others, all living, breathing, eating entities who must be fed, clothed, and quartered. So before we shipped out I took care, careful care, sir, to stock rations that I knew were palatable across the board, as it were, food that we can all live off.

"And another thing. What does an army do with its waste? Aha! Yes, what an army eats is turned into waste and you have to account for that in garrison and camp and depot! Ever consider that? No, I didn't think so."

Boulanger fell silent again, then went on: "I have been at all the staff meetings, you know."

"Yes?" Anakin answered, his attention focused on

the array of charts and lists and inventories that cluttered the screens in the quartermaster's compartment. "What?"

"I have been at all the staff meetings," Boulanger repeated. "What did you think of the logistics annex I wrote for your operations plan?" He leaned back, crossed his hands on his potbelly, and glared defiantly at Anakin, daring him to say anything derogatory about his work.

"Yes, Quartermaster, excellent work!" Anakin answered quickly. He kicked himself mentally for not having had the foresight to study the logistics annex before this visit. He'd given it only a cursory glance when it had been presented by his divisional chief of staff. And he'd never noticed Boulanger at the briefings.

"No one ever asks me any questions about my work. That's because they don't have to. I'm good at what I do."

"Yes, Quartermaster Boulanger, you are and you have and I thank you for your excellent work." Anakin nodded at Grudo and they both rose, shook hands with the quartermaster, and headed for their shuttle. Anakin resolved that as soon as he got back to his quarters on the *Ranger,* he'd call up that logistics annex and go over it as thoroughly as he had the other parts of the plan. Once done, he'd call for Boulanger, sit down with the logistician, and go over every detail with him until they were firmly fixed in his own mind. He would memorize how many metric tons, long or short, of supplies, fuel, and ammunition a force his size needed to sustain itself in combat, and how many ships it took to transport those commodities to the battlefield. He had to know what was on which ships, too, in case any were lost in the landing or fell behind the rest of the fleet because of mechanical problems. In his many talks with Halcyon about tactics and strategy and leadership, this subject had come up frequently and the older Jedi had emphasized its importance, but they had not discussed it in any detail. Anakin would now. He vowed to discuss logistics with Halcyon as soon as he'd boned up on it.

"Don't be the kind of commander who leaves the details to others," Grudo had warned him. He wouldn't.

"You have dealt with Captain Slayke, Grudo, tell me about him." They were in the shuttle going back to the *Ranger* after their meeting with Quartermaster Boulanger. "I would also like to know how you came to be friends with Master Halcyon."

"It would be better if you talked directly to Master Halcyon about those things," Grudo answered.

Anakin was silent for a moment. "I have asked him, but he's been very vague about it. I know the three of you were involved in the incident on Bpfassh. I've asked him, indirectly, about Slayke, but all he would ever say was that he held no grudge against him and would work with him as his comrade once we reach Praesitlyn."

"Yes, that's Nejaa Halcyon! Fair in all things."

"I know, Grudo. But I must work with Slayke, too. I have to know more about him, and since Master Halcyon is reluctant to talk about what happened, I have to ask you."

"Is that an order, sir?" Grudo asked formally.

"Yes," Anakin replied just as formally. "If that's the only way I can get you to talk, it's an order."

"Very well. Slayke is a warrior. A great warrior, too, not some fat-faced man with milky-smooth skin. He's a very big man. He fights with head, heart, strong right arm! He's a being of principle, and brave, too. Handsome for a human, or so I'm told."

"You don't have to tell me what he looks like—I'm going to see him soon enough."

"Maybe you'll see him," Grudo said darkly, "maybe not. Everyone dies, more die in combat."

"Yes, Grudo, as you have told me. More than once—as I've seen many times for myself over the past two and a half years," Anakin said sharply. "Please continue."

Zozridor Slayke had established his reputation prior to the outbreak of the Clone Wars as the commander of a Republic corvette, *Scarlet Thranta*. His background was obscure, and it was assumed he had worked his way up in the navy to command his own warship through talent and ability. Profoundly dissatisfied with the Senate's dilatory approach to dealing with the Separatists, Slayke had decided to do something on his own. Without orders, he'd detached his vessel from its command and proceeded to launch a series of stunning raids on Separatist shipping and naval forces. He was immediately labeled a pirate, and a bounty of forty-five thousand credits was put on his head.

But Slayke didn't see himself as a pirate. He mistreated neither the civilians nor the military personnel he captured during his raids, and the proceeds from prize ships and their cargoes were evenly distributed among his crew or donated to worthy causes. The last transmission he'd sent to navy headquarters from *Scarlet Thranta* set the tone for his subsequent enterprises: "While the Senate sleeps, a great evil threatens the peace and freedom of the peoples of our galaxy. Our politicians, who neither work nor sacrifice, have forgotten, if they ever knew it, that freedom is not free, that the price of freedom is constant vigilance. We, the crew of *Scarlet Thranta,* are the children of your beloved Republic! We are your sons and daughters. We are the Sons and Daughters of Freedom! Follow us!" This message became a clarion call for oppressed beings everywhere in the galaxy, and in a very short time Slayke had put together a small but formidable fleet that not only caused considerable embarrassment to the Republic Senate, but served as a thorn in the side of the Separatist powers, as well.

"I know this because I was with Captain Slayke," Grudo said. "You see, Slayke has the right personality to command, the personality to lead. Soldiers follow him."

At loose ends, as he often was between wars, and entirely on his own at the time, Grudo had volunteered for service with the Sons and Daughters, not out of sympathy with their political views, but because the group was illegal and the prospects of some good battles looked promising.

"Tell me about Slayke, the man," Anakin asked.

Grudo's snout twitched. "Captain Slayke is a commander you can talk to. He listens to every soldier, and there were many times I heard him tell his soldiers that the only difference between him and them was ceremony, privileges of rank, you know. He said that every soldier who fights alongside him is his sibling, that rank has no privilege in combat. Not with the Sons and Daughters, anyway."

"And Halcyon?"

"He came to arrest us."

At the special request of the Senate, the Jedi Council had selected Jedi Master Nejaa Halcyon to command an expedition to apprehend Slayke and bring him to Coruscant to stand trial for piracy and treason, not necessarily in that order. To his credit, Halcyon had protested the order. In his opinion, Slayke was only doing what the Senate should have done on its own. When asked what he would do if the decision were up to him, he'd answered boldly, "I'd go to his aid." But the Council's decision was that no matter how just the cause, the threat to the Republic could not be met by renegade captains operating on their own without the authority of the Senate. Orders were orders, and Halcyon obeyed.

Halcyon's ship was *Plooriod Bodkin*. He shadowed Slayke's fleet for weeks, waiting for an opportunity to pounce on his flagship and arrest him. He knew, rightfully, that once Slayke was in custody, the Sons and Daughters movement would dissolve and no longer be able to interfere in galactic politics. He thought Slayke had made a fatal error when he dispersed his fleet to various ports to refit and recruit and, aboard his own flagship, *Scarlet Thranta*, made for Bpfassh in the Sluis sector. Halcyon followed.

"But Slayke didn't make a mistake," Grudo said. "You see, we knew we were being followed. Slayke also knew there was a Jedi in command of the force sent after him. How he knew this, I don't know, but Slayke told me that himself. He also told me that those who command the Force are very dangerous, but that he, Slayke, uses his brain, which is more powerful than the Force." Grudo hooted softly. "I don't know, but that time Slayke was right."

"How did Slayke manage to capture Master Halcyon's ship?" Anakin asked. He couldn't imagine anyone being smart enough to steal a Jedi Master's ship. But Slayke had.

"That was my doing," Grudo told him.

Taking refuge on the double planet Bpfassh was a brilliant move on Slayke's part; with its complex system of moons, sparse population, and vast wilderness areas, Bpfassh was an excellent place to hide a starship. Besides, the inhabitants, while not sympathetic to the Separatists, were not exactly allies of the Republic, either. As far as any of them were concerned, Slayke was a pirate, and that would assure their silence if questioned by his pursuers. Slayke had no intention of disabusing them of that notion.

"It took time for Master Halcyon to find us, but he did." Grudo tapped a suction-cup-tipped finger against his snout as he contemplated a spot in a far corner of the compartment. In his mind he was on Bpfassh again, reliving the event. He sighed. "I fought Nejaa Halcyon in personal combat. Just him and me. It was wonderful, wonderful." He lapsed into a happy silence; it was some time before he continued.

Halcyon's plan of attack had been simple and direct. Once he'd located *Scarlet Thranta,* he simply swooped down on the camp, disembarked his force, and rushed the place. Slayke's defensive plan was also simple and direct. He had dispersed most of his crew to lose themselves in the Bpfasshi towns and cities, keeping with him only enough men to operate a starship—and Grudo.

The only being Halcyon found in the camp was Grudo, armed with every weapon in a bounty hunter's armory, hooting challenges at the Jedi and his landing party in Rodian, which few of them could understand, but which made clear that he was not going to come along peacefully.

"Where is Captain Slayke?" Halcyon had thundered.

In answer, Grudo had hurled two knives in his direction. Everyone ducked except the Jedi Master. The weapons *thunked* into the ground between his legs, a clear challenge to combat. Grudo eschewed the use of the blasters slung on his hips and drew another pair of knives. Brandishing the weapons, Grudo advanced menacingly a few paces.

A lieutenant took aim at the Rodian with his blaster, but Halcyon ordered him not to fire. "I'll take care of this," he told the man. He picked up the knives, tested their balance, and went out to meet Grudo in individual combat.

"I never knew why he did that," Grudo reminisced. "His mission was to take *Scarlet Thranta* and capture Slayke, not fight an individual combat. But fight we did, and everybody saw us. He never drew his lightsaber. When I dropped my knives and weapons belts, so did he, and we fought hand to hand. Ah, what a warrior! You know the business about Jedi not feeling anger or hatred, but that day—ah, Nejaa Halcyon needed a fight! He didn't fight like a Jedi at all. It was very strange, very wonderful."

Anakin shifted uncomfortably.

"I've never known how Slayke knew this fight would happen," Grudo mused. "When he left me in camp he told me, 'Grudo, let no one pass!' He told me it was very important that I stand my ground. He told me, 'Grudo, have no fear, the Jedi will never hurt an unarmed being.' Sooo, we fought, and what a fight it was!"

Halcyon had not wasted any time maneuvering to get a position of advantage over the Rodian; he just waded right in, and Grudo advanced to meet him. Halcyon's party formed a large circle, and some of them took bets on who would win. Their attention was fully focused on the contest before them.

"Halcyon seemed unwilling to use Jedi tricks"— Anakin assumed he meant the Force—"and fought like an ordinary warrior. So I used his momentum against him. Many times I flipped him to land jarringly on the hard gound. But Halcyon sprang back up every time and came right back at me." He hooted a soft laugh. "He was fast enough to get through a few times, and he hit hard enough to bruise—including a couple of bone bruises."

Covered in perspiration, his clothes torn in many places where Grudo had grabbed him to throw, Halcyon had pressed home his advantage of speed and dexterity while the Rodian, hurting from the many blows the Jedi Master had rained upon him, managed to keep out of Halcyon's grasp. Each time one or the other struck a blow or made a throw, *Scarlet Thranta*'s crew sent up a roar of approval. Soon the ground the two fought on had been churned into a morass. Both contestants had lost any sense of time, and as the fight dragged on they began to stumble and miss opportunities as physical exhaustion began to take its toll.

"The fight stopped when Slayke stole *Plooriod Bodkin*. You should have seen Halcyon's mouth drop, like a door opening: *plop!* Everyone stared as the ship rose up on a pillar of fire, getting smaller and smaller and then disappearing. Halcyon froze, eyes on the sky. Nobody moved. I could have killed him then, but I didn't. I knew the fight was over, that Captain Slayke's plan had worked. There's no honor in killing an opponent when he's looking away, and I respected Nejaa Halcyon for fighting like he did—he never once called on the Force during the fight, as far as I could tell." He hooted softly for a moment, then said, serious again, "I don't understand why he didn't kill me after his ship was taken, but he didn't."

Slayke had disabled the drives on *Scarlet Thranta*, leaving Halcyon and his men stranded on Bpfassh for several months until a repair ship could arrive. Grudo had been taken without further struggle as Halcyon's prisoner—the only quarry to show for the whole mission. As the weeks dragged by in idleness, they had gotten to know each other fairly well. Finally one day Halcyon said, "Grudo, I'm letting you go when we get back to Coruscant. I'd be the laughingstock of the whole galaxy if I returned from this mission with only one prisoner. Here's the deal: for your freedom, you stay put until I can find some use for you."

In the meantime the Senate relented on its charge of treason and piracy, and Supreme Chancellor Palpatine, bowing to the inevitable and making the best of the situation, commissioned Slayke to continue raiding Separatist shipping and outposts.

"So," Grudo concluded, "I found rooms at the Golden Slug and there I waited until you and Halcyon came for me."

The shuttle had been parked in the loading bay on the *Ranger* for some time before Grudo finished his story, its pilot fuming in the cockpit.

"Strange, isn't it, how fate arranges our lives?" Grudo pondered. "Here we are now, very near to where I first met Halcyon and where I last saw Captain Slayke. Two very great men, and I have been honored to serve them both. Now, soon, we all meet again, and this time we're all allies. Life is good!" He paused for a moment, then said, "I wonder what Captain Slayke is doing down there on Praesitlyn right now."

13

They could smell the battlefield before they ever got in sight of it. L'Loxx pulled his speeder into the shadow of a rock outcropping. "Now's where it really gets hairy," he told Erk and Odie. "There's about a kilometer of open terrain we've got to cross to get to our positions. It's constantly under observation, and the enemy is always directing harassment and interdiction fires onto it. Our labor droids have built a series of bunkers connected by deep trenches throughout the area—once we get inside our defensive perimeter, we'll be all right. But it's that race across the open ground where you'll have to really be on your toes. I've done it several times. Zig and zag a lot. Follow me—I know where to cross our lines. The challenge for today is *widow* and the countersign is *orphan,* in case we get separated."

"What *is* that smell?" Erk asked, wrinkling his nose.

L'Loxx smiled wryly at the pilot. "Right, you don't have any experience with fighting up close." It was the disdain of the infantry soldier, who lived and fought and bled in the mud, for those who slept in beds and fought in what foot soldiers considered clean environments. "You don't know. There are tens of thousands of troops down there, all stuck in one area, without running water. They start to smell after a while." He looked away, and his face went blank for a moment. "Besides, we haven't had time to bury all our dead." He shook it off and returned to the matter at hand. "Here's what we'll do. I'll go in first on Jamur's speeder. They'll recognize me as friendly. Once I'm in, you two come on the seventy-four-Zs. You can't see it from here, but there's a redoubt down there that's got this whole area covered in case the enemy flanks us and comes in from the rear. I'll tell them not to fire on you, and the other outposts will direct counterbattery fire on the enemy guns. That should distract them enough so you can get through with no problem. Remember the passwords because they *will* challenge you. Can you handle that speeder there, flyboy?"

"Sarge, one of these days I'll get you in the backseat of a fighter and show you some real handling," Erk said.

L'Loxx grinned. "I look forward to that day, Lieutenant. One final thing. We've determined that whoever's controlling the enemy guns only reacts to movement, so if you fall or are wounded, lie still and you won't be a target."

"How long do we lie there?" Odie asked.

"Until we come out and get you. Ready?"

Slayke's army had dug in along a dry riverbed that faced the plateau on which the Intergalactic Communications Center sat. Various strongpoints connected by a trench-and-tunnel complex had been constructed. The remains of uncounted thousands of destroyed battle droids and war machines littered the complex, mute evidence of the heavy fighting that had been going on. Right now the lines were relatively quiet. Occasionally high-energy weapons directed their beams into the defenses, or Slayke's artillery lanced out at the enemy positions, but otherwise there seemed to be no movement at all.

Almost from the instant L'Loxx headed down the slope, high-energy ranging weapons began to take him under fire. It took him a full thirty seconds to cross the intervening open space, zigging and zagging without any apparent pattern, and disappear into the safety of a trench line where he was protected from the enemy guns.

"Ohboy, ohboy," Odie muttered, putting her speeder into gear and roaring down the slope. She made it halfway to the trench line before the enemy opened fire, confused momentarily by the presence of one of their own speeders crossing no-being's-land. Obviously, whoever or whatever was operating the enemy fire-control system was slow to make the connection that the bikes couldn't belong to their side, since no lone recon trooper would be making a dash for the enemy lines. At that point Slayke's own artillery responded to the enemy fire, which had slackened considerably by the time Odie made cover.

Erk swallowed nervously. The palms of his hands were sweaty on the speeder's controls. He'd quickly learned how to operate the machine on the long trek across the desert, but what was required of him now would be a degree of skill in riding that he wasn't sure he possessed. One mistake he would *not* make was to exit his position in the same place as the other two had; by now every enemy gun would be trained on that spot. Carefully, he guided his speeder down the ridge about a hundred meters. That meant he'd have to aim for the trench line at an acute angle. Would the terrain look so different approaching from that angle that he'd miss the entrance? Would the violent maneuvering disorient him?

He gunned the speeder, cleared the ridgeline by ten meters, and slammed down on the other side with enough force to jar his teeth. Caught off guard, the enemy gunners didn't fire at him at first, but after a few seconds beams began lancing down all around him, slagging the ground where they struck. Erk zigged and zagged, left, right, right, straight ahead for a few meters; stop for a one-second count; then straight ahead for a few more meters, executing sharp turns every few meters. He could feel the heat of the near hits as the enemy gunners tracked him. They could have laid down a curtain of fire between him and the trench but didn't. Instead they kept tracking him as an individual target, as if trying to score points in a game.

Erk never saw the depression in the ground. Just as he crossed the depression's forward edge, a bolt struck the speeder's fuel cell and it exploded in a violent orange blossom, but he had already pitched headlong over the controls and slammed down into the ground with enough force to knock him unconscious. Those few seconds saved his life because the enemy gunners, or whoever was controlling them, seeing him lying on the ground and not moving, apparently thought he had been killed in the explosion.

The next thing Erk knew someone was hauling him to his feet. "Come on! Come on!"

It was Odie. Groggily, he straddled the machine she guided him to and held on to her for his life. The speeder leapt forward at top speed, almost throwing him off. She swerved sharply to the right and again to the left, the speeder cutting the turns so close that his knee dragged along the ground. In seconds they were inside the trench. Odie switched off her engine, and willing hands emerged from the bunkers to help the pair off.

"Fine work!" Sergeant L'Loxx shouted. "Flyboy, I sure hope you navigate that fighter of yours better than you did that speeder! You should have a medic see to that knee."

Erk nodded dumbly, still dazed from being thrown. Then he gathered himself and asked, "Where's the aid station?"

"Fifty meters or so that way there's a connecting trench." L'Loxx pointed to the right. "Follow it, you can't miss it." He turned to one of his soldiers. "Frak, show him the way. Wait for him and bring him back. If the docs can't take care of him right away and you think he's all right, bring him back—he can get treated later."

While the sergeant was instructing Private Frak, Erk pulled himself to his feet. He looked to see how high the lip of the trench was. Confident that he was protected from direct fire, he followed Frak down the trench.

Odie's concerned eyes followed Erk for a moment, then decided he was going to be all right and asked a more immediate question. "Any chance of getting something to eat?"

"That's what all of us would like to know," L'Loxx answered. "What I can do is offer you a place to rest out of the elements." He showed her into a small bunker with a cot. Odie didn't care that the cot was filthy from the many unwashed soldiers who had slept on it—at least it was off the ground. She was asleep as soon as she closed her eyes.

Sergeant L'Loxx woke her an hour later. "Come on," he said. "Captain Slayke wants to see you and the flyboy."

Odie sat up and rubbed her eyes. She mumbled something—the only word L'Loxx could make out was "Erk."

"He's back and he's been taken care of. Let's go. The captain's waiting for us."

Slayke's army, composed of volunteers from all over the galaxy, was a polyglot conglomeration of species. As far as possible, Slayke had organized his units to keep individuals of a species together. As the trio negotiated the narrow trenches, at one point they squeezed past a squad of Gungan engineers rebuilding a caved-in bunker; in another sector a company of Bothans staffed observation posts. And everywhere was the detritus of war: destroyed battle droids, discarded weapons, abandoned personal items, and empty supply containers of all kinds littered the positions; engineer and labor droids scurried everywhere, collecting weapons and ordnance for salvaging, rebuilding damaged walls, helping living beings scavenge for supplies.

The command post was in a bunker deep underground. It was a hubbub of organized disorder, officers and noncoms taking reports from the outposts, others passing on orders, staff officers dealing with the myriad details required to keep an army operational in combat. At the center of it all was the commanding figure of Zozridor Slayke.

Sergeant L'Loxx approached the captain, came to attention, and saluted. "Recon report, sir," he announced.

"Omin, I see you made it back again." Slayke nodded for him to proceed, and L'Loxx made his report, concluding with the discovery of Erk and Odie and the trip back to their lines.

Slayke held out his hand. "Welcome to my victorious little army. Do you know if there are any other survivors of General Khamar's force?"

"Nossir," Erk answered. "That doesn't mean there aren't any, just that we didn't see anyone else."

Slayke shook his head. "Too bad. We could use the reinforcement, but since you're all there appears to be, you'll have to do. You're a fighter pilot, Lieutenant? I'd like to assign you to an aircraft, but we're all out of them just now. But you, trooper, you're recon? Reconnaissance is my eyes and ears. I rely heavily on troopers like Omin here." Odie was surprised at how Slayke used or even knew the first names of his soldiers. "The enemy is constantly trying to outflank us and take out positions from the rear. That's why recon troopers are so important to me. I need someone to replace Corporal Nath. He was a good man, Jamur, but he's gone now. Would you be willing to take on the job?"

With Slayke standing there looking straight at her with his penetrating eyes, it was very difficult for Odie not to shout out *Yessir!* but she didn't. Instead, she said, "If you don't mind, sir, I'd rather stay and fight alongside Lieutenant Erk." She swallowed hard but couldn't stop her face from turning red at the words. "He's a pilot, sir—he doesn't know how to fight on the ground. He needs someone to hold his hand." She blushed more brightly when she realized how what she said could be taken.

Slayke raised his eyebrows, glanced at Sergeant L'Loxx, who just gave a noncommittal shrug, and turned to Erk.

"Um, she's my copilot, sir, sort of, that is," Erk said.

"Oh?" Slayke answered. "Come over here with me." He gestured at a hologram map table behind where they stood. On it was a three-dimensional display of Slayke's troop dispositions. "Here, this dry riverbed is no-being's-land, the dividing line between our armies. The lines are very close together there." He grinned wolfishly. "I had us move in so close that his ships in orbit don't dare fire because they'd destroy his own droids. That's assuming any of his ships can break contact with my fleet to pay attention to what's happening down here. He caught on quickly and keeps his forces just as close to mine so my ships can't fire on his ground forces.

"This redoubt," he said, pointing at a fortified outpost, "is the most advanced part of our lines. It's called Izable, and it's there to warn us of any change in the enemy's dispositions, any preparations he might be making to attack us. About six hundred meters behind

Izable, but out on the flanks, are two more forts, Eliey and Kaudine. Here, where we are now, is the main position in our defenses. About six hundred meters behind us is the final redoubt, Judlie, where you came into our lines. Judlie covers our rear. These five strong-points are massively dug in, and each has a three-sixty-degree field of fire, fully interlocked with the fields of fire from the other positions, so if the enemy gets through anywhere along our lines all the forts can bring fire on him. Here, here, here, and here are ar-tillery positions, equally well dug in, but their guns are registered on every square meter of our own lines, so if the enemy breaks through they'll be taken under direct fire. The redoubts are connected by a series of tunnels and trenches to allow us to shift soldiers and supplies from one point to another as needed. This place is an engineering marvel. We built it in just two days while under fire. That's thanks to our engineers and hun-dreds of labor droids. Engineers saved this army.

"On the other side of this riverbed are the enemy's positions, occupying this large, flat plain. This mesa, back here, is where the Intergalactic Communications Center is located. That was the enemy's objective, and I'm sure he's holding it in considerable strength. I'm sure that as members of General Khamar's army you're familiar with how this place is laid out. Whoever's in command over there is smart. He tried six times to take us by storm and we beat him off each time. Not without losses on our side, but we cut his droids down by the thousands. He took Izable twice, and we took it back from him each time. Now he's content to probe our lines looking for weak spots, attempting to outflank us, and digging tunnels. Yes, he's got one going right now, at a depth of about one hundred meters, headed straight toward Izable. When he gets there he'll set off a mountain of explosives and blow Izable sky-high. So we're digging a countermine to go under his and blow it before it reaches Izable. Be interesting to see who gets there first, won't it?" Slayke grinned fiercely.

"What are our chances?" Erk asked.

"Before we attacked I sent a message to Coruscant asking for help. Maybe it'll come in time, maybe not. Until then we're on our own, but we've really messed up this guy's timetable." He gestured at the enemy positions on the holomap. "My guess is he's waiting to be reinforced, too. Whoever's opposing me over there was sent here to secure the center, not garrison it, so there's got to be a large follow-on force coming along soon. If it gets here before we're reinforced . . ." He shrugged.

"What are you planning to do until then, sir?" Odie asked.

"Do? Well, I'm going to kick them as hard as I can." The officers standing around the map laughed. "And you two—I can always use a pair of gunners up at Izable. How about it?"

"Yessir."

"Sergeant L'Loxx, get them fed, issue them some equipment, and get them up to Izable. They can report to Lieutenant D'Nore for further assignment. Good luck." He held out his hand and they shook.

The meal they were given consisted of field combat rations designed to sustain life at a high rate of metabolism, not to satisfy epicurean tastes. When they were finished eating, L'Loxx gave them each an equipment belt. "They're standard infantry load-bearing equipment harnesses, but we've added some extra tools we've found useful in the field. Check out the pouches first chance you get and familiarize yourself with their contents. Could save your life in a pinch."

Lieutenant D'Nore was a harassed Bothan struggling with the responsibility of maintaining his outpost on 100 percent alert. It was he who had led the assault party that had most recently recaptured Izable from the battle droids. Since then, the only sleep he'd been able to get was in brief snatches. "I'm not letting them retake Izable," he told his two new fighters. "You'll work in an advanced listening post covering sector five." He didn't bother to indicate where "sector five" in the outpost might be before he was off to confer with the soldiers in sector three, shouting over his shoulder as he left, "I'll talk to you two more later. I had three people down there, but they were all wounded and evacuated. So whatever you do, don't fire your weapon unless you're attacked. I don't want the enemy to know we've reoccupied the listening post." With that he disappeared down a communications trench.

A sergeant standing nearby said, "Come on, you two, I'll take you down. Be sure not to expose yourselves above the trench line, or you'll get zapped for sure." Crouching low, the pair followed him off in the opposite direction from the one the lieutenant had just taken. After some twistings and turnings, the trench ended at a fortified embrasure. "Sector five," the sergeant announced. Bloodstains and shreds of clothing marked the spot where medics had treated the last crew operating the gun.

"I've never even seen a weapon like this, much less know how to operate it," Erk said, looking at the E-Web repeating blaster.

"I've been trained on all types of infantry weapons," Odie replied. "I'll fire the blaster, you monitor the power generator." She turned to the sergeant. "When will we be relieved?"

"When you're relieved, and I don't have any idea when that will be," he answered. He handed them each a ration packet. "Make them last—they're all we have left. Sleep in shifts. One of you monitor the tactical net at all times. Comm check every thirty minutes. Don't miss one. Fire your weapon only when you have a target. You aren't down here to stop an assault, only to give us a warning if one comes and slow them down a little. When they start closing in, that's the time to go back up that trench to the main defensive position as quick as you can. It's up to you to decide when to bug out, but don't wait too long. Your communications call sign is *Hope Five;* the command post is *Izzy Six.* Synchronize your chronos—it's sixteen fifteen. Check in at sixteen forty-five." With that, he scuttled back up the communications trench.

Despite her brave words, Odie hadn't trained exhaustively with the E-Web repeating blasters, and it took her several minutes of examination to refamiliarize herself with the system. When she felt confident enough, she began explaining it to Erk.

"This blaster should be connected to the other ones in the outpost by its built-in long-range secure comlink," she said, pointing out each component as she mentioned it. "That means if we come under attack, the targeting systems on the other blasters will automatically zero in to give us supporting fire and vice versa." She rapidly checked the comlink. "Good, it's working. Everything's still powered up, so we don't have to go through that sequence—that can take up to fifteen minutes."

"What'll this thing do?" Erk asked, looking at the blaster. He unfastened his equipment harness and tossed it in a corner.

"Might want to keep that on, Erk," she warned. "You never know when you might need something in there."

"Yeah, I've glanced at it—mostly groundpounder beauty aids, most of which I don't even know how to use. So what's in those pouches?"

"Neat stuff. I haven't had a chance to inspect everything yet but—"

"I want you to teach me how to use this blaster, Odie. I don't need all that junk slung over me to do that—it'll only get in the way. You tell me if there's anything hanging on here I might need, all right?"

"Sure. Well, this blaster, see, it's a pretty deadly anti-personnel weapon. Its effective range is only two hundred meters, but its maximum range is out to half a kilometer. With the interlocking fields of fire, I don't think any droids will get through. Your job will be to monitor the power flow so the gun doesn't overheat during action. If I get disabled, just switch to the power generator's preset mode—this switch here. That'll prevent dangerous surges, but it also reduces the weapon's rate of fire considerably. I'll teach you everything you need to know about how to use it, then we can spell each other."

"How'd you learn all this stuff?"

"Recon troopers are infantry, too," Odie answered, "so I've been trained on weapons, even if I don't carry a blaster rifle."

The embrasure had been drilled out of the rock in a way that allowed for plenty of overhead and flank protection. Forward observation was through narrow slits cut in the stone. Erk peered through one of the viewing ports. In the fading light he could still clearly make out the blasted ground between sector five and the dry riverbed, which was littered with destroyed droids. He wondered what had happened to the defenders of this position when it had been overrun. For the first time, a feeling of hopelessness began to possess him. How could anyone expect them to survive in this position? "We'll have to sleep with our headgear on," he remarked, "since we'll need infrared capability once it gets dark."

"Right. The blaster has an infrared target acquisition system. Before it gets too dark to see, I'll show you some more things about it."

The night passed quietly. The lines were probed in other sectors, resulting in intermittent blasterfire. At those times the tactical communications net came alive with reports and orders, and both Erk and Odie became fully alert, but once the shooting died down they took turns trying to catch some sleep. They divided the night into two-hour watches. Odie had taught Erk enough about their weapon that he could operate it by himself and deliver immediate fire if anything moved in their sector. Even watching through his night-vision devices, Erk's eyes played tricks on him: irregular mounds seemed to move if he stared at them long enough. He found himself rubbing his eyes and shaking his head frequently to clear his vision. He fought to stay awake. As a fighter pilot he knew very well how fatal inattention could be, but he wasn't in a high-performance fighter now, he was sitting in a damp, rocky crypt that smelled of blood and feces, hunger gnawed at his stomach and made him faint, he hadn't slept in ages, and he ached all over. His knee, in particular, throbbed painfully.

He sighed, shook himself, blinked. First light would be in a few minutes, then dawn. Usually he loved this time of day, before the rest of the world was awake, and everything was quiet, clean, peaceful. He shivered. The nights in this part of Praesitlyn were very cold and the days scorching hot. He looked down at Odie. She had drifted off to sleep as soon as it was her turn. He smiled. She could've been out there with the recon troopers, doing what she did best, riding free like the wind, but instead she had volunteered to stay with him, and here she was in this hole, the only thing between her and the invading army a thin wall of rock. When they got out of this mess . . .

Erk's heart fluttered. Something out there had moved! His palms on the aiming handles suddenly grew sweaty. He nudged Odie with his toe, and she snapped awake instantly.

"Something's out there," he whispered. He was fully alert now, as every fiber in his body reacted to the adrenaline surging through him. He was surprised to hear himself chuckling in anticipation. "Come on, come on," he whispered, focusing the gun's optics, impatient for the action to begin. He could see as clearly as day through the sighting system. Then the entire field of vision through the firing port seemed to heave up and come at him.

"Izzy Six! Izzy Six! Hope Five. Here they come!" he said urgently.

Erk began firing into the mass of oncoming battle droids. He was aware of Odie at his side, monitoring the power surges as the blaster roared.

A tiny voice inside his helmet asked, "Hope Five, Izzy Six here. What is the enemy strength? Repeat, what is the enemy strength? Over."

"Thousands of them," Erk shouted. "Thousands!"

14

My Dearest . . ." No, that wouldn't do, too impersonal. He started over. "My love . . ." No, no, too, too ordinary. He thought uncertainly about what to say next. Try this: "I miss you more than I can say. My heart is overflowing with love for you, my dearest, sweetest . . ." He wrote in this vein for a while on a sheet of flimsiplast, then paused and reread the paragraph. No, no, no, he sounded like a lovesick adolescent! This was his wife, a Senator, a heroine, a woman who was the life mate of a Jedi Knight, or a man who soon would be one—or dead.

Anakin Skywalker sat in his cabin on board the *Ranger*. In a few hours he would transfer from the *Ranger* to the *Neelian*, a corvette accompanying the transports. Halcyon would remain on the *Ranger* to lead the attack while Anakin commanded the landing force. Then Halcyon and the heavy cruisers would smash a hole in the enemy blockade, a hole through which Anakin and the ground forces would make planetfall on Praesitlyn. They knew through IFF—identification-friend-or-foe—systems unaffected by the communications blackout that at least some of Slayke's fleet had survived the initial contact and were still in orbit around Praesitlyn, in contact with the remaining Separatist ships.

When Slayke had been pardoned for raising his own force to attack the Separatists and commissioned to act on his own as a privateer, he had been given his own set of IFF codes. These codes contained all the information on file about each ship in his fleet, its name, class and armaments, ship's complement, and so on. Each ship had been equipped with a transponder that, when queried with the appropriate IFF code, would respond with its proper identification, thereby establishing that it was a friendly vessel, hopefully avoiding the kind of "friendly fire" incident that all too frequently occurred in the heat of battle. Halcyon was confident that once the attack commenced, Slayke's vessels would join them, and together they'd over-whelm the blockading force. So far the cordon placed around Sluis Van did not appear to have been dis-turbed. If those ships moved to participate in the bat-tle, things could get complicated.

The landing zone on Praesitlyn had already been marked out: a piece of rugged terrain behind a dry riverbed on the plain just below the plateau where the Intergalactic Communications Center sat. Halcyon had picked that spot rather than one on the plateau it-self because he felt a pitched battle that close to the center would be more likely to result in its destruction and the death of the technicians who were presumed to be prisoners of the Separatists.

Halcyon, Anakin, their commanders, the troops, and the crews who staffed the fleet had done all they could to prepare for the coming battle. Now it was time to rest. In a few hours the fleet would arrive at its initial point, the sector of space surrounding Praesitlyn that the captains had selected as the area where they would bring their ships into attack formations. The enemy fleet had to know they were coming by now; they had been inside the dead zone where communications had been cut off with the rest of the galaxy for some time. In fact, Halcyon had been in the middle of a report to the Jedi Council when the equipment had gone dead, a sure sign that they had entered the hostile zone of influence.

Anakin crumpled the flimsiplast and fed it into the shredder. He pulled out another. A Jedi did not feel fear, despair, loneliness. He knew that the coming battle would be won and that his division would acquit itself well: Grudo had told him so many times, and Grudo knew armies and commanders. In fact, Anakin had been a phenomenally quick study in the art of command, throwing himself into the task every waking hour of each day the fleet was in transit. He had immersed himself enthusiastically in all aspects of military management, as well. Neither did he feel despair; he looked forward to the coming battle. They had right and justice on their side, and they would prevail. He eagerly anticipated meeting the legendary Captain Slayke. And he didn't feel lonely, either. His relationship with Halcyon, who treated him like a younger brother, had grown even closer. And Grudo, the faithful, solid, reliable old Rodian, had stuck so close to him during the voyage that they had become inseparable companions.

Anakin Skywalker was no stranger to fear, pain, despair, and rage, but all that was behind him now, in another life. He began to write again: "You are with me now, my love. I feel the warmth of your breath on my cheek and smell the scent of your hair and clothes as you press your body close to mine. We faced death together, my love, and conquered it. Tomorrow, though I face death again, your love is with me and will sustain me . . ." He wrote for some time. Often on this voyage he had wished he could use his considerable Force sensitivity to look in on Padmé. But even if he could, he knew he wouldn't: that would be an inexcusable abuse of his powers as a Jedi, and because he had already broken his oath by marrying Padmé, he was determined not to do it again to satisfy his personal desires. Still, as he wrote, in his mind's eye the walls of his spartan compartment seemed to fade away, and once again he was reunited with his beloved Padmé by the beautiful lake on Naboo where they'd consecrated their vows of eternal love and companionship.

A lump had formed in his throat by the time he finished the letter. He reread it. His handwriting was not easy to decipher, but something like this could not be committed to an electronic medium that might be read by someone else. It was private in the extreme and would remain that way. He shook his head and smiled. "I can't believe I wrote this." He brushed away the tear that had formed in the corner of his eye, then blinked and looked around. Well, there they were again, the steel bulkheads of his tiny compartment. The gentle throbbing of the *Ranger*'s drives coming up through the deckplates warmed the soles of his feet. Reality.

Carefully, Anakin folded the sheet of flimsiplast several times and then sealed it tight. He wrote across both sides, PERSONAL FOR SENATOR AMIDALA, and placed it lovingly inside his cloak. Before he left for the assault, he'd leave it and his other personal things in the custody of the captain of the *Neelian,* to be delivered in the event of his death.

He lay on his bunk and closed his eyes, but sleep just wasn't there for him now. Halcyon had agreed that instead of taking a shuttle to the *Neelian,* Anakin could take his customized Delta-7 Aethersprite. Well, if he couldn't have his Padmé, he'd have his starfighter and spend the next few hours tinkering with her.

A battle fleet never sleeps. Crew on board the ships might sleep when off their watches, but a battle fleet is always awake, always alert, and on the eve of going into action soldiers sleep in shifts at their battle stations. A tension runs through a battle fleet so that the individual vessels and their crews are like the components of a vast living creature, a predatory animal on the verge of leaping onto the prey it has tracked through the depths of space. But in this case the prey could fight back. Perhaps even the clone troopers felt the tension—not that it affected their mental states significantly—and Grudo felt it, too. For Jedi Master Halcyon, it was a familiar and exhilarating sensation, but nothing to lose any sleep over.

Halcyon had finished his last war council with his captains, and they had departed to their separate commands. All was ready. Now the final waiting had begun.

When Halcyon woke from a brief sleep he sat in his quarters and wrote, "My Dearest Scerra and Valin . . ." This was just the latest in a series of letters he had written to his wife and son to be delivered in case of his death—but hopefully in person once this expedition was over. He was writing them by hand, to protect them from prying eyes and to keep safe—for now—the secret of his violation of the Jedi oath. Finished, he folded and sealed the letter and added it to the packet he'd been keeping, a dozen letters in all. The thought of his wife and son warmed him.

He put the thought of his loved ones out of his mind. He had endured the separation from them for so long now that the pain had subsided into a dull throb deep in his vitals. It was no good to think of such things. He stretched. He'd go find Anakin, give him a last-minute pep talk, bolster both their spirits. The young Jedi was proving to be a commander in his own right. Oh, everyone knew he was brave—what he'd done at the Battles of Geonosis and Jabiim and in other desperate situations had proved that. On Jabiim he'd been personally ordered by Supreme Chancellor Palpatine to leave the battlefield after more than a month of hard fighting, forced to leave his friends, to help with the evacuation. And Anakin had obeyed the order, however reluctantly. He was no stranger to pain, death, defeat. He *knew* he had a destiny. He was destined to command. The young Jedi possessed a great Force sensitivity; he was bright, bright to the point of genius. Halcyon was sure Anakin would be a Master someday and even sit on the Council. And now he had demonstrated his aptitude for command, the ability to lead, that ineffable quality of personality that convinces others that one knows what one is doing, and if they follow, they will succeed. Observing him daily, Halcyon was sure Anakin had put his emotions behind him.

Halcyon stood. There was only one place Anakin would be at this late hour.

"How's it going, Anakin?"

Startled, Anakin stood up in the cockpit of his starfighter, *Azure Angel II.* "Just making some last-minute adjustments." He hopped down from the fighter and wiped his hands on a rag. "I'm ready."

It was quiet in the docking bay; the other machines, shuttles mostly, had been secured against the impending action. The pair sat on some empty crates.

"Just a few hours and we'll be in it," Halcyon said. "You have ten thousand troops under your command. How do you feel?"

"Ready." Anakin slapped his knee. "Ready."

"Is your arm all right?"

"Never felt better." Anakin flexed his fingers to prove it. "Master Halcyon—I've been meaning to ask you something . . ."

Halcyon looked closely at Anakin. "Sure. What is it?"

Anakin hesitated, then blurted, "Grudo told me about your run-in with Slayke and, well, I thought I'd ask you . . ." He shrugged. "Why—that is, why did you fight him that day? Not so much why did you fight him, but why did you fight him the way you did?"

"I've wondered about that myself." Halcyon took a deep breath. "I never wanted to go after Slayke, you know. Others thought him a rebel at best, a pirate at worst. But I thought he was only doing what the Republic should have been doing all along. I had plans to go home to—" He caught himself. "—to visit with friends, take a rest, but the Council appointed me to lead the judicial corvette they were sending after Slayke, and I had to follow my orders, do my duty, do what I am sworn to do. We Jedi have no personal lives, no families like other people." His voice took on a tone of bitterness that surprised Anakin. It was a bit how he felt himself right now. Unconsciously he touched the spot beneath his cloak where he was carrying the letter to Padmé.

"So," Halcyon continued, "when we got to the clearing where Slayke's ship had landed I knew he was not aboard, and I half suspected that Grudo standing there with his knives was part of some kind of diversionary scheme. At the time I thought it was designed to draw me away from the woods where Slayke and his crew were hiding." He laughed harshly. "But at that point I just didn't care," he said with feeling.

Anakin was taken aback by the emotion in the Jedi Master's voice.

"Anakin, can I trust you?" Halcyon blurted then.

The Jedi Master sounded terribly serious, and his eyes looked shadowed by sadness. Anakin wanted to tell him, *Of course you can trust me,* but suddenly he didn't know if that was a reassurance that was his to give. "Go on," he said uncertainly.

After a moment, Halcyon continued. "You know the reason we Jedi aren't supposed to have any emotional connections with other people, don't you?" Anakin didn't answer: the question was rhetorical. "It's because emotions cloud a Jedi's judgment, make it difficult for him to see his duty, to do the hard and difficult things he's sworn to do. Well, I failed the test."

Nejaa Halcyon told Anakin about his wife and son.

At first Anakin couldn't speak, could only gape mutely at the man who had become a mentor. Halcyon chuckled and tapped Anakin under the jaw.

"Dropped so fast I thought you'd dislocated it," he said. He sighed. "So there it is. You're the only one who knows. Are you going to tell the Jedi Council when we get back?"

Anakin didn't know what to say. "No," he croaked, trying to control his voice. "I suspect Yoda already knows, or guesses. Not much gets by him." Then guilt and honesty overcame him. "Besides, if I report you, you can retaliate by reporting me," he said all in a rush. And then he told Halcyon about his marriage to Padmé.

It was Nejaa Halcyon's turn to gape. When he could talk again he said, "Married? You?" He shook his head wonderingly. "So you married her when you went to Naboo together, didn't you?" he said slowly. "And even Obi-Wan doesn't know?"

Anakin reddened as the shame of his lie rose up from its hiding place deep in his heart. "It has been . . . difficult," he admitted. "Obi-Wan is my Master—and my friend. I hate lying to him!"

Halcyon just nodded. "I know, I know. We have gone against everything we have ever been taught—against what it means to be a Jedi . . ." His voice trailed off.

"But it doesn't feel wrong!" Anakin burst out. "I mean—the dishonesty, yes, but not the love! Not the caring! I feel no less a Jedi for my love of Padmé!"

"I, too, have struggled with that." Halcyon frowned. "I wonder sometimes if Yoda does know about me— about us. But if that's the case, then why did the Council pick me to lead this expedition? And why did they allow me to take you as my second in command, when they knew it would throw us together—two who share such a secret? It's not because we were the only Jedi available. There were others at the Temple—or they could have recalled some from other commands. So why do it this way?" He looked at Anakin, and his shoulders straightened. "I'll tell you what I think. I think we're being given a chance to prove ourselves— they as much as told me that. And I've come to think this assignment may be more of a trial even than that." He seemed to be about to say something more, then clamped his mouth shut and stood up. "It's about time for you to shove off, young friend." He stood. "Time to show them all what we're made of."

"I guess so." Anakin also stood, and as they shook hands warmly, he wondered what greater trial the Council might have in mind.

15

"Attack! Attack! Attack!" Tonith pounded the control panel. "Attack all along the line! Throw in as many battle droids as we need to break their defenses! We've already captured their forward bastion; press on now, press on!"

Tonith had established his command post near the communications center on the plateau that overlooked the battlefield. This gave him a commanding view of what was going on, while it placed him and his staff far enough behind the lines to avoid serious danger from the fighting.

"But Admiral," B'wuf, the senior control technician protested, "we've already lost upward of one hundred thousand droids in our previous attacks. And we've taken the forward bastion twice before and lost it twice. Our losses have been enormous. I'm sorry, sir, but I seriously advise that our better course is to hold the line here until we're reinforced, and then overwhelm them with sheer numbers."

"My dear B'wuf, assets that just sit in the bank only earn interest. You must invest to make a fortune." He regarded the controller carefully. B'wuf had the annoying habit of speaking in a slow drawl, as if always looking for just the right words to express himself, as if he was afraid of saying the wrong thing and getting himself into trouble. In Tonith's experience, he was typical of the technical breed, out of his depth when dealing with anything in the real world of business affairs. This man would give in when he should stand firm, and he'd stand firm when he should give in. Tonith had dealt with his kind before, but despite his shortcomings he had his uses.

"I—" B'wuf began.

Tonith cut him short. "Do you own these battle droids? Did you pay for them? You're acting as if they're your own personal property. They're assets, my dear B'wuf, assets in an active market and worthless unless invested wisely, do you understand? It's my job to make that investment and yours to obey my orders. To the letter, B'wuf, to the letter. Now—" Tonith noticed that the entire control center staff had stopped work and was listening to them. "You, get back to work!"

As one, the technicians spun back to their consoles. Tonith turned back to B'wuf. "We are being reinforced very shortly. When they arrive I want this situation cleared up. Keep your infantry moving forward, closely supported by armor and artillery—"

"But sir, our air assets were severely depleted in the battle with General Khamar's army. You know success is possible only if guaranteed by, well, full employment and integration of arms."

"They don't have any air assets, either!" Tonith clutched his hands together in frustration.

"But sir, our fleet—"

"Our fleet is useless. Our ships watch theirs and none dare engage the others, because if just a few are lost, the balance of power will swing to one side or the other; and none dare come to our aid here, because if any are taken out of orbit, the other side has an advantage. Blasted credit pinchers," he swore. "So none can interfere, we're on our own until reinforced. When reinforcements arrive, their ships will overwhelm what's left of the enemy fleet—"

"But sir, we have ships blockading Sluis Van. They could lay mines and come here to—"

"We don't need them. Now get—"

"But sir, for every one of them we kill, they knock out hundreds of our droids!" B'wuf protested, his face coloring.

"Well, do the math! How many of the enemy are there? How many of our droids? Once we crack their defenses, their casualties will increase, and when they're at last routed, we'll wipe them out to the last fighter. Now hop to it!"

"But, Admiral . . ." B'wuf drawled.

"Blast it, stop arguing with me!" At the end of his patience, Tonith signaled for two guard droids to approach. "B'wuf, see that corner over there? Sit down there. You," he said, turning to the droids. "If he moves, kill him."

"Yessir. How much movement before we kill him?"

Tonith shook his head in desperation. "If he tries to, oh, get up, kill him. Otherwise I don't care if he scratches his back all day long. Oh, and B'wuf, while you're over there, keep your blasted mouth shut. Now move."

White-faced, B'wuf trudged over to the corner and sat down. The two droids placed themselves directly in front of him. Slowly, B'wuf raised a hand to his head and scratched. Nothing happened. He sighed.

Tonith strode into the center of the control room. "You heard my orders. Carry them out. As of right now I am taking personal control of all operations. Now press on, press on! Never mind casualties. A little more effort and we'll crack their lines. Victory is almost ours!"

A serving droid rolled up with a pot of tea. Eagerly, Tonith poured. "A spot of tea, anyone?" he asked, holding out the pot to the technicians at their arrays. Everyone pretended to be busy. "Very well." Tonith shrugged and sipped from his cup. He grinned. His teeth were as purple as ever.

"*Eeeeyaaaaaa!* Get some, get some! Come on, get some!" Erk yelled, firing indiscriminately through the bunker ports. He couldn't miss. Every shot disintegrated an infantry battle droid. But they kept on coming, rank after rank. Artillery lanced into them, but they just closed ranks and marched forward, firing at the muzzle flashes ahead of them, laying down a withering field of fire as they advanced.

"Erk! We have to go! They're overrunning us," Odie screamed, but Erk just shook his head as if she were an annoying insect and kept on firing. He had never seen such a target-rich environment, and it drove him into a frenzy of wild destruction.

She seized him by the shoulder and tried to pull him away from the blaster. He bounced her off with his hip and kept firing.

She could see hundreds of droids surging around their bunker. "They're flanking us! Get off that blaster and get your belt on. We've got to get out of here," she shouted. Scrabbling noises came from the bunker entrance. Odie snatched up her weapon and ran to the entrance just in time. Two droids came clanking down the short steps; she blasted them both. Erk never noticed. He yelled and cursed and fired and fired and fired.

"Tank droids," Odie shrieked. "Tank droids!" She could see two of them through the firing ports, lumbering along behind the infantry. The tank droids—"crawlers," because they moved so slowly over the surface of the ground—were heavily armored, fully automated tracked weapons platforms used to support infantry in combat. Their two synchronized forward-mounted blaster cannons had a 180-degree arc of fire and were used with deadly effect on troop concentrations, vehicles, and bunker complexes. Dorsal anti-aircraft weapons and grenade launchers supplemented the cannons. Ideally they were employed in echelon, like a set of stairs, as they moved forward, the machines farther back protecting the flanks of the ones farther forward.

The ground shook beneath the tank droids as they rolled toward the bunker.

Odie could see the energy bolts of Slayke's artillery being deflected off the behemoths. "Cease fire," she yelled, beating her fists on his helmet as hard as she could—but he remained impervious to her warnings. He fired on the nearest tank droid. Immediately its blaster module swiveled in the direction of the bunker, but before it could unleash a devastating bolt, the ground behind it erupted upward and flipped it forward to land on its back on top of the bunker.

The countermine Slayke had ordered dug beneath the Separatist mine had intersected its target and gone off just in time to break the tank droid charge.

The last thing Odie heard before everything went dark was someone screaming.

Slayke looked at his staff officers. "Time is very short," he began. "I shouldn't waste it on speeches. You all know what to do; we planned for a last stand from the beginning." He paused. "Well, this is it," he told them, but it was obvious to them all that their situation was desperate. Izable, Eliey, and Kaudine had fallen, and the forward artillery had been withdrawn, along with the survivors of the overrun outposts, to a line centered on Judlie, behind the main command post. This was the plan that had been prepared even before Slayke had landed on Praesitlyn. The enemy had temporarily halted their assault to straighten their line and bring up reinforcements.

"That's the only break we're going to get," Slayke said. "We'll have time to form a last line of defense at Judlie. Withdraw your remaining forces there immediately." He grabbed his blaster and turned away from the chart table.

He stopped and turned back to his officers. "We all knew this might happen when we intervened. I'm sorry it did. I thought Coruscant would come to our aid. Maybe they're on the way. No matter. We're here, they aren't. When help does arrive we'll have worn these nerfs down to the point where a single Jedi Padawan will be able to kick them to pieces." He paused. "Surrender is no option for us, not against this army, we all know that." There was one more thing he had to say to his comrades. "If we've got to die, this is as good a place as any. I am proud to have had the privilege of leading you, of sharing your hardships and your friendship, and I am blessed to have people like you accompany me into the next world. Let's not go easy."

The dozen officers gathered around the chart table snapped to attention, raised their right fists, and shouted, *"Oooorahhh!"*

Erk slowly became aware of an enormous pressure squeezing down on him. He opened his eyes, but couldn't see anything. Was it was pitch dark, or had he been blinded? Fighting panic, he managed with difficulty to free his arm from the debris pinning it to the bunker floor and brought his wrist in front of his eyes. His chrono glowed comfortingly in the dark and he sighed in relief—he hadn't lost his sight. It was difficult to breathe with that weight pressing down on him. He moved, and the load shifted and groaned. It was Odie—she slipped off to one side, and the two or three large rock fragments that had been pinning her onto him rolled to the floor.

"Oof." He could breathe again.

Odie groaned. "Th-thanks for getting us killed," she gasped at last.

At first Erk didn't know what she meant. Then: "Oh, yeah. I got a lot of them, didn't I?" He flexed his arms and legs and sat up. Despite multiple bruises and contusions he was still in fighting order. He felt around in the dark, found Odie, and lifted her by her armpits. "Where are you hurt?"

"Uhn. I have a big, er, feels like a big bruise on my hip. Otherwise—" She ran a hand through her hair and over her head. "—I think I'm all right." What felt like blood crusted one side of her face. With her fingers she could feel a big gash on that side of her head. "We must've lain here for a while," she said, experimentally feeling the gash. "The blood's clotted." She felt around her equipment belt and unhooked the glow rod fastened to it. She pressed the activation stud, and the bunker filled with blessed bright light. That was the good news. The bad news was that the blast had caved in the front of the bunker and loosened a huge slab of rock in the ceiling that had broken into two fragments when it fell, imprisoning the pair inside a space that tapered, like a rocky tent, to about two meters high and three meters wide at the floor. Odie pressed a hand against the rock. "It's as solid as—rock," she said. "We're lucky it didn't fall right on top of us, or we would have been squashed." She pressed her hands against one slab and pushed. "It seems solid enough now, though. Must be gravity and resistance are keeping them upright."

"Well, we're not squashed. We have air, and we're secure and comfortable in this rocky bower," Erk commented wryly.

"Seems we're spending a lot of time underground together recently."

"Yeah. That's the only way I can manage to find some time alone with you. How long will that glow rod last?"

Odie shrugged. "It runs on power cells. I recharged it maybe ten days ago, and I don't think I've used it much since. I should be good for seventy-five or a hundred hours."

"We'll be out of here long before then." He picked up his helmet and tried to put it on. No good: when it had been knocked off his head, debris had smashed it. He shook it experimentally, then turned to Odie. "Try yours."

"I would, if I could find it." She looked around the confined space. "It's probably under that rock somewhere. Fine. We're without communications with the command post. If it still exists."

"It does. Count on it. All right, you've kept me in suspense long enough. What's your plan for getting us out of here?"

She sniffed. "Well, we both start whistling as loud as we can, and when we reach the right pitch of sympathetic vibration the rock will just crack open and we'll emerge into the sunlight, like insects coming out of a chrysalis."

Erk stared at her for a moment and then broke into laughter. She joined him. They laughed until the dust floating in the air made them cough.

"I'm scared," Odie confessed after a while. "We're trapped in here for good, aren't we?"

Erk didn't answer immediately. She had expressed

his own fears. "Well, I guess we *are* sealed in here," he said after a slight pause, as he pressed a hand against the rock slab.

"The Republic never did send anyone, did they?" Odie asked, not really expecting an answer.

"They sure weren't here when we needed them."

"We're going to die in here, aren't we?"

"Sure looks like it." With a sigh, he reached down and took her hand.

"We'll die of thirst before we starve, won't we? To think of all we came through to end it like this." She couldn't keep the bitter taste of despair out of her voice. She turned the glow rod off to preserve its power.

Hours passed in the darkness. They whiled away the time reminiscing about better times, friends and relatives, music they liked, their homes, fine meals they'd eaten. Erk was the more experienced in the world through his travels, and he was a good raconteur: he made Odie laugh with his wild tales. They ate the remainder of the small allotment of rations the sergeant had given them when he'd dropped them at the bunker. At least they each still had a full canteen of water.

They were quiet for a time after they ate and quenched their thirst. Then Erk drew Odie closer to him and kissed her. They held each other tightly, until fear and exhaustion overcame them and they fell asleep in each other's arms.

When Erk awoke at last his chrono told him it was late at night. He swallowed a mouthful of water from his canteen, then nudged Odie awake. "We missed supper," he told her. She sat up and ran her hands through her hair. "Odie, I am not going to die in here! You hear me? We are not going to die in here!"

"How are we going to avoid it?" Odie pressed her hand against the rock. As before, it was still solid to the touch.

"I don't know, but we will!"

Daylight was fading fast now. With the exception of just a few weapons—no more than a battery—Slayke's heavy artillery pieces had all been knocked out. His aircraft had all long ago been destroyed; he didn't even have a shuttle craft to get back up to what was left of his fleet in orbit, not that anybody was thinking of going anywhere. The enemy's troops had paused after taking over the forward positions in Slayke's defensive line, ostensibly to consolidate their position and shorten their lines for the final attack and to bring up reinforcements for the final, overwhelming push. It could be only minutes away now. That was the only break Slayke had been given since the assault began. It would give him the time he needed to prepare for a last stand.

Slayke sat with his eyes glued to the optics that gave him a 360-degree surveillance of the terrain in front of Judlie.

"Sir, here are our dispositions."

A staff officer handed him a display, and he glanced at it quickly. "Tell all commanders to hold their positions at all costs. But tell them I give the ranking soldier in each unit permission to disperse before being overrun. If there's any chance for our troops to scatter and escape into the desert, they can try it. Make that clear." The officer saluted and turned to the communications console.

Slayke thought they'd only die out in the desert, but even so, he consoled himself, they might live a while longer.

A long, rolling artillery barrage began to envelop their positions, shaking the ground around them.

"When that stops, they'll be coming," Slayke said to his command staff. "When they overrun us, anyone who wants to try can attempt a breakout. No way am I going to stay here and fry."

The optics were no use now; the ground between the two armies was being churned and battered into dust, making it impossible to see anything. He turned to his staff. Their cheeks and eyes were hollow and their faces drained of blood, but each still attended to duty, some talking to the infantry and artillery units, others checking weapons, equipment, water, and rations. Dust from near hits hung suspended in the close, humid air around them; an enormous blast shook the bunker and some officer shouted, "Missed again!" and several of them laughed. Someone coughed. The officers muttered among themselves, going through the motions of leading an army that virtually no longer existed.

An enormous ripping, tearing roar engulfed them, distant and muted at first, but rising quickly to a deafening crescendo so profound it made their guts vibrate. It was clearly coming from somewhere behind them. Slayke pounded a fist into his forehead. Nobody had any doubt what it meant: it was their death knell.

"He's been reinforced!" Slayke said. "Grab your weapons and equipment."

"Lay on!" an officer shouted as the staff scrambled for the bunker exit. "At least we'll die fighting!"

Slayke raised a blaster rifle over his head. "Follow me!" he ordered.

16

Anakin paced the bridge of the *Neelian,* clenching and unclenching his fists as he observed the battle cruisers deploy into attack formation. "I should be out there with them," he muttered.

"No, you belong here," Grudo answered. "That's the plan; everyone agreed to it—*you* agreed. Commanders, too, must follow orders. Once the battle plan is approved, everyone must follow his or her orders. That way, everything works according to the plan. Please, sit. You're making the crew nervous."

At that moment Captain Luhar, the *Neelian*'s captain, glanced up at Anakin. He patted the gravity couch beside him. "Commander, have a seat."

Reluctantly, Anakin lowered himself onto the couch. "I hate just sitting here," he grumbled.

"You'll have action soon enough," Luhar replied. He was not sure about Anakin, whom he felt might be too young and inexperienced—Jedi or not—to be second in command of a fleet. He hoped that nothing would happen to General Halcyon. "Increase magnification," he ordered his navigator. Immediately the

Ranger came into sharp focus on the viewscreens. "She's a beautiful little ship," Luhar said.

Luhar was a distinguished-looking officer, middle-aged, Anakin estimated, with a full head of silver-gray hair. Anakin had admired the man's calm professionalism from the moment he had first stepped onto the *Neelian*'s bridge. But the *Neelian*'s role was to guide the troop transports to safe orbit and oversee the landing operations, not engage the enemy fleet, and despite the great responsibility Anakin had accepted when he'd been given command of this operation, the young Jedi was controlling with difficulty his natural urge for action.

The enemy commander had ordered his ships into a vast boxlike formation in orbit above the hemisphere where the Intergalactic Communications Center was located. "We'll have to break that square to get through to planetfall," Anakin observed.

Luhar nodded. "It's a strong defensive formation, sir. But we'll break it by lining up in a column three ships abreast and attacking at speed. Our ships will concentrate on one side of the square at the same time, in echelon, like a set of moving stairs, to bring the concentrated firepower of our entire battle fleet to bear against that one sector. That's when we go in. Once we're through, we'll disperse the remaining enemy vessels and destroy them individually. Have you ever been in a battle fleet engaged against an enemy, sir?" They'd been over this plan innumerable times, but he knew Anakin would be comforted discussing it again, only minutes before it was to be put into action.

Anakin nodded. "Yes," he said, "but not from the

bridge, not watching everything unfold. I got this—"
He tapped his prosthesis. "—in individual combat.
Have you ever gone one-on-one against someone who
was out to kill you, Captain? Have you ever killed anyone up close?"

"Can't say as I have. It's the commander's job to get
others to do the killing, not to go in and do it himself."

Anakin shot him a look, suddenly annoyed with the
captain—from his tone, it seemed to the young Jedi
that he didn't consider individual combat much above
the level of starship pilots brawling in a tavern.

"Ah! There're Slayke's remaining vessels." Captain
Luhar sat forward in the couch. "They see what we're
doing, and they're forming up to attack the port side
of that square. You watch, we'll crack that square in
no time. Blast it, I wish we had communications with
those ships."

"If that jamming platform is anywhere in orbit, sir,
we'll get it," the fire-control officer said, looking back
over his shoulder from the console where he sat.

Anakin concentrated on controlling himself. Drawing on his Jedi training, he slowed his heartbeat and
made himself relax. He knew he shouldn't have taken
Captain Luhar's remark so personally. It was only natural for these older military professionals to question his
ability to command them: they had minds of their own
and a long list of campaigns to prove their coolness in
combat. He would just have to prove he could do it.
He deepened his breathing, forced the tension out of
his muscles, and put all troubling thoughts out of his
mind. Now he could more clearly observe the activity
on the bridge. The crew were going about their duties

quietly, with the confidence born of long experience. He switched his viewing console to cover the deployment formation of his transports. They stretched out in columns far behind the *Neelian*. Escort ships, alert for any approaching danger, cruised about the periphery of the transport columns in apparently aimless courses, but Anakin knew that the commanders of those ships were actually very carefully patrolling their assigned sectors, alert for any approaching danger. Even if they totally destroyed the enemy fleet—and that seemed inevitable now—if anything happened to the troop transports, the expedition would be a total failure.

A brilliant flash lit up the viewing consoles.

"All right, there they go: the *Ranger* just got off the first salvo," Captain Luhar said calmly, as if the commencement of a major engagement were an everyday occurrence. "Torpedoes, I do believe. Now we'll see how well they work. Mark the time! All stations report." He listened carefully as each of the ship's stations reported they were ready for battle. "Commander, it's up to you now. As soon as you're sure the enemy's fully engaged, you may send in the transports."

Anakin knew what he had to do. The nervous tension that had bothered him only a few minutes earlier was gone. In his mind he could see the attack plan unfolding. He thought of the thousands of troops in the transport ships, buttoned up in their landing craft, weapons and equipment at the ready, patiently waiting for launching to the planet's surface. The signal for the transports to advance into orbit would be the *Neelian* moving to a predetermined position. It was Anakin's responsibility to give the *Neelian*'s captain that order.

"Prepare my landing craft," he ordered. As soon as the transports were on the way, he would follow.

"Landing craft prepared," the boatswain replied immediately.

"All stand by," Captain Luhar ordered. "Commander, we wait on your command."

"Not yet. Not yet. Give me more magnification on the *Ranger,* please."

Nejaa Halcyon stood on the bridge of the *Ranger,* the slightest shadow of a smile on his lips. He stood easily, balanced on the balls of his feet, relaxed, in perfect control of himself. He was minutes—seconds—away from embarking on the most important mission of his life, but calm and confident in himself and the people around him. He was not troubled by thoughts of failure or death; if anything happened to him or the *Ranger,* Anakin was fully capable of leading the expedition. If he was to fall now he'd do it in the discharge of his duty and die an honorable man. The *Ranger*'s energy screens were up, her crew were at their battle stations. They were ready to engage the enemy at last.

"Commander, we are two minutes from initial point," the *Ranger*'s commander, Captain Quegh, announced.

"Sir, General Halcyon?" It was the fleet intelligence officer. "Please look on your screen. That bright blip at the center of the enemy's defensive formation is the jamming platform they've been using to cut us off from Coruscant."

"We got the blasted thing at last!" Quegh pounded the arm of his gravity couch.

Halcyon broke into a big grin. "Are you sure, Intel?"

"Positive, sir. That's her. She looks like a droid control ship, sir. The Separatists can afford technology we can't. Wish we had their resources."

Captain Quegh laughed outright. "In less than a minute we're going to have their tails."

"Okay, Intel, good work, very good work. Captain, you have the target for your first salvo."

"Copy, sir. Gunnery officer, mark that target for proton torpedo salvo. Deactivate the homing system. Use line-of-sight guidance system. I want these babies dead on." The *Ranger* carried a battery of two MG1-A proton torpedo tubes. They were new weapons, auxiliary to the ship's batteries of laser cannons, not yet tested in battle but potentially devastating, with a range of three thousand kilometers, a velocity of twenty thousand kph. Unaffected by energy fields, they could go straight to their target without interference. Using line-of-sight guidance would prevent the missiles from homing in on other ships as they closed in on their primary target.

"Target marked, sir. Range one thousand kilometers."

"Thirty seconds to initial point," the navigator intoned.

"Fire when ready, Captain," Halcyon commanded. He strapped himself into the gravity couch beside Quegh and waited.

"Fire control," the captain said, "on my mark—"

"IP reached, sir," the navigator said.

"—fire! Watch officer, mark in the log the time the first salvo fired." He turned to Halcyon. "General, we are engaging the enemy."

A bright flash filled the viewscreens. "We got him! We got him!" the navigation officer shouted. Immediately the communications consoles blinked into life and the bridge was filled with a cacophony of voices from the other ships in the fleet.

"Get some control there," Quegh told the communications officer, who immediately got busy reestablishing the ship's command-and-control net. "Tell the fleet to follow me and execute the attack plan." He turned to Halcyon. "This is all we needed to give us the edge over the enemy."

"Captain, can you try to establish contact with Slayke's forces? Also, set me up with a line to Coruscant. I want to report that we have opened contact with the enemy. First salvo to us."

"Second to them." Captain Quegh pointed to a screen. A nasty red glow began to blossom on a heavy cruiser on the extreme starboard flank of the attack formation. It grew quickly; then a bright flash consumed the ship. He shook his head sadly. "That was the *By'ynium,* Lench's ship. He was a good captain. Good crew on that vessel." But now bright flashes began to appear all over the enemy's ships as Halcyon's fleet closed in.

The *Ranger* lurched suddenly to port. "Everyone stand fast. Damage reports!" The ship's stations reported no significant damage. "Near hit," Quegh said with a sigh. "They're ranging in on us, so hold on, everyone." All the *Ranger*'s batteries began firing as the enemy ships loomed bigger and bigger in her view-screens. Halcyon noted with satisfaction that many of them were burning.

"Give me an external view of our hull," Quegh commanded. When he switched to the port side he shouted, "No, wait, that was no near hit—we're being boarded!"

A huge explosion suddenly rocked the *Ranger*. Her powered movement began to slow, and then she began drifting. "Tell the other ships to continue the attack," Halcyon shouted as he unstrapped himself from his gravity couch. "What's our status, Captain?"

"We've been breached somewhere aft. I think it took out our propulsion unit. There's a small vessel fastened onto our stern. They're coming in through a breach back there. Ship's stations, damage reports."

There was no report from the propulsion unit.

"Captain," the executive officer reported, "not all the air lock doors are working. I'd like to go back and inspect the damage, sir."

"Go to it."

"I'm going with him," Halcyon said. "You two—" He gestured at the pair of guards standing beside the aft hatch. "—unsling your weapons and follow me." He pulled his lightsaber from his belt.

The guards did as they were told, grinning broadly. "It's about time," one of them said.

"General, what are you doing?" Quegh asked.

"I'm taking these guards and your executive officer and going aft, Captain. If we have boarders on us, we're going to repel them." He turned to the ship's exec. "Commander, arm yourself."

"How the—"

"I can handle this. Alert the crew to prepare to defend themselves."

"General, we have to get you out of here!"

"No time for that, Captain. Send a message to the *Neelian*. Inform Commander Skywalker that he has command until he hears from me, and that he should commence deploying the landing force. Seal this hatch behind us and don't open it unless you know who's there." He turned to his three companions. "Come on, let's get aft and deal with the boarders."

"The *Ranger*'s been hit!" Anakin shouted. Everyone on the bridge started.

"I believe you're right." Captain Luhar leaned forward. Then he looked at Anakin. "Commander, that means—"

"Sir! Message from the *Ranger*. She reports her propulsion unit is damaged and they have been boarded. General Halcyon directs Commander Skywalker to assume command of the fleet and to commence deploying the landing force."

"Look there!" another crew member shouted. "She *is* being boarded." On the screens they could just make out a dim shape attached to the *Ranger*'s stern. "There's another one."

"They're skirmisher ships," the captain announced. "The enemy commander's put them out in advance of his position to ambush us. Blasted things remained cloaked until they attacked. Comm, warn the rest of the fleet. Commander, shall I give the order to land the landing force?"

Anakin struggled to control his emotions. He was in

charge now, and he would be every bit the commanding officer.

"Thank you, Captain. Please give the order to land
the transports. Inform General Halcyon's deputy division commander that he is now in command of his
division and, until further notice, I shall be field commander in place of General Halcyon." He turned to
the Rodian. "Grudo, our troopers are ready for battle.
Let us join them."

Anakin stood before the screen for a moment.
Smoke, debris, pain, and fear—he could see it all. But
Halcyon was alive and fighting. Anakin smiled. *Too
bad for you, boarders,* he thought. He tried to send a
thought to Halcyon: *Good luck.* As he and Grudo
made their way back to the flight deck he realized how
little he had used the Force since they'd set out from
Coruscant.

There was vast confusion aft of the *Ranger*'s control
room.

"Commander," a chief petty officer exclaimed, running up to the ship's executive officer, "good to see
you, sir. They're in the propulsion unit. I assume the
crew there is all dead. We've sealed the air lock doors
just forward of the propulsion room, but they're cutting through and we have some doors in the forward
compartments that won't seal. Better suit up."

"General, follow me." The exec led them into an
equipment compartment that was full of crew getting
into low-gravity gear. "If we're going to have a fight
inside the ship, sir, we can't rely on hull integrity.

Quickly, quickly!" Several crew members, already suited, rushed up to help Halcyon into his own gear.

"Have you issued weapons yet?" Halcyon asked.

"Taking care of that, sir," an ensign replied.

"Good. What is your job, Ensign?"

"I'm a structural engineer, sir."

"You know this ship, then, don't you?"

"Yessir."

"Commander, I'll go forward with the two guards and this ensign, assess the threat, and hold them up. I want you to organize the crew and form them into an attack force to follow me. Clear?"

"Clear, sir."

With his suit secure and life-support systems running, Halcyon raised the ship's bridge. "Captain, Halcyon here. We are going aft to assess the situation. I'm leaving your exec here to organize a party to repel boarders. What can you see from up there?"

"The propulsion room has lost atmosphere. Someone's in the next forward compartment, cutting through the air lock. Please be advised, a malfunction has prevented us from sealing the air lock between where you are and the propulsion unit. Be prepared for loss of atmosphere momentarily. Droids don't need it, but we do."

"We're all right. Everyone's suited up and armed. Will keep you informed." Suddenly the atmosphere rushed out of the *Ranger*'s aft compartments with a roar so violent it nearly knocked them off their feet. Just as suddenly the wind and roar ended in the deep, still silence of airless space. Halcyon had counted twenty crew on the bridge and fifty more behind them who'd been suiting up. That meant a hundred crew members were unaccounted for, dead if they hadn't been killed in the attack or failed to don their zero-atmosphere suits in time. "Ensign, I'm only familiar with certain parts of this ship. I need you to guide us to the stern. Guards, are you ready?"

"Yes," one responded.

The other added somberly, "The rest of our detachment is back there somewhere. Yeah, we're ready."

Halcyon held up his lightsaber and activated it.

"Pretty light," one of the guards commented.

"You should hear it sing," Halcyon replied.

"I've never seen a Jedi Master or one of those things before," the other guard said.

"Well, you're seeing us now. I'll lead the way. Ensign, you stay close behind me. Guards, ready your weapons and bring up the rear. Don't fire unless you have a clear target, and whatever you do, don't shoot me!"

"I'd never shoot a Jedi, sir. Don't know about a general, though."

"When we get through this, I'll have both of you assigned to my personal staff."

"We don't deserve a reward like that, sir," the one protested.

Halcyon laughed. "That's no reward. After a while, you'll wonder what you did to deserve such punishment. Come on, stay alert."

They passed the ship's medbay. The medical staff hadn't had time to suit up. "Poor guys," one of the guards whispered.

"I'm afraid that's only the first of many," Halcyon

said. "Ensign, are we going the right way? By the way, what is your name?"

"Yessir, right way. Six compartments ahead there's a hatch that leads us to B Deck, then back six more compartments and we're there, if they haven't moved ahead. Uh, my name, sir, is Dejock."

"Captain, update, please," Halcyon said into his comlink.

"As far as we can tell they're having trouble with the hatches. We couldn't seal them airtight, but the crew did manage to close some of them manually and dog them and they're having to cut through."

"Guards, what do I call you?"

"I'm Corporal Raders, sir."

"I'm Private Vick, sir."

"Call me General. And no more jokes from here on out."

They came upon the battle droids just as three of them entered the crew's compartment. Halcyon didn't hesitate. His lightsaber flashed in a whirl of energy, easily deflecting the bolts from the droids' laser rifles. He slashed into them, one-two-three, and the machines disintegrated before his companions could point their blasters at the intruders. Halcyon stood flat against the bulkhead and, as the next three battle droids came through the hatch, disposed of them in turn. In six seconds he had turned the compartment into a junkyard.

"Blast through that hatch!" Halcyon ordered. "Exec, we've got them stopped. Bring up the rest of the force."

The two guards advanced using fire-and-maneuver, one directing bolt after bolt of energy through the open

hatch while the other rushed to the left, to continue de-
livering fire when his companion broke to the right and
took cover up against the bulkhead. Ensign Dejock followed the second guard. "Sir, this next area is a storage
compartment. The one directly aft of that is a repair
shop and then the propulsion room."

Halcyon went through the hatch. The compartment
was full of battle droids, all of which opened fire at
the same time. Halcyon parried the blaster bolts with
his lightsaber. Most of the bolts arced back onto the
droids that had fired them. Halcyon pressed forward.
The two guards followed him. In seconds the repair
shop was a shambles, but the droids in it were all destroyed.

Halcyon's suit was nearly melted through in places
from near hits; one of the guards had sustained a bad
burn on his thigh, but the self-sealing material in his
suit had saved his air supply.

"We have them on the run!" Ensign Dejock shouted.

"Yes, we've pushed them back. Come on, let's clear
out the next compartment." Halcyon started forward.

"Hold it!" The ship's exec stepped through from the
crew compartment, followed by twenty heavily armed
men. "You don't look so good, sir. Your suit's sustained some damage." He looked around the compartment, littered with destroyed droids, and glanced up at
the hull. "It'll take some time to repair that damage,"
he said. "General, you'd better get back up to the
bridge and get out of that suit before it fails. Take these
others with you. We know what to do. We'll finish
what you started." He looked around the compart-

ment again and whistled. "You really did a job on them."

Supporting the wounded guard between them, the trio staggered back up to the bridge. Within a few minutes the ship's exec and his team had cleared the boarding party. The crew sustained no further casualties. Damage control was already working on restoring hull integrity, and atmosphere was being restored in some of the forward compartments—but the *Ranger* was out of the battle.

"I'm very sorry about your ship and her crew, Captain," Halcyon said.

"They were good troops and she's a good ship, sir, but I've already made arrangements to transfer to another vessel. We'll scuttle her. General, if it hadn't been for you, we'd all be dead now." Quegh held out his hand and they shook.

"Take good care of those two guards, Captain. When I get to the ground I want them assigned to my staff. Hard to get good help these days."

"Commander Skywalker is already deploying his troops, sir."

"Good! Get me down there, or he'll have the war won by the time I can land and claim the glory."

17

Using ground-skimming navigation, Anakin expertly guided the troop landing craft, letting it roar along at a scant ten meters above the ground. Grudo sat strapped into the copilot's seat, gripping the armrests as Anakin delicately shifted the steering yoke just enough to clear the top of a hill that flashed beneath them. "Just missed that one, Grudo! Check our troopers, would you?" He was delighted to be flying the transport, and perversely amused that at last he'd found something that made the Rodian soldier nervous.

Glad to have an excuse to take his eyes off the terrain that was whipping past too close beneath them, Grudo slid the cabin door open and glanced back at the fifty clone troopers strapped into the troop compartment. They sat there calmly, silently, as if they were riding a bus to a picnic. The platoon commander glanced at Grudo and gave him the thumbs-up sign. Grudo turned back to Anakin.

"The troopers are doing well. Can you slow down a bit, or do you enjoy giving me heart failure?"

Behind them, at somewhat higher altitudes, the sky was dark with other craft, each carrying fifty combat-loaded soldiers. The plan was to approach the pre-designated landing zones from about one hundred kilometers out, flying close to the ground to avoid detection, instead of landing straight from orbit where the landing craft's entire trajectories would be subject to observation and direct enemy fire. From orbit, the armada could easily be discerned by the huge cloud of dust it kicked up as it passed over the planet's surface.

The combat engineers had already landed, and thousands of labor droids were preparing defensive positions for the infantry. Once Anakin's force had landed and reinforced the engineers, the rest of the army would touch down in huge transport ships.

"Relax, Grudo! I've been flying like this since I was a boy!" Anakin shouted. "One day I'll give you a ride in my starfighter." He glanced over at the Rodian.

"Please," Grudo groaned, "keep your eyes straight ahead."

"Get ready!" Anakin warned the hundreds of pilots following him. "We are zero-three from touchdown. I'll see you on the ground." He turned to Grudo. "I just hope some of Slayke's army has survived."

Identification codes are essential to distinguish between friend and foe. The Republic forces were issued a standard datapad called a Signal Operating Instruction, which was updated every month. The datapad contained a sign and a countersign for each day of the month that would be used by all the major units of the Republic forces to identify themselves. The dates were cross-referenced to those on Coruscant where the codes were made up, so no matter where one was in the galaxy the same signs and countersigns would be used. For instance, on the day Anakin Skywalker landed his army on Praesitlyn, the sign was *Jawa* and the countersign was *Eclipse*. These codes were different from identification-friend-or-foe, which were highly secret code messages used to determine if military vessels were hostile or friendly.

The encoding process used to protect these datapads was infinitely complicated, and thus far the Separatists had not been able to compromise it.

So as soon as the droid ship blocking communications was destroyed, Halcyon's fleet communications officer transmitted *Jawa* repeatedly to Slayke's communications system, but since Slayke had destroyed his equipment prior to abandoning his command post and retreating to strongpoint Judlie, there was, naturally, no response. Thus Anakin landed the army without certain knowledge that anyone from Slayke's force had survived.

The landing on Praesitlyn was to proceed in four waves: first, the combat engineers, supported by infantry and other arms to prepare defensive positions; then Anakin with his division, followed by Halcyon's division. Each division was assigned its own landing zone in an area thought to be far enough away from where the enemy force was entrenched to afford the troops ample opportunity to land, deploy, and take defensive positions before they could be attacked. Once the entire force was on the ground, with or without whatever might remain of Slayke's army, they would commence operations against the enemy.

*   *   *

"A withdrawal in the face of the enemy is one of the most difficult tactical maneuvers there is. You are the commander on the scene and the choice of tactics is yours, but can you do such a thing?" Count Dooku's image shifted before Pors Tonith's eyes.

"Droids do not panic, Count Dooku, and the enemy has not yet consolidated his forces. If I withdraw now to the plateau, I can do it essentially without interference. That will give me the advantage of occupying the high ground, as well as tightening my grip on the communications facility. They'll have to be very careful about using their heavy weapons to dislodge me, and when they finally attack, they'll have to maneuver uphill. If I stay where I am now, their combined force will overwhelm me. Of course if I was reinforced—"

"Surely you understand that we are committed on a broad scale across the entire galaxy. As important as your mission is, there are other commanders similarly engaged in strategic maneuvers. I have to weigh one priority against another. You shall be reinforced when the forces are available. Has any of your fleet survived?"

"Yes. Those ships have fled to join the fleet at Sluis Van. I will not commit them until I am reinforced. Otherwise they would be severely outnumbered and destroyed. The droid control ship that was blocking communications from here was destroyed also. They now have open contact with Coruscant."

"No matter. That investment worked well for as long as we needed it. We do not need it anymore."

"Prisoners tell me I am facing a Zozridor Slayke. What can you tell me about him? He has conducted a brilliant defense up to this point. Nevertheless, I was on the verge of wiping him out when the relief force from Coruscant arrived."

"Zozridor Slayke is an extraordinary man. We could use one like him." Count Dooku went on to recite Slayke's recent history.

"A renegade? I'm not surprised, sir. The man's troops fight like pirates with their backs to the wall."

"I'll tell you something else. The force now opposing you is led by a Jedi Master, Nejaa Halcyon, and a young Padawan named Anakin Skywalker." He went on to tell Tonith something about the history of the two Jedi. "Nejaa Halcyon, you will find, is careful and predictable, but beware the young Jedi—he is volatile. This is both a danger to you and a possible weakness you can exploit."

"Jedi can be killed, Count Dooku, but it's Slayke I think I should worry about, if he can fool a Jedi like he did. I imagine the two might have some problems sharing their command."

"Don't count on it. Jedi are not likely to let their personal feelings interfere with their duty. But if either is liable to succumb to his emotions, it is Skywalker."

"There is one more matter, Count. Reija Momen. I want to use her for propaganda."

Count Dooku's eyes narrowed to tiny slits as he steepled his fingers. "What do you propose?"

"Sir, I will put her on a HoloNet transceiver transmission to the Republic Senate, a live hookup. She will read a prepared statement to them. To wit: 'Remove your troops from Praesitlyn or Admiral Tonith will kill us.'"

Dooku made a rude noise. "They'll never believe you."

"Not all of them, no. But the Senate is a squabbling, democratic body. I know some of them are disposed to our cause, for whatever reasons, and others are, shall we say, not warlike. The broadcast will at least instill doubt into their deliberations."

"You cannot kill the hostages, you know that."

"Oh, but I will! Before I let myself be defeated, I will not only kill them, I will destroy the Intergalactic Communications Center. I've already made preparations to do exactly that. But don't forget this: Reija Momen is respected and well known on Alderaan, as well as on Coruscant; she's a handsome matron, too, an icon—everyone's mother. To see her begging for her life, for the lives of her workers, will definitely let them know how serious I am."

"Will she cooperate? After all, didn't she assault you when you first took her prisoner?" Dooku's smile was ice cold.

Tonith was amazed that Count Dooku knew about Reija striking him; he felt a sting of embarrassment at the memory of the blow, and a surge of elation. He could see that Dooku's interest had been sparked by his proposal. "I was caught off guard; it won't happen again." He bowed at the image. "She will cooperate, I will see to it."

Dooku was silent for a moment. "Very well. You may proceed." He smiled. "You should have been a politician."

"I am a banker—that's even more vile." Tonith laughed. "One more thing. When will I be reinforced?"

"Back to that again? You will be reinforced when you are." A distinct tone of exasperation was evident in Count Dooku's voice.

"I would like the record to show that not only have I fulfilled to the letter the plan you established for this invasion, but I would also have been totally successful if you had reinforced me as per our battle plan."

"Have you been listening to anything I've told you?"

"I have faithfully carried out my end of the bargain. I have had success snatched out of my grip because you or someone—"

"Admiral Tonith, are you questioning my judgment? Defy me, question me, and you are dead." Count Dooku's hologrammic image wavered.

"Yes sir, I understand that," Tonith said. "But I am no fool. No one else could have done any better here than I have, not even your vaunted General Grievous, the killing machine." Hands shaking, he slowly poured himself some tea. He sipped eagerly and sighed, then wiped perspiration from his forehead with a sleeve. He knew a remark like that could get him killed, but at this point he no longer cared. For all his considerable faults, Tonith was no coward, and he didn't like to be pushed around.

Count Dooku smiled. "In time. All in good time.

"Now. I approve your propaganda effort and your defensive plan. Put them into effect. Do not contact me again. I will contact you." The screen went dead.

"Sir, they're withdrawing. The droid army is withdrawing," an astonished officer shouted at Slayke, who had been observing the ships landing behind strong-point Judlie.

Slayke grinned broadly. "Yes, Lieutenant, and take a look at those ships: they're ours. Talk about being saved in the nick of time!" Certainly the ships were those of the Republic, for each clearly displayed the distinctive black-on-white logo of the eight-spoked wheel within a circle. "I don't think I've ever seen a more beautiful sight." Slayke clapped the officer on his shoulder. "Tell our people to cover the droid retreat. I'm going out and see who's in charge."

Slith Skael moved defensively to protect Reija when Tonith entered the room where they were being held prisoner.

"Remove him," Tonith told the droid guards, "but keep him just outside the door. I may have some use for him in a few moments." The droids unceremoniously grabbed the Sluissi and dragged him, protesting, out of the room.

"What do you want?" Reija gritted.

"Are you being treated well?" Tonith smiled and took a seat opposite Reija. "Are we not looking after your welfare, madam?"

"If you can call murder, unprovoked warfare, beastly—"

"Shut up, woman!" Tonith's voice cracked like a whip. "Listen to me very carefully. I'm going to put you on a HoloNet transmission to the Republic Senate on Coruscant."

Reija started at the news.

"Sit there and be quiet," Tonith snapped. "There's

more. You will read a prepared statement. If you do
not agree to this proposal, or if you try any tricks while
reading the statement, I will kill your Sluissi friend.
Here, read." He handed her a short script. "Read it
aloud."

Reija glanced at the short paragraph and smiled. "I
knew they would come," she whispered. Her lip quiv-
ered as she spoke, and her eyes grew moist, but then
she grinned broadly. "You're in trouble, aren't you?"

"Shut up, you arrogant . . ." Tonith visibly drew in
his anger. "Read the statement. Read it back to me.
Now."

Slowly, Reija read the statement.

*I AM REIJA MOMEN, DIRECTOR OF THE PRAE-
SITLYN INTERGALACTIC COMMUNICATIONS
CENTER. MY STAFF AND I ARE BEING HELD
PRISONER BY AN ARMED SEPARATIST FORCE.
THE COMMANDER OF THAT FORCE DEMANDS
THAT YOU ORDER THE TROOPS NOW OPPOS-
ING HIM TO WITHDRAW FROM PRAESITLYN
IMMEDIATELY. FOR EVERY HOUR YOU DELAY
ISSUING THAT ORDER, ONE OF MY STAFF
WILL BE EXECUTED, ENDING WITH ME. I
BEG YOU, FOR THE SAKE OF MY PEOPLE, TO
COMPLY IMMEDIATELY.*

"Add a little more emotion toward the end. Otherwise, very good. Now we shall proceed to the communications room—"

"You'll never kill all of us. You need us as hostages.
As long as we're alive the Republic forces won't mount

a massive attack on the center, and you hope you can delay that until you're reinforced."

Tonith sighed and snapped his fingers. A droid entered the room. "Make ready to slice off her left ear," he ordered. The droid seized Reija with one hand and deftly gripped her left ear in strong, mechanical fingers. Those fingers squeezed—hard—and Reija fought not to scream. "Now get her to her feet," he commanded the droid. "We don't want to keep the Senate waiting."

They pushed Reija down the corridors to the control room. She did her best to get a grip on herself and to ignore the painful burning sensation that engulfed the left side of her head as the droid continued to put pressure on her ear. "You must know that the Senate isn't even in session," she gasped.

"No matter. We will transmit to the transceiver in the Senate Communications Room, and I guarantee you, one minute after it's received the Chancellor will be calling the Senate into emergency session." Tonith laughed outright.

A hologram pod had been set up in the main control room of the communications center, and a chair placed in front of the pod for Reija to sit in. She was unceremoniously thrust into it by the droid. As the droid retreated, she pressed a hand to her burning ear.

"Remember, my dear," Tonith sneered, "if you try to get smart with me during the transmission, I will have that ear removed. I must say," he continued pleasantly, "you look charming—or you will when you put your head down and compose yourself. The Senators will be impressed. Here is the script. Read it slowly and verbatim. Wait for the signal from the technician." He nodded to a technician at the controls.

Reija studied the script. "When will you begin the executions?" she asked.

Tonith shrugged. "When enough time has gone by without a response. When I'm ready. We may not have to execute anyone at all if you do this right." He nodded at the technician.

"Begin," the technician said.

Reija looked calmly into the middle distance. "I am Reija Momen, director of the Intergalactic Communications Center on Praesitlyn," she began, her voice steady and well modulated. "My staff and I," she continued, "are being held prisoner by an armed Separatist force. The commander of that force demands you order the troops now opposing him to withdraw from Praesitlyn immediately. For every hour you delay issuing that order, one of my staff will be executed, ending with me." She paused for a full three seconds. The technician glanced nervously at Tonith, who, smiling, held up a hand indicating he should let Reija finish her statement.

"I beg you, for the sake of my people, *Attack! Attack! Attack!*" she screamed.

18

The flag of the Republic wrapped around his neck, Zozridor Slayke leapt gracefully over the ramparts the labor droids were erecting and looked around. His heart raced. For almost as far as he could see the sky was full of landing craft; others, already landed in vast clouds of dust and sand, were disgorging squads of armored troopers. An older human male with brown mustaches and brilliant blue eyes looked up as Slayke approached and nodded to his companions, who appeared to be studying maps or plans. They turned as one and stared at the battle-scarred figure rapidly approaching, a huge grin on his face.

Slayke stopped before the older man, came to attention, and saluted him smartly. As his hand came up to his right brow at a forty-five-degree angle a tiny cloud of dust puffed off his arm. "Captain Zozridor Slayke, commanding the force opposing the Separatist invaders of Praesitlyn, sir. I hereby offer my full assistance in your campaign to liberate this world."

The older man, an embarrassed expression on his face, slowly returned Slayke's salute and said, "Well,

I'm here to tell you!" He gestured at a Jedi standing next to a—a Rodian?

"Who is that?" Slayke asked, startled.

Anakin stepped into full view. "Jedi Anakin Skywalker, Captain Slayke. I'm in command of the landing force. This," he said, nodding at Grudo, "is my sergeant major. I am very pleased and honored to make your acquaintance."

Slayke looked over at the older man he'd mistaken for the commander, but that gentleman shrugged.

"The Republic's so low on soldiers they're robbing the cradle now, eh?" Slayke slammed a fist into his thigh. A cloud of dust puffed up. "What was your name again, Jedi General?"

"Anakin Skywalker, sir." Anakin bowed slightly at the waist. "And it's Commander, not General. Sir, I have heard a lot about you and am honored—"

"Look, Jedi Commander Anakin Skywalker, I have only about two thousand soldiers left of all those who landed here with me. We fought them hard and upset their plans. But you're honored? Don't talk to me of 'honor,' Jedi. We're nothing but blood, guts, and sweat here and—" He shook his head as he looked over the landing force. "If there's anything more useless in this galaxy than a Jedi's brain, it's a clone trooper. They're one step above a droid—in fact, I'd prefer droids over these ugly clones anytime. You can't tell clones apart, and they all have the same personality."

"Now, see here!" the older officer protested. "We've heard quite enough from you, Slayke. I'm here to tell you!"

"Who is this, since he's not the general?" Slayke asked Anakin.

"My quartermaster, Major Mess Boulanger."

Slayke roared with laughter and pointed a finger at Boulanger. "You mean I was dumb enough to try to report to a blasted box kicker? Oh, that's rich! Well, Major, rather you commanding this force than this beardless wonder here."

Anakin held up a hand. "Captain Slayke, right now I'm busy landing my troops. We're going to establish a defensive position. I suggest you remove your forces to this spot and consolidate with us. As soon as General Halcyon joins us—"

Slayke groaned and slapped his forehead. "Halcyon, did you say? *Nejaa* Halcyon? He's commanding this fleet?"

"Yessir. As soon as he joins us—"

Slayke laughed. He turned his eyes skyward and raised both arms over his head. "Why is this happening to me!"

"Captain, I know you and General Halcyon, er, had some, uh, differences once—"

"Oh, you do, do you, young beardless Jedi?" Slayke laughed louder. "I never met the man." He scowled. "I was too busy stealing his ship. So the best the vaunted Republic can do is send me a boy and a certifiable idiot with an army of—of—test-tube soldiers," he sneered.

"We'll do," Anakin said shortly, controlling his annoyance with effort.

"All right! All right!" Slayke held out both palms. "I'm going back to my troops. You see that slight rise over there? That's my command post. When *General*

Halcyon gets here, you and him come on over and we'll talk. I'm the one who's been fighting the droid army. You want to know what it's been like, you come on over and see me." With that, he spun on his heel and stomped off.

"Whew," one of the officers standing nearby sighed. "He's what we call a hard case where I come from."

"Well," Anakin answered slowly, "he has been through a lot. Did you hear what he said? He only has two thousand soldiers left of the army that landed here with him? That's a fantastically heavy casualty rate! No wonder he's bitter." He turned to his officers. "Let's land the rest of our force, and when General Halcyon gets here, we'll go on over and pay Zozridor Slayke a formal visit."

The landing continued unopposed.

Supreme Chancellor Palpatine's expression did not change as he watched the short transmission from Praesitlyn. "Reija Momen is from Alderaan, isn't she?" he asked Armand Isard, who had been enjoying drinks with the Chancellor when Lieutenant Jenbean, the Senatorial Communications Center watch officer, delivered the transmission.

"I believe so, sir." Isard also had watched Reija Momen's statement without evident emotion.

"Hmmm." Palpatine replayed the transmission. "A brave woman."

"Shall we call an emergency session of the Senate? Or perhaps we should respond? The first hour in the ultimatum will be up soon."

"To view this? I don't think so. What good would it

do? The hostages? They won't kill them. This is a bluff, and a blackmail bluff at that. The Republic will not, cannot, permit itself to be bullied like this. Lieutenant Jenbean," he said, turning to the watch officer who had brought Momen's statement directly from the communications center, "have you showed this to anyone else?"

"Nossir. I brought it directly here as soon as it was received. The technicians on duty have seen it, sir, but that's all."

"Good." Palpatine paused. "Do you know Momen personally?" he asked then.

"Nossir, not personally. I know her by reputation. She is one of the most highly respected persons in our profession."

"I understand. I will keep this with me until I decide what to do. Until then, you are to treat this as absolutely top secret, is that understood? Have your log entry show only that a transmission came in from Praesitlyn, nothing more. If anything else like this comes through, I want you to bring it directly to me. Inform your relief that if anything comes in from the communications center on Praesitlyn he's to do the same thing."

After Jenbean left, Isard turned to Palpatine and asked, "Do you really think he'll keep this to himself?"

"No. Armand, where emotion rules, the wise man will hedge his bets every time. Did you see the lieutenant's expression as we watched the transmission? You know he'd seen that thing several times before he brought it to me. That woman, Reija Momen, she's an icon; she looks like the ideal mother. Only old hard cases like us can resist an appeal like that to our basic instincts. What about Tonith? Is he serious about killing the technicians?"

"Yes, Supreme Chancellor, he is fully capable of that once they lose their value to him. Or he may not kill them. It depends on how he calculates his odds for personal survival. He's a cool one, very dispassionate— what you'd expect of a banker; a living calculating machine, profit here, loss there, balance the account and so on. What will you do with this situation?" He nodded at the recorder.

"Nothing for now. Our young communicator friend will do it for us." Palpatine smiled enigmatically.

"May I ask how you know?"

Palpatine inclined his head in a slight bow. "Trust me. I know. All I had to do was look at that young man's face. May I refill your glass?"

Lieutenant Jenbean was incensed, and the farther he got from Chancellor Palpatine's residence the angrier he became. They had just sat there watching that transmission without even a change of expression. How could those politicians have taken this so lightly? Didn't individuals count anymore in this Republic? Wasn't the Republic the guarantor of the freedom and lives of each of its citizens? Surely nobody would expect Palpatine to call off the relief expedition, but shouldn't he have shared this information with the commanders, demanded a plan to free the hostages?

When the transmission had come through, everyone on his shift had watched it several times, thinking at first it could only be a hoax. None of the communicators had much knowledge about what was happening on Praesitlyn except that the Separatists had captured it and the Senate had sent a relief force to liberate it. But they all knew Reija Momen—everyone in the field knew her. And there she was—he shook his head and clenched his fists—a prisoner of some fiend, being forced to make this transmission.

Although it was not clear to Jenbean just what Chancellor Palpatine—or anyone else—could do about Momen's situation, he was incensed that the Chancellor proposed to do nothing at the moment. In just a few minutes one of the technicians on Praesitlyn would be murdered; maybe it had already happened. He shuddered at the thought of further transmissions showing people he knew lying dead in the Praesitlyn Intergalactic Communications Center.

Before he put in place the caveats on the transmission that Palpatine had demanded, Lieutenant Jenbean, staking his entire future on doing what he thought was right, would retransmit Momen's broadcast to someone who could do something to save her.

Anakin smiled as Halcyon stepped into his command post. They shook hands warmly.

"You've done an excellent job landing and deploying the army," Halcyon told him. "What's happening?" He nodded toward the high ground.

Briefly Anakin filled him in on the tactical situation. "Our landing went off unopposed. The enemy is withdrawing to the plateau, and we haven't been able to take advantage of the movement because we weren't fully deployed when it began. Now they occupy the high ground, and I'm sure they're fortified up there, using the communications center and its staff as hostages to prevent us from mounting a full-scale attack. It's going to be hard to dislodge them."

Halcyon nodded. "That's why we've got to be flexible. I've got a couple of ideas. Have you met Slayke yet?"

Anakin smiled. "Yes. He wants us to visit him in his command post as soon as you're ready."

"I've never met him in person, you know. He was too busy stealing my ship the only time our paths crossed." Halcyon grinned. He unfastened his cloak, sat on the nearest chair, and ran a hand through his hair. "I'm tired, and the battle hasn't even started yet."

Anakin sobered. "How badly damaged was the *Ranger*?"

Halcyon shrugged. "We had to scuttle her. We lost a large number of her crew, as well. It was close."

"For Captain Slayke, too," Anakin told him. "They put up a great fight, but his army was almost destroyed."

"Not good, not good," Halcyon said, shaking his head. He was silent for a long moment. At last he took a deep breath and stood up again. "Shall we go pay the Great Man a formal visit in his lair and get this army moving?"

19

Their courses inexorably set, the vast armada sped through the cold, eternally dark reaches of space. Aboard each ship systems pulsed with energy as its computers, carefully attended by an army of perfectly functioning droids, kept it on its predetermined course. Weapons systems that could destroy whole fleets were at the ready.

These were dead machines, almost as cold inside as the vacuum of space outside their hulls, kept just warm enough to prevent metals and plastics from weakening and lubricants from freezing. They had no names, only numbers and nomenclatures. Nowhere except on the flagship—a monstrous killing machine in its own right—was there to be heard the voice of a single living being; no laughter, no cursing, no complaining, no life; just the muted whispering of machinery. And on the flagship itself, grim-faced beings went about their duties with the calm born of an ingrained military discipline as rigorous as the technology that controlled the droid infantry in the transport ships following the battle cruisers. In those transports silence pervaded the compartments crammed with hundreds of thousands of battle droids folded motionless in their racks, waiting for the signal that would turn them into dispassionate, efficient killing machines.

Had there been living beings on board these transport ships, and had they walked through the storage compartments where the droids awaited the call to battle, it would have been like visiting a vast crypt where the bones of a monster species sat patiently entombed while awaiting resurrection. The huge bays were silent except for the constant pulsation of the ships' drives sending their vibrations through the deckplates. The droids were lined up perfectly in their serried ranks; occasionally a slight course deviation or a change in the ships' rate of speed caused them to sway minutely in their racks to the soft *click-click-click* of metal on metal. And were a visitor to stare too long and too closely at those skeletal miracles of mechanical invincibility, especially were his attention to be drawn into the black sockets of their optics, he would shudder with the vision of his own mortality reflected there, and scurry back into the world of warmth and fellowship and hope that distinguish the living from their machines.

This fleet was the long-awaited Separatist reinforcements, the armored fist reaching out to smash the world known as Praesitlyn.

"Welcome to my humble and last remaining strongpoint," Slayke boomed in greeting as he bounded to his feet. His officers stood around silently, staring at the two Jedi and their three companions. Slayke narrowed his eyes at the companions but said only, "Let me introduce my staff." He introduced each officer, who bowed slightly to the visitors.

"I presume, sir, that you are the—" Slayke hesitated for just a brief instant, but that hesitation spoke volumes to Nejaa Halcyon. "—inestimable General Halcyon?" He extended his hand. At his full height, with his broad chest and shoulders and shock of flaming red hair, Slayke was an imposing figure.

"The same, Captain," Halcyon answered. They shook. As they made physical contact each looked into the other's eyes, two wary rivals sizing each other up. Anakin tried to keep his own expression neutral; he realized he was very much the junior partner in the triumvirate Halcyon was about to propose, and he knew instinctively that silence right now was the best asset he could bring to this situation.

"What do you have that I can steal from you this time?" Slayke asked, a wry, challenging expression on his face.

Halcyon ignored the question. "This is my deputy, Commander Skywalker."

"We've met." Slayke bowed slightly. "And those two strapping lads over there?" he asked, indicating the two guards Halcyon had brought along.

"Corporal Raders and Private Vick, my confidential advisers on military affairs," Halcyon answered.

Slayke nodded. "It's a smart commander who listens to the voices from the ranks. I'm beginning to like your style." The two guards stood self-consciously among Slayke's officers.

"I see you've dragged him along, too," Slayke

sneered, nodding at Grudo, who was trying to remain inconspicuous at the rear of the crowd.

"Grudo goes where I go—that's the way it's going to be," Anakin answered at once.

"My, my, this sprout certainly has a mind of his own." Slayke chuckled. "I like soldiers who have minds of their own—they're much harder to steal than, say, someone's starship." He laughed enormously.

Again, Halcyon refused to acknowledge the jibe. "Can we talk in private?" He nodded at the officers standing about.

"No. Whatever we have to say, my officers can hear. I don't keep vital information from my troops." Slayke motioned to a sergeant standing nearby to clear off a field table. "Excuse the disarray, but, ah, we moved in here on rather short notice, and my cleaning staff hasn't had a chance to tidy things up." He grinned. "The detritus of battle," he said, gesturing around the room, "which includes my troops and me, I'm afraid. But you and your army are unbloodied, vigorous, straining against the traces, eager for battle! Take your seats and I'll tell you a thing or two about the battle we've fought here."

Halcyon and Anakin joined Slayke at the table.

"I'm sorry that I don't have refreshments for my honored guests," he told them, "but we're fresh out of ale and cakes. Now . . ." He rubbed his big hands together. "I have devised several maneuvers that I'm confident, with the timely arrival of your troops, I can use to successfully assault the enemy's positions on the plateau. Please observe the schematic of the terrain on that screen. What I propose we do is—"

"Excuse me, Captain," Halcyon interrupted. "I'm very anxious to hear your battle plan, but first there's something we've got to get straight."

Slayke pretended surprise. "Please proceed, Nejaa—you don't mind if I call you Nejaa, do you?" he asked, his voice dripping with sarcasm. The command post, crowded as it was, had gone utterly quiet, the silence broken only by the static-laden voices of Slayke's unit commanders making their reports, the muted background music common to military command centers.

"You can call me what you like, as long as you mean *sir*. I was sent here by the Senate to take command of this operation, and take command I will. You will place your remaining troops under me. While I value your opinion and look forward to hearing your advice, I'll make the final decisions on any plans for the employment of this army, is that clear?"

Anakin realized instantly that Halcyon had taken the wrong approach with Slayke, but held his tongue. There was more going on here than the mere execution of orders.

Slayke leaned back in his chair and puffed out his cheeks. "Well, that's a mighty big speech from a guy"—he leaned forward across the table—"who can't even keep his pocket from being picked." He grinned evilly.

Halcyon still refused to be drawn in. "Captain, I have the authority of the Senate—"

"Tell them to kiss my sweet toes," Slayke retorted.

"—I have a fleet in orbit and I have an army of fresh troops—"

"Blasted faceless clones," Slayke spat. "Look around

you! This is an army—these are soldiers, battle-hardened veterans who've withstood the worst the enemy has thrown at them and still have fight in them! You think your clones can match spirit like that? Ha!" He placed his hands behind his head. A susurration of agreement swept through Slayke's assembled staff officers. "And, I might add, you took your sweet time getting here!"

"Captain." Anakin leaned forward so he could speak confidentially. "You would never have survived that final attack. I'd say you owe us, not the other way around."

"Oh, ho, ho, the nursery speaks!" Slayke roared. Several of his staff snickered. "General Halcyon, maybe you'd like your *Plooriod Bodkin* back? I'll trade her for your own flagship. Now that I've bloodied the enemy's nose, I think I need a vessel fitting a man of my considerable skill, don't you agree?" He roared with laughter and pounded the frail table with a massive fist.

"My flagship was scuttled and most of her crew killed when we broke the cordon and restored communications, Captain," Halcyon answered, his voice flat and hard.

"Yes? And while you were taking your time getting here, we were fighting and I lost thousands of good troops! Do you think any of us care in the least about your flagship's crew?" Slayke's face had flushed with anger. "We didn't have the 'Force' to help us, either. I suppose you called on it to extricate yourself?" He sneered.

"Yes, and this." With one smooth motion made so fast nobody—not even Anakin—saw it coming, Hal-

cyon drew his lightsaber and activated it. The on-
lookers gasped at the sight of the brilliant blade of pure
energy.

Slayke's eyes narrowed and his body tensed, but he
didn't move or even show any degree of surprise. "Any
more tricks?" he asked in a normal voice.

Halcyon deactivated the lightsaber and hooked it
back onto his belt. "I rather like these things," he said
pleasantly, patting the weapon affectionately. "They
come in handy when you're outnumbered a hundred to
one. You were saying?" He smiled engagingly.

Slayke laughed. "I have to admit, I'm coming to
admire your style!"

At that point Anakin lost his patience with the ver-
bal sparring. "We don't have much time to get organized," he interrupted. "Let's get on with our strategy
session. What happened on Bpfassh was then; this is
now. Let's put that behind us and concentrate on the
job at hand." He paused, letting them see the dark fury
in his eyes. Both Halcyon and Slayke stared at him.

"Well . . ." Slayke leaned back and regarded Anakin
for a moment. "Yessir!" He gave a casual salute.

Halcyon cleared his throat. "He's right, Slayke," he
said. "We've got to cooperate—" Halcyon's personal
comlink interrupted him. "This must be something important. Excuse me, please."

It was the fleet communications officer. "Sir, I have
just received, well, the most, um, interesting transmission from the Senatorial Communications Center on
Coruscant. I believe you must see it at once, sir."

The room went completely silent. Slayke raised an
eyebrow.

"Can you tell me what it's about?" Halcyon asked. "I'm in a conference now in Captain Slayke's command post."

The communications officer paused. "General, I think you should see it and, well, you'll see what I mean. Do you have a HoloNet transceiver available at your current location?"

Halcyon looked up at Slayke, who said, "Right in there," gesturing toward a partitioned-off corner of his command post.

"Yes I do," he said into his comlink. He turned to Slayke. "What are your codes?"

Slayke held out his hand for Halcyon's comlink. After a second's hesitation, the Jedi handed it over. Slayke spoke quietly into the comlink, then returned it and said, "We'd better go take a look."

They reached the HoloNet transceiver just in time to see Reija Momen's image flash on the monitor.

"I am Reija Momen, director of the Intergalactic Communications Center on Praesitlyn. My staff and I are being held prisoner by an armed Separatist force. The commander of that force demands you order the troops now opposing him to withdraw from Praesitlyn immediately. For every hour you delay issuing that order, one of my staff will be executed, ending with me. I beg you, for the sake of my people, *Attack! Attack! Attack!*"

The last *attack* echoed through the totally silent room. Slayke swore under his breath, then ordered, "Play it again!"

"Gutsy woman," Halcyon said with admiration.

"She's asking us to attack even though it means her life and the lives of her people. That's like calling in a laser cannon barrage on your own position to save it from being overrun."

"No kidding," Slayke agreed. "So she's the one we came here to rescue."

Anakin couldn't utter a word. There was something—else—about that woman.

Halcyon looked at his second in command. "Anakin?"

Anakin stood with his fists clenched, the muscles in his jaw working. The monitor was blank now, but he continued to glare at it as if Momen's image were still there.

"Anakin?" Halcyon asked.

Someone behind them was cursing in the most foul terms. Someone else said something softly and the curses stopped.

"Anakin?" Halcyon clamped a hand on Anakin's shoulder and shook it.

"What?" Anakin blinked, as though returning from someplace different.

"Anakin, it's over."

"Y-yes. I—it's just . . ." Anakin shook his head again and took a breath. "That woman, she reminds me of— well, I don't know . . ."

Slayke stood. "Listen up, everyone," he announced in a voice so loud several officers started. "Listen up," he repeated in a softer tone. "If our comrades who died here fighting these Separatists could see what that woman has done, they would know—" His voice cracked. "—they would know their lives were not sacrificed in vain." He paused and took a breath. "If we ever needed a cause to keep us going, we have it now!"

He walked over to Halcyon and offered him his hand, then extended it to Anakin and shook warmly. "I put myself and what's left of my army completely at your disposal. What are my orders?"

20

One of the many hardships of being in an army during wartime, aside from the possibility of getting killed, is lack of sleep. In wartime, the commander who waits to make a decision usually doesn't live until tomorrow. All military movements and operations seem to occur during the night—and to last all night—and anyone who can sleep on the eve of an attack is either a veteran or so tired he just doesn't care anymore. Of course, the constant pumping of adrenaline into the soldier's system will keep him active, but sooner or later exhaustion sets in.

The strategy session that started at strongpoint Judlie continued for hours. Eventually they moved to Halcyon's command post, which was bigger, better equipped, and offered refreshments that Slayke's depleted supplies could not afford.

Drawing up a battle plan is no easy task. It has to be both detailed and concise, but at the same time flexible enough to accommodate the instant changes required by a fluid battlefield situation. Halcyon's operations officer was given the task, under Anakin's supervision, of writing the plan. Each staff specialist in Halcyon's army was given a portion of the plan, an "annex" to execute: the personnel chief, operations chief, chief surgeon, intelligence chief, ordnance chief, the artillery, infantry, armor, and air commanders, and last but hardly least, quartermaster and transportation—none other than old Mess Boulanger. Each portion of the plan would be integrated into the whole. Time was short, however, and nobody could quite agree on the best course of action.

After several hours it finally got down to two basic approaches.

"Frontal assaults are out of the question," Slayke roared. "You ought to know that an attacking force incurs casualties at a rate of at least three to one against a fortified position. That's what he's hoping for, so he can cut us down to size!"

"I know, I know," Halcyon replied. "I'm just advising a feint at his center while a strong force swings around one of his flanks. Grab him in the center of his line, hold him fast, make him think that's our main axis of attack, and hit him around the flank and come down on his rear."

"How about a vertical envelopment?" Anakin suggested. "We have the transports. We could land a force in his rear and attack from there, while our main force advances on the center of his line."

Slayke cocked an eyebrow. "What do you think?" he asked Halcyon.

"I don't know," the Jedi Master replied cautiously. "What's his anti-aircraft capability?"

"We've made an assessment," his intelligence officer responded. "We sent remotely piloted vehicles over his lines an hour ago in anticipation of this question, sir. We sent several—none came back. But they transmitted enough information for us to determine that his anti-air defenses are particularly dense. We spotted quad laser cannons, as well as ion cannons that they must have off-loaded from their ships and installed as air defense weapons. We estimate at least thirty-five percent casualties just going in, sir—and even higher casualties coming back out."

"Prohibitive," Slayke said softly. "I'm sorry, Anakin, vertical envelopment won't work. I think the only viable tactic is to swing around one of his flanks." Which had been Halcyon's opinion from the beginning.

"Don't forget, he can reinforce every part of his line on a very short axis, while we'll have a much longer way to go to move troops and supplies, especially if we're successful in getting around one of his flanks," Anakin pointed out.

Slayke nodded approvingly. "The young Jedi is becoming a strategist."

Halcyon smiled. "Anakin is a man of many surprising talents."

Slayke laughed. "Anakin, you just may have a future in this trade."

"Then we'll follow the plan to attack the center simultaneously with a strong force swinging around his flank," Halcyon said. "But first we've got to know how strong his positions are."

"I have just the man," Slayke said. "Omin, front and center! Sergeant L'Loxx is one of the best recon men in the business. He'll probe their lines and find any weaknesses there might be."

The sergeant approached the officers and came to attention. Halcyon stood and shook his hand. "It's nearly midnight, Sergeant L'Loxx. Can you complete a reconnaissance of the enemy line by dawn?"

"I can't do the whole line in the same night, sir," the sergeant answered, "but yessir, I'll reconnoiter wherever you want and be back here well before dawn. I can be ready in fifteen minutes."

"Let's send three probes, then—center, left, and right. But I think we should send clone commandos," Anakin said.

"Begging your pardon, sir, but I'm the best there is for this job, only I can't do the whole line myself. Give me whatever sector you want and I'll get the information you need."

"Very well. Sergeant, you take the right flank." Aside, Halcyon told Anakin, "You select commandos to do the center and left flank." Then back to L'Loxx: "The former strongpoint Izable will be your jumping-off place, and that'll be where you'll come back through our lines. How many troopers will you need?"

"Just me, sir."

"Only yourself?" Halcyon looked at Slayke, who shrugged. "What if something happens, Sergeant? How will we get your report?"

"Nothing will happen to me."

"I'd like to go with him," Grudo said, stepping up beside where Anakin was sitting.

"Ridiculous!" Slayke snorted.

"A Rodian should be good on patrol, sir," Sergeant L'Loxx said. "They're experts at getting into places where they aren't wanted—and getting back out again."

Anakin nodded. "Grudo's in, then."

"We want to go, too," someone said. It was one of the guards from the *Neelian*, Corporal Ram Raders.

Halcyon stood up quickly. "What is this? I send out one man on a recon, and half my army wants to go along. We may as well mount the assault right now without any idea what's out there. No, and that's final." He sat down.

"Please, sir," Raders pleaded. "That's the sort of thing we're good at. Besides, all we're doing here is standing around. We can be a great help to the sergeant."

"I'll take them," Sergeant L'Loxx said. "If I'm not satisfied with how they move, I'll leave them at Izable. But that's it. Four's maybe too many as it is."

"Very well," Halcyon said. "Anakin, coordinate all this with the clone commandos. All of you meet back here in fifteen minutes for a briefing."

Anakin turned to the operations officer. "Would you start writing up the operation order? I want to talk to Grudo privately for a moment." He excused himself and went outside with the Rodian. They sat down on some ration boxes in the dark. "I don't want you to go out there, Grudo, but if your mind is set on it, then I won't stop you."

"I'll be all right," Grudo replied.

Anakin didn't speak for a while, not sure what he wanted to say. "Are you married?" he asked at last.

Grudo hooted a laugh. "Many times."

"Did you love your wives?"

Anakin could feel Grudo's shrug in the dark. "I was good to them, they to me. But a soldier, just like a Jedi, must put duty first, learn to live without the things other men yearn for. Why do you ask?"

"Just curious."

"Don't worry. I'll be fine." Grudo laid a hand on Anakin's shoulder, and the two were silent.

"That woman we watched earlier, do you know her?" Grudo asked, changing the subject. "I saw you. I think you must know her."

"N-no . . . ," Anakin replied. "She just reminded me of my mother, who was killed."

"That must have been hard," Grudo said softly. "But you know, I've watched you, and I can tell you this much: she'd be proud of you now, your mother. I've never seen someone as smart in as many ways as you are. You're quick in everything: to learn, to decide, to act. You will be a great commander, and I'm proud to have helped you." He stood. "I must go now. The sergeant is waiting, and dawn comes quickly tonight."

"Good luck, then, friend."

"Yes, luck. Every soldier needs luck, but remember, it's skill that counts in battle. But you wish me luck and I take it, with many thanks." Grudo took Anakin's hand in his own, held it briefly, then turned and disappeared into the night. Anakin was surprised at how silently the Rodian walked in the dark. He stood there for a long moment, then turned and went back into the command post.

"They won't be foolish enough to attack us at the center of our line," Pors Tonith told his assembled commanders. "They'll send a force at the center, but it'll be a diversion. The main attack will come on one of our flanks. Therefore, I want a strong reserve here—" He indicated a spot near the communications center. "—ready to move to reinforce any part of our line on a moment's notice. Expect probes all night tonight and then an attack in the morning. I want you all out there all night long, checking your positions, registering your weapons, checking your fields of fire. Droids don't need sleep and you do, but tonight no one sleeps in this army."

"These hills on our left, sir, they command the approaches around that flank and we have troops on them, but they're still only lightly defended. I suggest we reinforce immediately."

"We must wait until the attack develops," Tonith said. "With a mobile reserve we can reinforce anywhere we need troops. You have your orders. We must hold this position until our reinforcements arrive, which I am confident will be very soon now."

After his commanders had left the command post, Tonith grinned at B'wuf, still sitting under guard, dozing fitfully. "Wake him up," he ordered the droid guards. "I said no one sleeps in this army, and I meant no one. Except me, of course. The brain needs its rest." He turned to one of the technicians. "Wake me if there are any developments." And he went to his quarters to sleep.

The briefing went quickly. There were three recon teams. Team one would cover the left flank; team two the center; and team three, Sergeant L'Loxx's team, the right flank. Each soldier on the three teams was given a comlink. "No voice traffic," the intelligence chief warned them. "The enemy is sure to be eavesdropping.

"Everyone, form up at Izable. As soon as the barrage starts, move out. When you're ready to come back in, press the talk button on your comlinks: one long and one short for team one; two long, two short for team two; and three long, three short for team three. When you've all reported you're ready to return, we'll lay down some more artillery to cover you, and that'll be your signal to come back in."

"I hate these things," L'Loxx muttered, looking at his comlink. "They always go off at the worst possible moment."

"All right," the intelligence chief said. "As soon as you're all assembled at Izable, Sergeant L'Loxx, give me one long squelch on that comlink you so heartily despise and I'll send in the artillery. And don't worry about anyone calling while you're out there. The comm is set on a secure channel reserved for this reconnaissance. Are there any questions?"

There weren't.

Izable was a shambles. The smell of death was everywhere. In one spot a tiny wisp of smoke filtered through a crack in a demolished bunker, a sign of a fire still smoldering; it showed a very bright glow through the infras, indicating that the fire must still be extremely hot. They wondered what was burning, and Grudo shuddered at the thought. The four team members huddled together a short distance from the other two teams, waiting for the barrage to commence.

The plan was that as soon as the attack opened up

they would dash forward to follow the dry riverbed around to the right of the mesa and then climb to the top. There were several talus slopes that could be used for that purpose closer by, but L'Loxx had decided to go far around to the right and emerge on the mesa almost behind the enemy line. "They'll be waiting for us, you can bet on it," he told the other three, "and their attention will be to their front." To cloak themselves from the enemy's night-vision devices, the four wore special protective clothing of L'Loxx's own design. It wouldn't give them total protection from infrared scanners, but with all the noise, confusion, and heat of the artillery barrage, it would give them enough cover long enough to get to a spot where L'Loxx counted on the enemy's lack of vigilance to protect them from discovery.

The night was pitch black, illuminated only by the stars above.

"Ooof!" Erk sat up so suddenly he banged his head against the rock. "Odie, I think I've got it! Give me your equipment belt!"

She handed it over.

"Some light, please?" He fumbled with a pouch. "Aha!" he exclaimed victoriously. "Just as I thought! Odie, this is our way out of here!" He held a vibroblade in his hand. "Mechanics use a version of this same thing to cut the hardest metals while working on starfighters! I think we can use it to—"

"—cut rock," Odie finished.

"You bet!"

"Are you sure? That's not an industrial version, Erk,

it's a vibroknuckler. We use those as backup weapons in case we get into a close scrape. Well," she amended with a smile, "we use them to cut open ration packs, too."

Erk fitted his fingers through the activation rings. "Don't look too closely," he said. He squeezed the rings and applied the blade to a section of overhead rock. After a few seconds the blade's action began to produce heat, and molten rock fragments began dripping down on the floor. He shut the device off quickly. The rock glowed faintly where he'd used the knuckler to slice a groove twenty-five millimeters long and ten millimeters deep in only a few seconds. "Say hello to the outside world!" he said softly.

"Whew! That thing produces fumes—how are you going to cut your way through all that without suffocating us or setting us on fire?"

Erk thought for a moment. "We'll take it slow and easy, give the heat and fumes plenty of time to dissipate. Time's all we've got right now. We've got a good airflow in here, so we should be able to keep the oxygen level high enough to allow us to breathe. Here, help me off with this." He shrugged out of his flier's tunic. "Ugh, haven't had this off in days." He laughed. "These are treated to be blast and fire resistant. All starfighter pilots wear them. We'll use it as sort of a shield while cutting. How much power do you suppose this still has in it?"

"Maybe ten hours? I don't know, Erk. Can you cut a hole big enough for us to get out in less than ten hours of use?"

"Well, we're sure going to find out, aren't we? I'll

start at the apex there, where the two slabs join the wall. That way whatever I cut out won't weaken the resistance that's holding all this stuff up."

"We'll take turns, Erk."

"Ah, I knew you'd come in handy!" He grabbed her and kissed her.

"I don't know about all this fraternization between an officer and an enlisted woman, Lieutenant," Odie said. She put a hand behind his head and kissed him full on the lips.

"When we get out of here I'm going to talk to you about doing some serious fraternization. Well, watch out rocks, here we come!"

21

Quickly but carefully, the four made their way along the dry riverbed, keeping close to the far bank to hide themselves as much as possible from observation by the enemy positions on the mesa far above. This proved to be a wise tactic, and in a very short time they had worked their way to a point where the ancient river had changed its course away from the mesa.

The friendly artillery barrage roared and split the sky above with bright flashes, and soon counterbattery fire began ranging down onto Halcyon's positions. The entire universe seemed to be consumed in the fiery holocaust. None of them had ever seen such a display, and they were both exhilarated and awed by it. Sergeant L'Loxx smiled to himself: the diversion was working.

They crawled one by one over the riverbank and picked their way over the plain that separated it from the steep mesa walls. There was evidence everywhere of the enemy's occupation—destroyed equipment, blasted droids, deep shell holes—all providing the cover they needed as they crawled and scuttled over the open ground. Every piece of equipment they carried had been carefully padded so as not to make any noise, and L'Loxx had brought along a piece of cord that connected each team member to the next so none would get lost in the dark. He'd also painted small luminous dots between their shoulder blades; by using the night-vision goggles, each could keep his eye on the one in front. Each carried a blaster pistol as his main weapon, but nothing heavier. After an hour they had made their way across the plateau to the slope of the mesa at a point L'Loxx judged to be somewhat behind the right wing of the enemy's positions. That was where they would negotiate the steep cliff to come out at the base of the hills that dominated that end of the line.

L'Loxx knew this ground, had been over it numerous times. This end of the enemy's defenses was anchored in the two small hills that occupied a commanding position on the mesa. A thin line of skirmishers had been posted just above the plain, but since the hills themselves could only be approached from the front through a forest of boulders, some bigger than banthas, the advance sentry posts, L'Loxx hoped, were considered sufficient security to warn of an attack. He signaled for a halt. When the other three had closed up to him he went to each and whispered, "This is where we go up. When we come out at the top we should be just behind the far right of the line. I'll go in first. Stay close behind."

Gradually the barrages ceased. An unnatural quiet descended on the battlefield, and it was plunged again into impenetrable darkness.

*   *   *

Lieutenant Erk H'Arman paused in his work. Cool air came through the tiny hole he'd been able to cut in the rock. Through it he could see the stars. "We're going to make it, Odie." He sank into a sitting position and removed the tunic that had been covering his arm and hand. "Shine some light on my arm, would you?"

Recon trooper Odie Subu gasped. "It's covered in blisters! I have a first-aid pac on my belt." She fumbled with some pouches and applied a dressing to Erk's wounds.

"You're an angel, Odie. Do you think there's a reason we were put together to go through all this?"

"I think there's a reason for everything, Erk."

Erk examined his tunic. "It's holding up pretty well. It's just those splatters of molten rock are pretty hot. Would you mind giving me a drink? My hands are mighty sore about now."

She unfastened her canteen and held it to his mouth. He drank greedily. When he had his fill, she said, "Let me do some of the cutting now. You rest awhile."

"All right. But let's both take a break for a minute, let some of this hot air dissipate. As soon as you begin to feel the heat, stop. I made the mistake of holding on too long. I've really messed myself up. Don't let that happen to you."

"It's a guy thing. You guys always want to do everything right now. Let this woman at it." They lay there, resting for several minutes, and then she donned his tunic and began cutting away at the rock. She worked steadily for ten minutes.

"Do you hear that?" Erk asked. The roar of the artillery came to the pair inside the ruins of their bunker somewhat muffled but still gloriously loud enough to tell them that a major attack was under way.

"We've been relieved?" Odie whispered. Starting to cry, she slumped down next to Erk. He put his good arm around her shoulders. The hole had widened enough with her cutting that she could put her hand through it.

They listened in the darkness. "It's either a relief force, or the final assault," Erk said at last. "Either way we're getting out of here."

"I'm sorry for crying like this."

Erk pulled her close and buried his nose in her hair, which smelled of atomized rock and sweat, but to him it was the most delightful fragrance he could imagine. "Forget it, Odie. It's a girl thing, you know?" They laughed. "Now stop this mooning around and get back to work," he said with mock gruffness. "We both need to get out of here and get a bath."

They entered the jumble of boulders. The rocks loomed over them like tall buildings. It was so quiet they could hear one another breathing. Sergeant L'Loxx signaled a halt. From far ahead, off to the left a bit and above them, they heard faint metallic sounds. Nobody needed to be told it was battle droids moving about. But how many? What were their fortifications like? Did they have heavy weapons? What would be the best way to attack them? Through his night-vision goggles L'Loxx could make out a small open space between the rocks. He stepped into it, followed by Grudo.

A droid stood up just to the sergeant's left, and before L'Loxx could react, Grudo drew a vibroblade from his equipment belt and took the thing's head off with one swift, clean blow. Just as quickly as he had drawn and struck, the Rodian grabbed the droid's falling body and eased it to the ground. But nobody caught the head before it tumbled onto a pile of debris. Sparks flashed from the head's severed circuitry.

Hearts in their mouths, they all froze where they stood. Then L'Loxx continued to lead the way carefully across the clearing. On the other side he crouched down and indicated that they should gather about him in a tight circle.

"Good work, Grudo." He punched the Rodian lightly on the shoulder. "Now listen up. I go on from here alone." One of the guards protested. "No, I'm better at this than any of you. Establish a defensive position here and wait for me." He pressed a stud on his wrist chrono. "It's zero three hundred hours now. First light is at zero six hundred. Give me one hour. If I'm not back by then, leave me."

"No way," Private Vick whispered. "We came in together and we'll all go out together, or not at all."

L'Loxx leaned close to the guard and whispered, "That's an order. If they get me, they'll get you, too, if you hang around. You do as I say or I guarantee you'll never be allowed on patrol again."

Private Vick couldn't tell for sure in the dark, but he thought the sergeant was grinning.

"You all know how to follow orders," L'Loxx told them, "so follow." He unclipped the cord that bound them together and vanished into the dark.

The three sat back to back and waited. Corporal Raders put his hand to Grudo's ear and whispered, "You do good work, Rodian. That droid never knew what hit it." Grudo nodded his thanks.

The minutes dragged by. Grudo felt at home now, with other soldiers on a dangerous mission, death or glory just a few meters away. It was what he lived for. He listened as the two guards whispered to each other. "Get me some," one said. "Yeah, bring them on!" the other replied. Grudo smiled in the darkness. Soldier talk, bravado to cover their fear—"Mocking the midnight bell," he'd heard someone describe it, the kind of defiant courage that gave warriors the strength and confidence they needed to fight. He loved it. No one was more alive than those who found themselves where they were now, on the thin edge of life and death. He thought of Anakin, whom he'd come to love during the time they had worked together. There was something about the young Jedi that Grudo had recognized the first time they'd met in that sleazy bar on Coruscant. He'd been unable to pin it down at the time, but subsequently he'd recognized it as the ability to get others to follow him.

In the darkness beyond, L'Loxx climbed up the reverse slope of the nethermost hill. The going was surprisingly easy. Cautiously, he peered over some rocks into the rear of the enemy defenses. Just ten meters to his left, no more, a group of battle droids huddled behind a hastily constructed rock wall. In his night-vision device they appeared as tiny glowing dots, the infrared signatures of their power cells and circuitry. As he watched, there was a small but bright flash from one of the droids, and then it disappeared from his vision to be replaced by a fast-fading glow. L'Loxx smiled. The thing had just had a short circuit. Delightful! They weren't being properly maintained. Good to know. Slowly, he scanned the line. He wished he had the telemetry to send what he was seeing back to head-quarters, but they had decided against using that option: there was too good a chance the transmissions would be intercepted. As he examined the position closely his heart began to race in his chest. This was it, this was the weak spot. The line could be turned at this point. He had to get this information back to head-quarters.

He crept back down the slope, expecting every moment to be subjected to blasterfire, but none came. In a few minutes he was back at the rocks, crouching down with his three companions.

"We're ready to go back in," he whispered, "and boy, do I have some intelligence." He withdrew his communicator and gave the signal they were ready to return. "While we're waiting for the all-clear, I've got to tell you what I saw up there. You won't believe this, but they—"

Two battle droids came clattering into the little clearing between the rocks. Vick drew his blaster and, kneeling, destroyed them both with two quick shots.

"Run! Run!" L'Loxx screamed.

"I'll stay here and slow them down," Vick yelled back. The other three ran between the boulders. A flurry of blaster bolts flashed in the night behind them.

Vick came running out from between the rocks. "Too many of them!" he shouted as he skittered past Grudo. Calmly, Grudo unholstered his blaster and drew his vibroblade with the other hand. As the droids came charging at him from between the rocks he cut one down with his blaster and slashed through the neck cables of another with his blade. In ten seconds he lay six of them low, forming a small obstacle the others had to clamber over to get at him. He stood calmly firing into the charging droids. Blaster bolts caromed off the rocks, singeing him; two hit him glancing blows and he staggered, but didn't go down. He piled the droids up. Thirty seconds into the fight there were no more droids to shoot at. Grudo stood panting for a moment. He holstered his blaster. Dead silence. No! Up ahead more droids were coming down from the hills. It was time to go. He turned and raced back in the direction of his comrades. At that point the artillery opened up again and the night turned to bedlam.

Odie stuck her head out of the hole she had cut in the rock. "A few more minutes, and I think I can get through!" She sat down beside him. "How's the arm?"

"Well, an ordinary person would be screaming and writhing, but me? Heck, I'm a hotshot fighter pilot and we train in pain." He grimaced, then turned serious. "I'm sorry, Odie, but I'll need your help to get up through that hole when the time comes. My legs feel a little rubbery, you know?"

"Give me ten more minutes and we're out of here!"

After the rock around the edge of the hole cooled

sufficiently, Odie lifted herself up to the rim. Erk gave her a boost from below and she was out.

The barrage started up again at that very moment. She slid back into the bunker. "Do you think we should go out there in this?"

"Who cares? Anything is better than another second in this tomb."

"Use your good arm to hoist yourself up, and I'll boost you from below. But be careful—it might be a tight fit."

The cannon fire was so intense it lit up the interior of the bunker. Erk's face showed pale and drawn in the flashing light. "Hope the crawlers don't run over us," he said weakly.

He managed to pull himself halfway through the hole, then got stuck. He grunted in pain. Odie grabbed his feet from below and with all her strength shoved him out into the clear. She tossed up her blaster rifle and followed him. They lay in the rubble, gasping for breath.

"We made it." The artillery roared and thundered overhead, but nothing hit the ground where they lay. "They're dueling," Erk went on. "Nicest display I've ever seen."

Figures emerged out of the dark. Odie grabbed her blaster and fired a shot.

"*Don't shoot!*" one of the figures shouted. "We're friends!" Someone rushed up to Odie and slapped her blaster out of the way. "Blast you!" he shouted, "you shot one of my troopers, you fool! Didn't anyone tell you we were coming through?" He looked at her in the strobing light of the barrage, then at Erk, lying on his back beside her. Both looked the worse for wear. "Hey, who are you, anyway?"

"Grudo's shot real bad," Corporal Raders said. "She hit him in the side of his head. Blast you people! What the—" He stopped abruptly as he took in the pair.

"I—I—we—we were trapped in a bunker, sir. I— I thought you were the enemy. My buddy is badly hurt, too. I—I'm sorry about your soldier. I—"

L'Loxx turned and knelt beside Grudo. The side of the Rodian's head gave to his probing fingers, but he was still conscious. His one good eye blinked in the gunlight. He tried to say something, but it came out as only noise.

"Let's wait for the ARC troopers," Raders suggested. "They can help us carry him back to the aid station. There's nothing we can do for him here."

"If we don't get him back right now he won't make it, and after what he's done this night, we're not waiting. You two," L'Loxx said, indicating Odie and Erk, "give us a hand."

"Sir, my buddy is badly burned—he can't help carry anyone."

"Okay, you help him along; we'll handle Grudo ourselves. And stop calling me *sir*, I work for a living— *hey!* I know you two! You're from General Khamar's army. We came in together. I don't remember your names, but I found you two out in the desert—"

"Sergeant L'Loxx," Odie gasped.

"How're you doing?" Erk asked from where he lay.

"I remember now," L'Loxx said, "they sent you up to Izable after we came in together. Well, I'll be—"

"Sergeant, let's get moving? We can talk when we get back to our lines," Raders suggested.

In moments they had rigged a stretcher from a net Odie found in her equipment belt and two long dura-steel rods they wrenched from the ruins of a bunker. Carrying Grudo over the rough ground was easier than they'd expected.

Sergeant L'Loxx came to attention and saluted Halcyon.

"Make your report, Sergeant."

"We didn't wait for the other teams to come in, sir, because I had two wounded and had to get them to the aid station. Their right flank is vulnerable, sir." He moved to a three-dimensional display. "First, this hill on the far end of the line is only lightly defended. I think they're counting on the rocks at the foot of the hill to break up any assault. Second, I didn't see any crew-served weapons up there. They haven't brought in artillery. And finally, I have reason to believe lack of maintenance might be reducing the droid fighting force. We put them through some exercises, and they'll lose combat strength through breakdowns."

"Who was wounded?" Anakin asked.

"I'm afraid the Rodian, sir."

"How badly?"

"Very badly, sir. But let me add this: we wouldn't have made it back with this information if it hadn't been for him. He stayed behind long enough to give the rest of us a chance to get some distance between us and the droid lines. I want to add also, sir," he said, turning to Halcyon, "that your two guards are solid soldiers. They held up their end."

"Well, who's the other wounded trooper, then?" Slayke asked. Briefly L'Loxx explained about Odie and Erk.

"I remember them. She went to Izable with the lieutenant," Slayke said.

"She's the one who shot Grudo," L'Loxx told Anakin. "In the dark and the confusion she thought we were the enemy. It was just one of those situations nobody could have anticipated. It happens, sir. Friendly fire."

"Very well, then." Halcyon had made his decision. "It's zero four hundred hours now. Commander Skywalker, at zero six hundred I want you in position to attack that right flank. Use Sergeant L'Loxx as your guide. Take two brigades of your division. Leave the third in reserve under the command of Captain Slayke."

"Shouldn't we wait for the commandos to report, sir?" Halcyon's operations officer asked.

"I'll be interested to hear what they've found out, but no. This—" He pointed to the display. "—is the pivotal point in our assault, and we'll attack there. I'll take my division and attack the center. I'll wait until you're in place before I commence my attack, Commander Skywalker. You wait ten minutes after I move forward before moving in. I believe during that time the enemy will bring in troops from his wings to reinforce his center. We've given him two artillery barrages so far tonight to soften him up, or I hope he thinks so, and when we hit him again while my division moves into position, he'll see that as the main attack, I'm sure of it. I think we might just carry this off." He turned to his operations officer. "Issue the order to all commanders."

"May I see him?" Anakin asked the medical officer who met him at the aid station.

"This way." The doctor's slumped shoulders and the deep lines that carved his face spoke more eloquently than the bloodstains on his surgical gown of what Sons and Daughters of Freedom had been through since they landed.

Grudo was lying on a field litter behind some curtains. Anakin caught his breath when he saw how grievously the Rodian had been wounded. *Friendly fire*, Anakin thought, that was what the sergeant had called the accident. He wondered who had invented such a ridiculous term. Some staff officer, no doubt, someone safe and secure in a headquarters, someone who jested at scars but who'd never felt a wound himself. There was nothing friendly about fire that caused that much injury, no matter who it came from. Anakin fought down a surge of anger, not at the hapless recon trooper who had shot Grudo, but at the kind of military mind that would call such a thing "friendly fire."

"Can he talk?" he asked the harried doctor.

"He's been muttering something, whether it's in his own language or just moaning, I don't know. It's astonishing that he's even semiconscious with a wound like that. I'm not that familiar with the Rodian brain, but look here, you can see through the skull—"

Anakin cut the doctor off. "There's nothing you can do, Doctor?"

The surgeon shook his head. "No, he's just too far gone."

"Can he hear us?"

"I don't think so, but his status is the same if he can hear us or not. With a head injury like that he won't last much longer. We can't even give him a sedative, unless, of course, you want me to end his misery—"

Anakin turned on him. "If I ever again hear you say something like that about one of my troopers, I swear . . ." He shook his head. "Now have the courtesy to leave me alone with my friend."

The doctor blanched, parted the curtains, and disappeared.

Anakin looked down at Grudo. "Can you hear me?" he asked. He bent closer. "Grudo, can you hear me?"

Grudo opened his one good eye. Something rumbled deep in his chest, and he coughed. "A-Anakin . . ." He let out his breath.

"Save your strength—you're going to be just fine," Anakin lied.

"No," Grudo whispered. "Time—to—go."

"No, no, Grudo! They're sending you to the *Respite,* a fine hospital ship where they have everything they need to help you—"

With great effort Grudo raised himself up on an elbow and with his free hand gripped the young Jedi by the shoulder. He brought his ruined face close to Anakin's. "Don't cry over me," he said, then fell back on the cot.

Anakin didn't need to touch Grudo to know the life force had left him. He sat by his side for several minutes, then stood and returned to the command post. There would be an attack in the morning, and he would lead it. Grudo would be avenged.

22

Often the success of a military operation depends on a mere chance event, such as someone coming to a place—a crossroads, a river, a bridge, a village—only a few minutes before or after someone else. That matter of moments can spell the difference between victory or defeat on a battlefield. Or sometimes disaster hangs on a decision by a commander who makes it without full knowledge of his enemy's intentions or dispositions; a good commander has to be able to make snap decisions, because delay can be fatal to a campaign. But so can the wrong decision, and even the very best commanders, pressed by the rapidly unfolding events of the modern battlefield to decide quickly on tactical matters, can make a mistake. Even with all the technology available to the warrior, the battlefield is still a confused and disorganized place where events move with lightning speed under a cloak of impenetrable darkness called the fog of battle. And no one who is not right there can penetrate it.

Thus the importance of the reconnaissance Nejaa Halcyon ordered, and thus the importance of the deci-

sion he made based on the information garnered by
only one of the teams sent on that reconnaissance.

Clone Commando CT-19/39, not Sergeant Omin
L'Loxx, good as he might have been, was really the
best reconnaissance man currently on Praesitlyn. His
own nickname for himself was Green Wizard, because
of his rank as a sergeant and his skill at patrol craft.
As soon as he was given command of team one to
cover the left flank of the enemy positions, he decided
to split it up so each commando could conduct his own
probe into the enemy lines and penetrate as far into
them as he could, to bring back as much intelligence as
possible.

Green Wizard made it all the way to the Intergalactic
Communications Center buildings without being detected. Carefully, he committed the position of every gun
he could find to memory, counted the droids staffing
the positions, noted their armaments, noted where the
enemy had dug in artillery. Of special interest to him
was the fact that several guns were evidently being
moved to the far left of the enemy line to strengthen
the positions on the two small hills at that end of the
defenses. In his opinion, however, the weak spot in
Tonith's line was on his right, not his left, because
Green Wizard had come through there so easily—and
especially now, since he could tell the general where
every gun was on that flank. It was clear to Green Wizard that the attack should fall entirely on the left, the
whole army thrown against that flank in echelon to
slam into it with tremendous force and fold it back

upon itself, breaking Tonith's hold and rolling up his entire defenses in one swift, irresistible blow.

The only trouble was that now Green Wizard had to get back to his own lines to report this information. He could call on his comlink, but General Halcyon had been very specific that no one was to break comm silence during the reconnaissance. Apparently his other two comrades had not had as much success as he at remaining undetected: there had been shooting all along the line, especially where they would have crossed—a lot of shooting—so Green Wizard was pretty sure they had been discovered and possibly had not made it back to their rally point just below the mesa. He wondered about the troopers who were supposed to probe the center. Would they have seen what he had? Had some of the shooting been directed at them? They were clone commandos so they were good, very good, but not as good as he, and everyone's luck ran out sometime. Green Wizard knew one day his would, too, and perhaps this night it had for his comrades. He had to assume he was the only one left now and it was up to him to get the intelligence he'd gathered back to headquarters.

The barrage came unexpectedly, catching Green Wizard still behind enemy lines. That didn't surprise him: such things happened often in battle. Someone had made a mistake, starting the barrage before all the teams had been accounted for, but that wasn't his worry—getting back was. Yet even as Green Wizard hugged the ground, he noted how accurate Halcyon's artillerists were. He respected accuracy and professionalism, and admired the artillery even as it came crashing and smashing down all around him, bouncing him up in the air, crushing the breath out of him, shaking his teeth loose.

At first Green Wizard felt no pain at all. He knew his leg had been severed, but he just tied off the artery with a length of cord and considered his options. He knew that soon there would be pain, followed by shock. He had to do something and quickly, because the intelligence he had was too important to die with him. If he stayed where he was, he would be found and executed. He could call in his findings now and his mission would be over, successfully completed; but his orders were not to use the comlink except to signal that he was ready to come back in. He gave the signal and for a moment, but only for an instant, he felt a flash of something like anger that someone back at the command post had not followed the plan for the night. The barrage continued unabated.

So his only option now was to try to get back to his own lines. With one leg gone, that would be difficult, but not impossible. Clone commandos were at their best when faced with obstacles that would be insuperable to any ordinary being.

Slowly, carefully, he began to crawl. At some point the tourniquet on his leg came loose and he started losing blood. He succeeded in making it as far as the dry riverbed, but that was where he finally realized he could go no farther. He had to make his report before he was too weak to do it, orders or no orders. He reached for his comlink, but somewhere along the way he had lost it. He chided himself for that. He had let pain and physical exhaustion distract him. It would be good if he did die here. He didn't want anyone to know how incompetent he'd become. But Green Wizard also felt a terrible sense of frustration, not because he was dying, but because he would die with information that was vital to the army he served. His last conscious thought was that he had done his best.

"We don't have much time," Anakin informed his commanders, "so here's the plan of attack." He called up a huge three-dimensional view of the battlefield. "The focus of our attack is this hill. Note the jumble of huge rocks at its base. They'll serve as cover for our infantry, and we'll mount our assault from there. The key is to get across this plain as quickly as possible, because there we'll be in full view of the enemy on the mesa. General Halcyon's full-divisional attack on the center will draw troops away from the flanks to meet it and weaken their positions elsewhere, in particular here on this hill, which we know from last night's recon is only lightly defended by infantry droids with no artillery. Once we occupy that hill, we'll enfilade the entire enemy position. First Brigade will occupy the hill, while Second Brigade will sweep around to the rear of the positions. We will be attacking from three directions simultaneously.

"We will be preceded by Clone Commandos, led by an ARC trooper, who will infiltrate the position on this hill and cause a diversion. Under cover of that diversion we will attack in strength. Now, as I said, it's vital we get across that plain quickly. We will be preceded by a battalion of crawlers that will lay down suppressing fire on the hilltop. Our infantry will follow in their armored transports. We'll use this dry riverbed to get into position—that will provide us cover until we're ready to attack across the plain. We won't mount our own attack until General Halcyon's division is fully engaged. Fire and maneuver all the way across, but move your soldiers quickly—I cannot overemphasize speed. You will be under direct observation until you get to these rocks. You'll be supported by artillery all the way, and it will continue to pound the enemy positions as you go up the hill, but as you can see, these rocks make the approach to this hill impossible for vehicles of any kind, so this phase of the operation will have to be accomplished on foot. This will be an infantry soldier's fight."

Anakin's commanders stood in full battle gear. Their troops had been assembled for the attack some time before and were waiting for their orders. He turned to the ARC captain in charge of his clone commandos. "You will depart immediately, Captain, and go in first. I want you to penetrate the enemy position and raise havoc up there. As soon as you're in, we'll follow. Remember, all of this starts ten minutes after General Halcyon commences his attack on the center of the enemy's positions. Everything we do must be coordinated to the second.

"That's it. You've all been assigned your sectors and objectives. Return to your units and brief your subordinates. We jump off in thirty minutes."

"Sir," one of the two brigade commanders said, "who will be battlefield tactical commander?"

"I will," Anakin replied. At the surprised silence that met his words, he straightened his shoulders and silently reminded himself to relax and remember Grudo's lessons. "First of all, I don't believe in ordering someone else to anything I'm not willing to do myself. Second, if any mistakes are made this morning, I'm responsible whether or not I'm there with you, so I may as well be there. And finally, you can't lead from behind. All right, let's get going. Dismissed."

"Sir, may I speak with you for a moment?" It was the ARC captain.

"Make it quick, Captain."

"Yessir. We lost six troopers on the reconnaissance, so we know nothing about what the enemy intends to do in his main positions."

"Well, Captain, I'm sure you lost your troopers because that part of the enemy line was impenetrable. That must mean that General Halcyon's decision to take the hills is the correct one. You heard Sergeant L'Loxx's report."

"Yessir. Why did the second barrage open before we knew if the men had made it back?"

Anakin hadn't expected that question. Was this clone questioning his commander's orders? He knew ARC troopers were several cuts above the ordinary clone trooper, but this line of questioning was getting very close to insubordination. "General Halcyon had to make a decision, Captain: leave L'Loxx out there until your troopers reported in, take a chance on losing all the recon men, or bring at least some of them in to make a report. In the event, he made the correct decision."

"But one did give the signal. Too late."

"Yes, yes," Anakin answered quickly, "I'm sorry

about that. Captain, you do realize that this entire attack depends on you and your troopers, don't you?
What do you say we get moving now?"

The captain saluted, made an about-face, and left
the command post. Anakin stood there thinking for
a moment. He had not expected a clone trooper—
even an ARC—to question orders. When Anakin had
craved a command of his own, he had not really
thought about the responsibility that entailed: responsibility for the lives of individual sentient beings who
would die on his orders, regardless of whether their
loyalty had been bought by the Republic, as was the
case with the clone army, or whether, like Khamar's
and Slayke's soldiers, they fought because they thought
it was their duty to oppose tyranny.

"A credit for your thoughts, Jedi."

Anakin whirled to see Slayke standing there, a big
grin on his face. "I was just thinking—"

"Thinking is dangerous for a commander." Slayke
laughed. "See where it's gotten me?" He paused. "You
are going to lead the attack personally, I hear."

"Yessir. I can't just send soldiers in there while I sit
safely back at headquarters. Besides, if anything goes
wrong, I want to be on the spot to correct it."

Slayke nodded and held out his hand. "You'll do just
fine. I wish I could go with you, but we're being held in
reserve. I've had a talk with your Third Brigade commander and we have an understanding. I'll hand it all
back to you when this is over. I'll be hanging around
here during the attack, keeping an eye on Halcyon.
Don't worry," he added, with a good-natured laugh, "I
won't let him goof things up. Well, good luck, Com-

mander." They shook hands, and then Slayke took two steps back, came to attention, and saluted Anakin.

As Anakin walked to his command post, he noted a spring in his step and couldn't help smiling. That brief conversation with Slayke had invigorated him. The old soldier, the rebel, the iconoclast, had actually taken the time to seek him out and wish him success. And had expressed his confidence in his leadership ability. That was a high compliment, and his spirits soared. Maybe Slayke wasn't such a bad character after all.

"Driver," Anakin shouted as he hoisted himself through a hatch, "crank this thing up. Time to move!"

23

Admiral Pors Tonith kicked the body gingerly with one foot and cast a wary eye at the armor that had been stripped from the corpse and piled off to the side. He was very nervous, being exposed like this in the open, but he'd been called out of his bunker to witness this grisly discovery and he realized it was important. It was still full dark and dawn was an hour away, but he was anxious to get back under cover again. "It's a clone commando," he said.

"We've found one more complete body and parts of others, possibly as many as five altogether," the officer said. "Evidently they were killed by their own artillery last night."

"Evidently," Tonith replied. "Evidently they made it all the way inside our lines without being detected. Evidently"—his voice rose an octave in anger—"they now know a lot about how my army is disposed. These weren't the only ones sent up here, you can be sure of that."

"We must strengthen our lines, sir," the officer said.

Tonith nodded in agreement. "That hill is the key to

our position. Did you move the troops and guns as I ordered last night?"

The officer shifted his weight nervously before he answered. "Some. We've experienced mechanical difficulties and—"

Tonith whirled on him. "You mean my orders weren't carried out?" he asked, his voice rising again.

"We are carrying them out, sir, but—"

"No buts." He was calmer now. "Here is what you will do. I want that hilltop reinforced. Right now. Shorten this line. Move troops from the right to the center; take some from the center to that hilltop. If they take that hilltop, our entire position will be exposed to their fire, and it's all over. If the coming assault threatens to turn our right wing, I want the army to fall back to a line about there—" He pointed to a spot some distance behind them, closer to the communications center. "They will take the enemy under fire as he advances across the plain below us, but if he makes it to the mesa, the right flank will swing backward like a door closing. That will shorten the line and consolidate our forces. Once he's on the mesa it'll force him to come at us over another stretch of open ground, where we shall cut him to pieces."

Tonith grinned, exposing his stained teeth. "And we have a little surprise for him down on the plain, don't we? Get artillery up on that hill right now. Also, warn all commanders to expect infiltration by ARC troopers. They will send them up here to penetrate our lines and weaken them in concert with a ground assault. They'll come at our center in full force, but the real objective of their attack will be right there." He gestured in the dark toward the hills again. "Now get to it and report to me in my command post when these dispositions have been made." He spun on his heel and stalked off to his command bunker, where it was safe and warm and where a simmering pot of tea waited for him. Where, he asked himself, were those reinforcements he'd been promised?

Anakin's assault force hugged the far bank of the dry riverbed, stretched out for nearly half a kilometer along the ancient stream. First light would be at precisely 0603, Praesitlyn time. It was now 0600. He sat at the communications console in his command transport. "This is Unit Six," he said. "Mark the time, three minutes and counting," he advised his commanders, all of whose eyes were glued to their chronos. He turned and grinned at the transport's commander, a clone sergeant. "Nervous?"

"Nossir," the tank droid commander answered automatically.

"Well, I am, and I hereby authorize you to be nervous, too."

He may as well not have said anything, for all the reaction he got.

"We have two minutes, Sergeant. As soon as the transport column goes over the top of the bank onto the plain, I want you to swing around on the flank, climb the bank, and park there so I can supervise the movements of my units." They'd been over this simple maneuver numerous times during the last hour, but just talking about it—about anything—had a calming effect on the troopers, and on Anakin, too.

"Yessir," the sergeant answered. The five sat silently, each thinking his own thoughts, each checking his chrono constantly, watching the seconds flash by.

"The worst part is to come," Anakin said. "We have to wait a full ten minutes after the attack—" He cocked his head. "There it goes," he whispered as Halcyon's preparatory artillery fires commenced. Within seconds, concussions from the dozens of guns of all types reached them inside the armor of the tank droid. They could feel the pressure of the firing in their eardrums. Last night the barrages ordered to cover the reconnaissance had been spectacular displays, but this morning the soldiers were right underneath the guns' trajectories and the noise was tremendous, especially when the enemy's own artillery opened fire on Halcyon's advancing troops.

"They're really catching it up there," one of the gunners commented. His voice showed no more emotion than did his blank-featured helmet. Over the command net they listened with rising anxiety to the cacophony of commanders' voices as Halcyon's troops dashed across the plain under the enemy's devastating fire. Someone in a transport screamed.

"Switch to the tactical net," Anakin ordered. They'd hear enough of their own troopers screaming soon enough—they didn't need any of that now.

And then he realized something important. These were clone troopers sitting around him now—bred to war, bred to discipline, bred to obey without question the orders of the powers that paid for their services. But though their faceplates were expressionless, minute perturbations in the Force told Anakin that these five were reacting to the impending attack like regular troopers, troopers who sweat, were afraid, who could imagine their own deaths. In his attitude toward the clones, had he himself prejudged them? They didn't act here, inside this transport that might soon be their funeral pyre, like they did in ranks. He wondered if Jango Fett had had a sense of humor.

The minutes dragged by. At precisely 0613, the vehicle battalion commander's vehicle roared over the bank, followed by scores of Republic transports.

"Get me up there right now!" Anakin ordered his driver, and the tank droid shot forward. The first dozen or so transports over the bank succeeded in cutting a deep furrow in the soil, and the rut deepened as more followed. This was planned for and would give the following troop transports cover as they negotiated the bank as well as an easy path to follow. But Anakin's vehicle surged over a bit to one side of the beaten path, and the going was very rough for the clones inside.

"Stop here!" Anakin ordered. He climbed into the commander's cupola.

"Sir," the sergeant protested, "you're exposed."

Anakin toggled his throat mike. "Better to see from up here."

"We should keep moving, sir. We're too good a target stopped like this!"

"Don't worry. The law of averages is with us. This

is a target-rich environment." The sight that greeted Anakin's eyes would never leave him: the entire plain was full of moving vehicles, huge clouds of dust and smoke, and burning fires. As he watched, a transport about a kilometer away suddenly blossomed into a ball of fire. He could see one of Halcyon's transports dimly through the drifting smoke and dust. It had suffered a direct hit from a blaster cannon. Burning clones poured out of the vehicle and whirled and twisted awkwardly in their armor, like living torches, before collapsing; the transport exploded in an enormous flash, and then, mercifully, battlesmoke closed over the scene.

Ahead, his own transports were making good headway so far. The battalion commander had positioned several machines along the route of attack, and they were already taking the distant hilltop under fire with their guns. The others were firing as they moved. "Get ready," Anakin told the transport commander waiting patiently in the riverbed for the signal to start advancing. Suddenly a dozen or more enemy tank droids surged forward out of a depression in the ground, guns blazing. Two of Anakin's vehicles were hit immediately. One was the battalion commander's vehicle. It started burning. No one tried to get out.

"Unit Six is taking over!" Anakin announced on the command net. "Concentrate your fire on those tank droids!"

Blaster cannon bolts flashed overhead from the enemy vehicles, bouncing off the ground and into the air over them, making sizzling noises as they passed. Anakin smiled. The Separatists had begun their counterattack too soon.

"Get me over on that firing line right now!" he ordered his driver. "Gunner, open fire when ready!"

Calmly Anakin's gunner announced the range—"Twenty-one hundred meters"—and fired his blaster cannon. The transport bounced and swerved as it moved forward, but the stabilized blaster-control system was unaffected by the motion and the second bolt hit one of the enemy machines squarely on its front armor. That bolt bounced harmlessly off the machine, but the second bolt disabled its right tread and it began to turn helplessly in a circle before several other gunners destroyed it with their own cannons.

"Sir, I suggest you get down from there before you're hit," the sergeant advised.

"If I'm hit, you take charge, Sergeant." Anakin reached down impatiently and tapped the driver on his helmet. "Come on, come on, get us over there!"

Odie and Erk sat in the aid station, listening to the thunder of the guns supporting Halcyon's attack. The assault had been going on for ten or fifteen minutes before the chief surgeon accosted them.

"You can walk now, Lieutenant, so shove off," he told Erk. "I'll need all the space I can get in this station in the next few minutes."

Odie, who'd been keeping Erk company while he was in the aid station, helped him to his feet. "Doctor, when will you be able to see him again?" she asked.

"I don't know," the surgeon replied. "Not for a

while. He may have to go into a bacta tank to regenerate the skin. We'll have to send him up to the *Respite* for that. In the meantime, he needs to keep that burn clean. If infection sets in, he could be in real trouble. Here." He grabbed a medpac and shoved it at Odie. "You don't seem to have anything better to do—take care of him for the next couple of days. Everything you need is in there, including painkillers. Hear those blasters? I want you out of the way before the casualties start streaming in here. Now go!"

"We need to hunker in a bunker, Odie," Erk said, then corrected himself quickly: "No—no more bunkers for us. Let's head over to the command post. Maybe we can be of some help there."

But before they could get out of the aid station, casualties from the ongoing assault started coming in and all the pair could do was step aside and wait for the flow of injured to stop. It didn't, and what they saw on the litters bearing the wounded was horrible. Odie gasped and put her hands to her mouth; Erk blanched at the sight of the mangled bodies. Never had either of them seen so much destruction of living beings. Erk had done all his killing at high speed in the soundless reaches of space or far above the ground in atmosphere environments. It had been a clean bloodletting, more like playing a hologame than actually killing anyone. Now he was seeing what weapons technology could do to living bodies up close, where he could smell the blood and burned flesh.

The surgeons established a triage. One had the job of examining each litter case as it came in and, depending on whether he thought the victim could be saved or not, determining where to put the soldier; these decisions were made in a matter of seconds. The unsaved far outnumbered the saved.

The worst were the burn cases, clones stripped of their armor, so badly incinerated that their limbs had been reduced to charred sticks, their faces to blackened skulls, uniform fragments fused to their flesh. Yet somehow they lived. None of these were put into the saved category. Others lay in pools of their own blood, limbs missing, internal organs exposed. Still others had obviously died before they were brought to the field hospital. They lay still on their litters, bodies bouncing as the litter bearers jounced them along. Over all was a dreadful silence; hardly any of the wounded screamed or moaned—they were all in shock, an orderly informed Erk as he brushed by.

Odie picked up two one-liter bottles of water from a nearby supply and shouldered her way to the unsaved. She knelt, lifted a badly wounded clone's head, and put the bottle to his lips. It was then that she noticed a huge gash on his back that went all the way from his shoulder down to his hips. She could see his spine and ribs. "Thank you," he sighed after he had drunk. When she put his head back on the litter her hand was covered in blood. She wiped it on her tunic and moved to another litter. When the bottles were empty she knelt on the floor in a state of nervous exhaustion and cried.

"Let's go," Erk said, kneeling beside her. "They've stopped coming in for now. Come on, we can't do any more here." He helped her to her feet using his good arm.

"They're clones, Erk," she whispered, "but they're still living beings—a-and they're put together exactly like us. They bleed, they hurt, they die, just like we do . . ."

"Come on, Odie, let's get out of here," Erk repeated. Outside, he stumbled, and Odie rushed to support him. He didn't get anything on her when he vomited.

The attack wasn't going as planned. As the first wave of the assault breached the mesa, the enemy troops had pulled back to prepared positions; the attackers were exposed to raking fire as they tried to close the gap. Nervously, Halcyon paced back and forth in the command post. Slayke sat unperturbed a few steps away, eyes glued to the battlefield monitors, listening intently to the reports coming in from the attacking units.

"They're pinned down on the mesa," Halcyon observed. "Anakin hasn't been able to take those hills."

"The last word we had from him, sir," an operations officer responded, "was that he was taking over the transport battalion. I don't even know if the infantry has been deployed to take the hill."

"Casualties?"

"We've several hundred so far, sir," the division surgeon replied. "More coming in every minute. May I have your permission to go to the aid station and help out?"

Halcyon nodded and the surgeon hurried out. Halcyon came over and sat down beside Slayke. "Our attacks have failed," he admitted. He smashed a fist into one hand to express his anxiety. "Somehow they stymied Anakin. His taking those hills was the key to our whole plan. I'm going to withdraw the troops."

"Anakin may have succeeded in taking his objective," Slayke reasoned.

"No, he hasn't. He's alive and still fighting, but not on the hills. We need to reassess the situation and try something else. I'm not going to exhaust my army attacking those heights in frontal assaults. There's nothing but dust, fire, smoke, and confusion over on Anakin's side, and he hasn't been in touch with us since twenty minutes ago when he announced he was taking over the transport battalion. I knew before we started if we couldn't crack that line within twenty minutes we'd never break it the way we'd planned."

"Now you know what it's like to command an army like this," Slayke said. "My troopers are ready. Give me the word and we'll support you wherever you need us. But I agree. I think we need to revise our battle plan."

"As soon as our troops begin their retrograde movement, move yours to the old riverbed. Establish a defensive line. It'll be tricky, our attackers passing back through your brigade, but you can handle that. Entrench there and prepare for a counterattack. Signals, issue an order for all units to break contact and withdraw to our lines as quickly as possible. Where are you going?" he asked Slayke, who had gotten up.

"To lead my troops."

Halcyon shook his head. "I suppose there's no sense

me trying to talk you into staying here with me. You and Anakin—you're fighters. Try not to get yourself killed." Halcyon knew Anakin was still alive and fighting, but that was all he knew. *Anakin,* he thought, *where are you? What are you doing?*

24

What are you doing here?" a harried staff officer demanded when he saw two strangers standing in the command center.

"We just came from the aid station, sir," Lieutenant Erk H'Arman answered.

"Well, get back over there, then, we don't need any hangers-on."

"He's wounded, sir," said recon trooper Odie Subu, "and I've been assigned to look after him." She displayed the medpac the surgeon had given her. "We thought we could help out here."

"Help us out? You look like you two should be on the *Respite* yourselves! Well, go see a doctor, then, but get out of here. We're busy."

At that point Zozridor Slayke happened to walk by. "Well, well," he said, "if it isn't my prodigal twins. What are you two up to?" He remembered Odie in particular, because she had volunteered to accompany the pilot to Izable. He'd also heard what had happened to them and how they'd gotten out of the collapsed bunker. "These are two good soldiers," he remarked to the staff officer. Realizing his commander knew the pair, the officer excused himself to go about his duties. Briefly, Odie outlined the situation at the aid station.

"Look, it's going to get real busy here in a minute and I've got to go fire up my commanders," Slayke told them. "Why don't you two go down to the Fire Direction Center? See Colonel Gris Manks, my artillery commander—he's big, you can't miss him. Tell him I sent you. See if he can use a hand." Slayke knew very well that the pair would be of no help to Colonel Manks, but after all they had been through, he felt they deserved a rest and a chance to avoid the crisis that was about to come. At least they'd be safe down in the FDC. With that, he was on his way.

The Fire Direction Center was literally "down," accessed by a sloping tunnel that labor droids had constructed under the supervision of Halcyon's engineers. The FDC itself was large and crammed with equipment that enabled the dozens of experts who staffed the place to communicate directly with the two divisional artillery headquarters and through them to coordinate and give missions to every single piece of artillery in the army. When the pair entered the FDC, Gris Manks was shouting loudly at a clone sergeant. He saw the newly arrived pair in his peripheral vision and whirled on them. "Who are you?" he demanded.

"Captain Slayke sent us to help out," Erk answered.

"Help out? You two? Lieutenant, you look all shot up—and you, trooper, you look all shot down. How can you help me?"

"Sir, I'm the one who was shot down," Erk answered, "and burned up, too. The trooper is my wingmate." He explained briefly how they'd gotten to the FDC.

Colonel Manks stared at the two in disbelief. "All right," he said at last, "the captain sent you? All right, then, you two go over there and sit by that droid. Don't pay any attention to what it might try to tell you. Keep out of the way and keep your eyes and ears open and you might learn something." He whirled, stomped over to a console, and began shouting loudly at a clone lieutenant.

The pair recognized the droid at once as a standard military protocol unit, the kind often found performing administrative duties in personnel offices and orderly rooms, and thought it strange to find one here in the FDC.

"Good day," the droid said as the pair sat down beside it, "I am very proud to announce that I am a modified military protocol droid. I have been modified to operate effectively at battalion-, regimental-, and division-level artillery fire direction centers—which, I am proud to say, I can run with expert efficiency. I know the nomenclature, ranges, maintenance requirements, and firing data of more than three dozen artillery pieces; I can prepare firing tables for all these pieces and plot ranges obtained from orbital satellites, forward observers, or maps; I can integrate and control their fires for destructive, neutralizing, and demoralizing missions in either concentration fire, barrages, standing barrages, box barrages, or rolling barrages. I am also qualified to arrange scheduled fires and fires on targets of opportunity, whether observed or unobserved. And, I might add, I am an expert on the employment of tactical fires whether in a supporting role, preparatory role, counterpreparatory role, or counterbattery role, or as interdiction or harassing fire. I am, in short, the top of the line of cannon operators."

The droid's voice had been programmed to sound like that of a young human female, and to hear the melodic tones spouting off artillery jargon was so unexpected that Odie began to laugh.

"I believe you are amused and I am pleased if I have in any way caused you to transition to that mode," the droid said. "But I have not yet finished my list of capabilities, for I was created and programmed to be a military protocol droid, which means I can function perfectly from the level of company clerk to battalion adjutant. I am an expert at running duty rosters for staff duty officer/duty noncommissioned officer; sergeant of the guard; corporal of the guard; guard mount; company charge of quarters and company runner, kitchen police, escort detail for fallen comrades, and refresher orderly; I am an expert at preparing morning reports and all types of personnel actions; I can maintain company punishment books or prepare charge sheets for summary, special, and general courts-martial and I can also act as recorder for those proceedings; I know the uniform regulations of every army in the galaxy as well as their awards and decorations manuals, and can prepare awards recommendations from letters of appreciation to the highest awards for heroism a world can bestow; I can prepare supply requisitions for every piece of clothing and equipment, ordnance, and weaponry authorized by tables of organization and equipment or tables of allowances; I can manage company funds; I can do everything, in short, required of a company clerk, company first sergeant, battalion sergeant major, or battalion adjutant. I can do all that in addition to arranging to demolish everything within fifty kilometers of where we are now sitting."

"Well, if you're so good, why aren't you over there arranging something?" Erk asked with a nod toward the bustling FDC staff.

The droid didn't reply immediately. "My commander, the incomparable Colonel Gris Manks," it confessed at last, "has declared me . . . *negatively uncooperative,* is how he put it."

They waited patiently for the droid to explain, but it just sat there staring at them. "Well, what does he mean by that?" Odie asked.

Again the droid didn't answer immediately. Then it bent close to the two and lowered its voice. It actually swiveled its clamshell head to see if anyone was close enough to hear. "It's not working," it whispered.

"What's not working?" Erk asked in a normal voice.

The droid made hushing motions with its hands. "Shhh. I don't want to go back to doing duty rosters," it whispered. "We do not have the proper mix of artillery pieces to conduct this campaign effectively. We do not have a sufficient quantity of indirect-fire weapons. We are attacking uphill, as it were. That requires the ability to conduct parabolic fires, not line-of-sight fires. Laser and ion cannons are wonderful weapons, but they fire line-of-sight. We can't use the batteries on board the ships in orbit because there would be too great a risk of destroying the Intergalactic Communications Center and all the noncombatants; we can't send in fighters to attack from the air because the enemy's air defense array is too powerful. Did you hear the barrage we mounted last night? All the really potent fires had to be directed against the forward edge of the mesa occupied by the enemy. It was the mortars that did whatever real damage was done."

"You mean like grenade mortars?" Odie asked.

"Yes!" the droid answered enthusiastically.

"But those are light-infantry, direct-support weapons with short ranges, aren't they?"

"Yes, the standard versions, but Captain Slayke had two full batteries of self-propelled heavy mortars constructed that have a maximum range of fifty kilometers. They can drop shells with warheads weighing up to one thousand kilos on targets on the reverse slopes of hills. You see," the droid said, leaning forward and tapping Odie on her knee, "proper employment of artillery requires the proper integration of all available fires. That's what an FDC does. To obtain maximum effectiveness from artillery, the fires must be coordinated to bring the most accurate and potent destruction on any given target in the Tactical Area of Responsibility, and that means the proper kind of artillery must be used. Of course, the mounted mobile mortars that accompany front-line infantry are not necessarily included in the FDC's menus because they are designed to operate independently, to give close support to targets of opportunity opposing the ground troops. But everything else an army relies on to bombard troop concentrations and fixed installations must be coordinated, and that is what I do." It leaned back and tapped its chest proudly.

"So why are you, ah, in trouble?" Erk asked.

"Because I told Colonel Manks he should have told Captain Slayke to invest in more large mortars."

"That doesn't sound like such a bad thing to tell your commander," Odie said.

"Yes," the droid answered, "but I thought it my duty to tell him that more than once. I told him fifty-two times, to be exact."

"Ah. I understand that could be trying. Why didn't he follow your advice?"

"Because, he said, one mixes weapons to cover all expected contingencies, and going too far with one weapons system at the expense of another would 'un-balance' our arms inventory."

The three sat silently for a while. All around them the FDC hummed with activity. "Things are not going well for us," the droid said at last. "We are calling off the attack."

"Calling it off?" Erk asked in disbelief.

"Yes, the attack on the enemy's flank has failed and he is holding fast."

"Now what?"

"We should put more artillery on him, enough so that he will go away," the droid answered. "I know. I am a modified military protocol droid. I have been modified to operate effectively at battalion-, regimental-, and division-level artillery . . ."

Erk turned to Odie as the droid droned on. "There's got to be a better way. All those casualties . . ." He shook his head sadly.

Odie rested her head on a hand and leaned close to Erk. Her voice quavered as she spoke. "It's one disaster after another. Will this never end? Does anybody know what they're doing? We're the only survivors of General Khamar's army, do you realize that, Erk? All those lives lost! Why did we, of all of them, survive? Why that Rodian I killed, the friend of that Jedi commander, Starwalker? Why did that have to happen?"

"Commander Skywalker," he corrected her. "I don't know—that's just the way it's turned out. But we made it; we made it this far and we're going to make it all the way." He put his good arm around her shoulders. "Commander Skywalker led the attack on those hills, Odie. I wonder what's happened to him?"

"I'm not sure I want to know."

25

The smoke and fires and the dust were so thick that the transport's infras couldn't penetrate it; the onboard radar was no longer effective at picking out targets, because the debris and fragments from exploding vehicles filled the air in a raging cauldron of destruction. It had become almost impossible to know if one was firing on friend or foe.

"Get us out of here," Anakin ordered his driver. "I've got to see what's going on and get those transports moving. My troopers are up there without infantry support. Move. Move!"

Suddenly Anakin's vehicle was rammed in the rear by another vehicle; everyone pitched forward in their harnesses, and the transport came to a stop. In that instant a bolt from a laser cannon struck the machine on the flank and drilled through into the crew compartment, which immediately burst into flames.

Without even thinking about it, Anakin reached down with one arm and grabbed the driver by the bottom of his back plate. With the other he sent a Force push that flung the cupola hatch open. The driver released his harness and kicked with his feet as Anakin hauled him out of his seat, up into the cupola, and over the side. They landed in a heap beside the transport, which began to billow greasy black smoke followed by a brilliant and intensely hot white flame that shot at least ten meters into the air. No one else made it out.

Dragging the driver, Anakin stumbled toward cover. He hadn't made it more than a few meters when another vehicle roared by, missing them by millimeters, almost knocking them down in its passing and nearly suffocating them in the thick cloud of dust that billowed behind it. Anakin flung himself and the driver into a shallow depression. All around them vehicles roared and churned, their guns flashing. The noise was deafening. Something came pounding at them out of the dust—a transport, headed straight for them. They burrowed as deeply into the depression as they could get and the machine roared right over them, half burying the pair in the caved-in dirt of the depression, which was now nothing more than a rut in the ground.

"We've got to get out of here," Anakin said, digging himself out of the dirt.

"Which way is out?" the driver replied.

He was right: Anakin realized he didn't know which direction was the front. He looked around and in only a moment located the transports.

"This way," he ordered. The driver followed him. They came to a transport that had stopped and was firing repeatedly at targets they couldn't see. Anakin recognized the faint markings stenciled on the front armor plate—it was one of his! He switched to his command net. "Aurek Trill Six Niner Slant Cresh, this is Unit Six. Open up, I'm taking you as my command vehicle." There was no response.

He reached for the small hatch that held a receiver-transmitter hooked into the vehicle's onboard communications system when suddenly it lurched forward, entangling the hem of his cloak in the track mechanism, jerking him off his feet and dragging him along. He was just millimeters from being pulled under the vehicle's treads when his driver leapt forward and severed his cloak with a vibroblade.

"Thanks, that was close," Anakin gasped as the driver helped him to his feet. He unfastened the cloak and let the fragment fall to the ground. Then he tapped the communications mechanism in his helmet and tried to raise the transport commander. He heard nothing but static.

"Come on, we'll have to get back to the transports on foot. They aren't far. Follow me."

They ran. Anakin had to hold himself back: the driver was well trained and in good shape, but even so, he couldn't match a Jedi at top speed. Anakin's blood pounded in his veins as he willed himself to keep his speed down a fraction when everything in him roared a single message: *Run!* But in a few seconds that felt like an eternity, he found himself in the rut the transport had made. The transports were there. He ran to the first one in line. Its hatch was open, and its commander stood in it with his armored head and torso half out of the vehicle. With an easy Force leap, Anakin bounded onto the vehicle's dorsal surface, surprising the clone commander, who drew his weapon, thinking he must be an enemy soldier.

Anakin seized the clone's arm. "I'm Commander Skywalker!" he said urgently. "Get down inside—I'm taking this as my command vehicle." The clone commander obeyed. Reaching down to pull his driver up behind him, Anakin climbed in.

Pors Tonith watched as the battle unfolded. He sipped from his teacup. Excellent! The enemy attack was proceeding just as he had anticipated. The attacks on his right and center were faltering, and the thrust toward the hills was being slowed by the crawler attack. They would have a big surprise when they reached the foot of those hills. "Are you ready?" he asked a technician.

"Yessir. We've penetrated their communications net. We have their commander's call sign, his voiceprint, and his authentication code. We are capable of issuing orders to all his troops."

"Good. Stand by." Tonith could now issue bogus orders to all of Halcyon's units to retreat or attack or stand still, but he wanted something more spectacular, and he was going to get it. He smiled.

"Give me your comlink," Anakin demanded of the battalion commander, ripping his own off and throwing it out through the hatch. "This is Unit Six. I am in the lead transport. On my command, follow me." He climbed back up into the vehicle's hatch. "Move this thing as quickly as you can. Listen carefully: I'll be giving you directions." He toggled to the command net. "All eyes on me, follow my light."

With that he drew his lightsaber, activated it, and

held it straight up in the air. He swept his arm forward; the vehicle lurched into the ramp and surged up onto the plain above, followed by a long line of transports.

"Hard left," he ordered, and the transport swerved to the left just in time to miss one roaring across in front. "Faster. Straight ahead. Right. Left. Open this thing up."

Laser and blaster bolts sizzled through the air. Anakin effortlessly batted them out of the way. Behind him some of the transports were hit and slowed to a stop, but the following vehicles sped around them, keeping Anakin's lightsaber in view. It was the only thing anyone could see at any distance in the dense dust and smoke hanging over the battlefield. Fortunately, Halcyon's transports had done a good job, and the enemy machines had all either been disabled or were retreating.

In a matter of seconds they reached the rocks at the bottom of their objective. "Dismount. Form up in battalions and follow me!" Anakin climbed out of the hatch and leapt to the ground. This was a maneuver the clones had practiced to perfection in countless training exercises. Squads, platoons, companies, and battalions rapidly took their prearranged positions, closing their ranks to cover the gaps left in their formations by the transports that had been hit on the way in. The surviving vehicles rolled up and began to lay down suppressing fire on the hilltop.

"Give us supporting fires," Anakin demanded of the Fire Direction Center.

"Copy that," a voice echoed in Anakin's headset. "Time on target five seconds."

Anakin counted *one-thousand-one, one-thousand-two, one-thousand-three, one-thousand-four, one-thousand-five,* and mortar rounds began exploding on the hilltop. It was a very satisfying display of firepower. He let the barrage continue as he took his place at the head of the lead battalion. He turned to the battalion commander. "That'll keep them down—nobody can survive under that pounding."

"I wouldn't be too sure, sir," the commander said.

Anakin looked at the officer disbelievingly, but just shrugged.

"We advance on your order, sir," the battalion commander said. "I advise that you stay here with the reserves until we've secured the hill."

Anakin hesitated only briefly before making his decision. He was ready for a fight; every fiber in his body tingled to lead the charge and put his lightsaber to work. But he was a commander now: his job was commanding, not fighting.

"Colonel, take that hill." He pointed at the hill that rose above the boulder-strewn field.

The battalion advanced by companies, the commander and his staff immediately behind the First Company. The field of boulders forced the clone infantry to bunch up to get through to the slope on the other side, and this made everyone exceptionally nervous. "Quickly! Quickly!" the battalion commander urged his troops, keeping his eye on the hilltop, which remained strangely silent. What were they waiting for? From just ahead came the sharp cracking of blaster rifles. "Droid skirmishers," the lead company commander reported. "We're brushing them aside."

The battalion commander heard only a very sharp *crack* when the mine went off, the instantaneous result of the concussion bursting his eardrums. He felt himself lifted off his feet and flung backward in a cloud of smoke, dust, shattered armor, and body parts. He slammed into a boulder and bounced off onto the ground. He felt no pain, just a dullness in his legs and back. He shook his head to clear it, but no good. He tried to get to his feet but couldn't: his legs had been severed just below the knees. He knew this because he could rise up on his elbows just enough to see that he had no feet. He tried to sit up, to reach down and stanch the bleeding, but he couldn't, because his back had been broken when he was flung against the boulder. Someone grabbed him under the arms and started pulling him back, and he lost consciousness. Much later someone, a woman, he thought, gave him some water.

The battle droids, rank upon serried rank, sat motionless in their bunkers. Their control systems were active, weapons systems charged, waiting for the command to attack. Only moments before, they had been ordered to take cover in the bunker complex to avoid the mortar barrage that began falling on their now-unoccupied positions. Labor droids had improved and deepened the bunkers the previous night so now they were impervious to the heavy mortar shells exploding in huge gouts of flame all over the hill. Not thirty minutes before, clone troopers had tried to penetrate their perimeter, but the droids had been ready for them. Now they sat safely in the bunkers, just waiting. The few sentient beings among them, their battle coordinators, hunkered in the bunkers expecting at any moment a direct hit that would penetrate the cover and destroy them all. But the labor droids had done their work swiftly and thoroughly, and although the concussions of the exploding thousand-kilo shells shocked and deafened them, they remained safe in their holes, waiting for the bombardment to cease.

The enemy infantry was approaching now, just as the admiral had said they would. The droid skirmishers were taking the leading units under fire. In a matter of seconds the huge mine laid in the remains of the blown tunnel to Izable would be detonated, and then the droids would be given the command to spring into action and deliver a withering fire on the survivors.

A controller sat with the detonating device in his hand, watching a monitor. As soon as the lead elements of the attacking force were bunched up between the rocks, he would explode the mine. The monitor went dead suddenly. No matter; he knew where the advancing infantry was. He counted: *One. Two. Three. Four.* He pushed the detonator button. The concussion from the exploding mine reached even those down in the bunkers, shaking them so badly that anything not secured was knocked over. The controller smiled. Now, when the mortars stopped falling . . .

The explosion threw Anakin to the ground. Ahead, where the lead company had just disappeared into the rocks, was a huge pall of smoke. The air was filled with dirt clods and rock fragments from boulders that had been shattered by the blast. Anakin leapt to his feet and ran forward. The sight that met him was straight out of a nightmare. Almost all the clone troopers in the lead company had been injured or killed outright in the blast. The wounded staggered about in a daze, their armor covered in blood; many were missing body parts. The ground was littered with corpses and the dying. Those not wounded physically were in a state of shock, weaponless, disoriented.

"Second Company, up," Anakin ordered over the tactical net. "Second and Third Battalions up. Follow me!" He ran through the carnage to the foot of the hill, drew his lightsaber, and activated it. He raised it over his head. "Form up on me—I lead the way!"

The remaining two companies of the First Battalion quickly recovered their wits and surged on through the rocks to where Anakin stood on the slope of the hill. By that time the rest of the transports had come up and were disgorging their troops.

"Send them in now," Anakin ordered the brigade commanders, who immediately formed their regiments.

There was still no fire from the hilltop. Good, the artillery was keeping them down. Thousands of clone troopers swarmed onto the foot of the hill and paused, waiting for the order to rush to the top.

At that moment their own artillery started falling on the transports.

"Adjust your fire at one-hundred-meter intervals. Roll back toward our lines. Pass this order to all units," Colonel Gris Manks called out. "The assault is being called off, and we must cover our retreating troops."

"Sir," one of the Fire Direction Center operators

called out, "I believe the troops on the right flank are just now assaulting the hill. If we adjust one hundred meters to the rear, the rounds will fall on our own—"

"Your information must be wrong. Adjust for rolling fires. I just got that order directly from General Halcyon. Received and authenticated. Order all pieces to target the plain according to our preregistered fire plan and support our line in case of counterattack."

The FDC directors dutifully passed on the order, and the blasters adjusted their fires accordingly.

Erk and Odie jumped to their feet. "*Received and authenticated,* standard practice," the droid commented, "means the commanding general has given the order and orders must be obeyed. I know because I am a . . ."

To Anakin, standing at the foot of the hill, the blaster assault from the top began as a bright, flashing row of fire from so many weapons that it was difficult to pick out the individual shooters. A wave of destruction rolled over the soldiers gathered around him. Without even thinking, he used his lightsaber to divert several bolts aimed directly at him. Troopers standing to his right and left were not so fortunate and were cut down in droves.

"*Forward!*" Anakin shouted and started up the hill. The companies, battalions, and regiments rolled forward behind him, firing and maneuvering as they went, but the line faltered under the devastating fire from the top of the hill, then stopped as casualties mounted and the survivors went to ground, seeking whatever cover the terrain offered from the destruction pouring onto them from above.

"Put artillery on that hill," Anakin ordered over the command net, forgetting the proper comm procedure in his excitement. "This is Commander Skywalker—give us back that artillery support! You're dropping rounds on our transports. Readjust your fire. We're being slaughtered down here. We are pinned down. Repeat, we are pinned down! Over."

Thinking this was some kind of trick—the order to adjust fire had just come from the FDC and presumably the army commander himself—the battery commanders assigned to support Anakin's troopers hesitated, then asked for confirmation from the FDC, and the shells continued dropping on the transports.

The fire from the droids only intensified. Few of the clone troopers were able to return it. Frustrated, Anakin toggled to Halcyon's command net. "General Halcyon, this is Anakin. What's going on? I'm pinned down here, my own artillery is firing on my rear, and the enemy in my front is killing us!"

Halcyon started when he heard Anakin's voice booming over the loudspeakers in the command post, and everyone stopped what he or she was doing. "Anakin, hold on." He turned to his artillery liaison. "Get me Colonel Manks."

"You gave me that order just a little while ago," Manks said when Halcyon asked what was happening. "*Adjust fires at one-hundred-meter intervals to cover our retreating troops—*"

"Our net has been compromised," an officer gasped. "You gave no such order!" He looked at Halcyon.

"Colonel, cover the retreat on the left but put fire on that hill on the right immediately. Anakin, as soon as the mortars start up again, get out of there—I'm calling off the attack."

When the mortars again started falling on the hilltop it was too late to do any damage to the droids—they'd already retreated into their bunkers.

Odie buried her face in her hands. "We're killing our own troops," she whispered.

"That," the droid said, "is what is called friendly fire. It happens all the time."

"I know what that is," Odie replied bitterly, "and I hope I never hear that term again."

"Your status, Tonith?"

It was that detestable Commander Ventress again. Pors Tonith put down his teacup. "You are calling at an inconvenient time," he sneered. "I am in the process of beating back a major attack."

"Yes, you look extremely busy, as you always do. Have you been successful, then?"

"Entirely," Tonith answered smugly, lifting the teacup to his lips and sipping contentedly.

"Casualties?"

"Ours? Light. Theirs? I haven't assessed them yet, but heavy, very heavy, indeed. You see, I was able to anticipate their moves perfectly—"

"Count Dooku will be pleased," Ventress interrupted, her voice a neutral flatness.

"I am sure this confirms his faith in my ability to command this situation and save it," he said, leaning back and grinning at the hologram image hovering before him.

"You shall be reinforced shortly. The fleet is on the way."

Tonith only nodded. "I may not even need them. I believe I'm faced by second-rate brains. Frontal attacks. Flanking movements. Jedi running about with their lightsabers. Pish! It's firepower and tactics that count, not heroics and posturing."

"I shall so inform Count Dooku," she replied. "One more thing, Tonith. When this is over we shall meet, and I will kill you." The image disappeared.

Tonith sat frozen for a second. Then he shrugged, drained his teacup, and poured another. "That will be the day," he smirked, but he knew she meant what she said.

26

I've never seen anything this fouled up," Private Vick, the former *Neelian* guard, commented to Corporal Raders.

The pair were standing in the rear of the command post, sandwiched together into a corner, trying to stay inconspicuous and out of the way.

"How do you know? I've got more time in the chow line than you've got in the guards," Rader replied, "and this isn't so bad. General Halcyon knows what he's doing. You've seen him fight up close and personal."

"All I know is things are falling apart out there and here we stand, sucking our thumbs. Let's go ask the general to let us loose."

"Yeah, but I don't want to work with any clones; those boys make me nervous. With those helmets, you can't see their faces."

"We need another mission, like that recon with Sergeant L'Loxx, he's someone I can really work with. We sure made junk out of some droids that night, didn't we? But bro, we don't want to wind up stuck down in the FDC, like those two lovebirds." Lieutenant H'Arman and trooper Subu had become known throughout the command staff as soft on each other. "You don't want that, do you?"

"No. Or standing around here, either. We should be out with that other Jedi, Skywalker. He's deep in it now. That's where I want to be. He could use a couple of good hands, I bet."

"You'd better watch out what you're asking for, buddy. But Skywalker, you know, I'm older than he is."

"Shows what you been doin' with your life."

Raders nodded silently. Then he said, "You know what I'd like right now?"

"I could think of a million things."

"I'd like a nice cold drink of water."

There was very little of that precious commodity on the battlefield. Major Mess Boulanger estimated, using standards established for soldiers of all species operating in every conceivable climatic condition found in the galaxy, that the clone troopers needed, to maintain top performance in combat in the desert-like environment found on the continent on Praesitlyn where the action was taking place, 8 liters of water every twenty-four standard hours, or 160,000 liters each and every day for the entire combat force under Halcyon's command, and that didn't count what was needed for the command, staff, and support units. The water vaporators, like those used on the farms on such worlds as Tatooine, could produce only a liter and a half a day, were very large, had to be spread apart certain distances to be effective, and were subject to constant bombardment by enemy artillery. Halcyon's engineers had drilled deep into the planet's crust and constructed artesian wells, but they were capable of producing only about ten thousand liters of water a day, and that supply had to be processed first to make it drinkable.

Thirst occurs in humans when fluid amounting to about 1 percent of body weight is lost. Death from dehydration occurs when that ratio reaches about 20 percent; less in an arid environment. Already in the attack just mounted against Tonith's lines, the clone infantry had sustained about 2 percent of their casualties from dehydration. And those infantry fighters were in top physical condition. Each had landed on Praesitlyn with a full combat load of more than forty kilos of weapons and equipment, including eight liters of water; by the time the attack on Tonith's lines was called off, most of them had consumed the water they'd brought with them.

Mess Boulanger had calculated this requirement very precisely and he had prepared for it. There was only one problem: the main supply, which was needed right now and required immediate and continuous replenishment, had to come from the fleet in orbit.

Far above the cauldron of death and destruction that raged about the Praesitlyn Intergalactic Communications Center, the crews of Halcyon's fleet in orbit labored mightily to keep his army supplied with the essentials of war. Grizzled bosuns directed massive loadlifters as they shifted cargoes and loaded them into transports. A steady stream of supplies proceeded from the ships to the planet's surface. Old Mess Boulanger had calculated precisely the amounts of ordnance, spare parts, and rations the army would need to operate at a high level of combat for a week, the period of time it was estimated would be required to break Tonith's hold on the Intergalactic Communications Center. He and his staff had also estimated the precise tonnage required to resupply that army per day to support it during heavy fighting. Boulanger had the troop transports that landed the infantry converted to combat delivery vehicles by modifying the troop compartments for storage and was using them by the dozens to move all this matériel. He had to use them because he needed speed and maneuverability to get the cargoes safely off-loaded. That was because there was one more big problem: nothing could be landed in the immediate vicinity of Halcyon's troops.

After the initial landings, which went off unopposed, Tonith's gunners began to take the landing area under heavy fire, destroying several transports and supply caches. This forced Halcyon and his commanders to establish a depot some thirty kilometers distant, behind a row of hills that shielded the incoming transports and their off-loaded cargoes from Tonith's direct-fire weapons, although making it to the depot was tricky because the ships had to make planetfall about three hundred kilometers away, and then proceed to the depot by flying low to the ground to avoid Tonith's guns. And then the transports had to run a gauntlet of fire to get to the troopers in contact with the Separatist droids. Many transports were lost.

Odie squeezed into the corner beside Raders. Erk joined her. "Hi, killer," Raders said.

Odie grimaced. "I don't like that name."

"Get used to it. You earned it," Vick said.

"It's getting mighty crowded around here," Raders said.

"Yes, why don't you two leave?" Odie responded.

"We were here first," Raders quipped.

Erk decided it was time to intervene. "We got tired of hanging around the FDC with no missions on schedule just now. Thought we'd come up here and stand around awhile."

"Yessir," Vick responded with a *who cares* shrug.

"Quiet back there," a staff officer snapped.

Anakin, a cold glass of precious water in his hand, sat in the command post making his report to Halcyon. "They were ready for us, Master Halcyon. My initial casualty reports put my losses at over six hundred killed, wounded, or missing. Among the missing is the entire team of commandos I sent to pave the way. None of them came back." He sipped his water.

"Our casualties in the other attack were over a thousand, and we don't know how many of those are missing or dead," Halcyon answered. "We're right back at square one."

"It was a good attack plan," Slayke offered. "Well coordinated, well planned, and well executed. Nobody needs to blame himself for what happened out there. Our opponent was ready for us, that's all. We'll have better luck next time." He had just returned from inspecting the defensive line he'd established at the dry riverbed. He laid a hand on Anakin's shoulder. "You and the clones fought bravely, Anakin. I'm glad you made it back. There's one bright spot: it's been hours now since our troops returned, and there's been no counterattack. I think that means he doesn't have the resources to mount one."

"We still have to get up there and dislodge him," Halcyon said. "But no more frontal attacks."

"Whoever's in command knows what he's doing," Slayke observed, "but no matter how good he is, he's no better than the three of us together. I suggest we call in our fleet and burn him off the mesa."

Everyone within hearing of the trio stopped what he or she was doing and listened to what was being said. They'd all been thinking the same thing.

"But—" Halcyon protested.

Slayke shook his head. "I know what you're going to say: we must try to protect the Intergalactic Communications Center and the lives of the surviving technicians. They're being held hostage, that's plain, but it's also plain the Republic doesn't make deals with criminals, which is just what these people are. If we want them off this planet, we'll have to blast them off. The center and the technicians, Reija Momen, all of them, will be collateral losses, is all."

"I've heard *friendly fire,* and now *collateral losses,*" Anakin said, finishing the last of his water. He ran a hand tiredly across his face. "I'm getting good at recognizing all these euphemisms for death and destruction. But after what the clone troops and I have been through, I think Captain Slayke is right. It's just . . ." He faltered as the image of Reija Momen sprang into his mind's eye. "Well, he's right." He nodded at Slayke but refused to look Halcyon in the eye.

At first Halcyon just stared at Anakin as if the young Jedi had uttered a horrible curse. He wanted to say, *What's come over you?* but caught himself at once. Anakin had been through a meat grinder. Still, he was a Jedi.

"The loss of life in this campaign has been terrible, I understand that," he said slowly. "Captain Slayke, you've been hit hardest of all, and I fully understand your desire to end this bloodshed as quickly and as decisively as possible. Anakin, you've just been through a terrible experience yourself. You are both brave and capable commanders, and I'm fortunate to have you with me. But understand this: under no circumstances will we sacrifice the lives of the noncombatants to achieve a quick or a pyrrhic victory." His eyes flashed as he spoke. "Remember, our mission is to save the people and the facility." He sighed. "Now, let's get to work and come up with another plan."

"Uh, excuse me, sir," Corporal Raders said from the back of the room. "We were just wondering when you were going to send us into action."

"Why not ask them to join us?" Slayke suggested, grinning. "You could do worse, asking enlisted people for advice. That woman and the officer with the dressing on his arm, I know those two, and they know the terrain around here better than any of us."

"Why not?" Halcyon responded. "All of you, come up here with us and keep your ears open."

"You're the one who shot Grudo," Anakin said as Odie approached.

"Yessir. It was a mistake. I-I—"

"Friendly fire, not your fault, happens all the time,"

Anakin said, not really believing it. He turned to Haly-con. "When we go back, I want them with me." He gestured at the two guards.

"Why?" Halcyon asked.

Anakin shrugged. "I just know I can count on them. They watched your back when you repulsed the board-ers on the *Ranger,* and I need someone to watch mine now that my commandos have been wiped out."

Halcyon didn't reply at once or directly. Something had come over the young Jedi, a hardness that hadn't been there before. "Yes, we're going back, Anakin, that's for certain. And we're not going to sit here lick-ing our wounds." He turned to a staff officer. "Get those ops people up here and let's get to work."

Mess Boulanger drew himself up to his full short-ness, stroked his mustaches, and replied, "Comman-der, I estimate it requires two thousand metric tons of matériel and supplies to keep your army running at the level of combat you achieved today. I have stockpiled more than that at our off-loading point, but as long as the enemy occupies the high ground, I've only been able to get a thousand tons a day in here, and that was with an unacceptable loss of transport landing craft, I'm here to tell you. We have enough on hand to mount one more full assault, and then you'll have to fall back and regroup."

The officers around the table considered this infor-mation silently.

"We can't wait for resupply," Anakin said. "And there is the chance that enemy reinforcements are on the way. If that happens the entire balance of power will shift to his advantage."

"Agreed. We must attack at once and end this siege," Slayke said. "What does our fleet commander say?" He turned to Admiral Hupsquoch, commander of the ships in orbit.

"We're keeping a sharp eye on the cordon around Sluis Van," Hupsquoch replied. "They have made no attempt to interfere with our blockade here, and if they did we're more than capable of handling them. My concern is the same as yours, Commander Skywalker: the possibility that the Separatists have sent for strong reinforcements from somewhere else."

Halcyon nodded. "It would be very unlike the Separatists to mount an operation like this without a contingency plan to reinforce their army. What precautions are you taking against a surprise, Admiral?"

"I have a screen of fast corvettes and cruisers spread out to a distance of one hundred thousand kilometers in every direction. The crews aboard all my ships are on full alert, half their complements constantly at battle stations."

"You?" Halcyon turned to his intelligence officer.

"Sir, I've been in touch with Coruscant constantly since we broke the enemy's jamming. All the intelligence services at the Senate's disposal are operating throughout the galaxy. None of them has found any indication that a major force is being assembled to come against us. That doesn't mean the Separatists aren't going to do that, only that we haven't spotted it yet. And our communications integrity has been completely restored, sir. No more incidents like the one this morning."

Halcyon nodded. "Look at this display." He flicked on a three-dimensional graphic of the terrain within a hundred kilometers of their position. "Reconnaissance shows that the enemy's perimeter is very tightly drawn up there. He's shortened his lines to consolidate his assets to better defend a three-hundred-sixty-degree perimeter, and he's drawn it in close to the center because he knows how we value it and the lives of the technicians there. That is why," he stated, nodding at his officers, "I will not permit the fleet to employ its weapons against him. It would mean complete destruction of everything up there."

"But our attacks, and in particular Captain Slayke's campaign before we got here, have weakened him," Anakin pointed out. "And remember what Sergeant L'Loxx noted during his reconnaissance: there's a lack of maintenance among the battle droids. That could count in our favor at a critical moment."

"He can't be resupplied at all," Mess Boulanger added.

"That's right," Anakin continued. "And in this environment, maintenance is key to combat power. I had no fewer than sixteen of my transports fall out of the fight this morning because of maintenance problems, but their crews have already gotten them back into commission. I don't think he can match that. During our retreat—"

"We don't 'retreat,' Anakin, we perform a retrograde movement." Slayke grinned, and several of the officers around him laughed.

"We weren't actually 'retreating,' we were just attacking in a rearward direction," Anakin shot back. "Anyway, on the way back we found two dozen of the enemy's tank droids out on the plain, abandoned. They'd just stopped functioning. So despite our losses, we've still got a lot of fight left in us, more than he has, I think."

"We can't envelop him vertically; his lines and security are too tight to permit infiltration; we're not going to waste our assets in another frontal assault; and I can't use the fleet's gunnery to dislodge the droids," Halcyon said, summarizing the obvious options.

"And he's sitting up there waiting to be reinforced," Slayke added.

"So what do we do?" Halcyon looked around the table.

"I know what to do," Anakin answered, almost in a whisper.

No one said anything. After a moment Halcyon nodded to Anakin to continue.

The young Jedi stood up and looked around the command post. His face and hands were still filthy from the morning's fight, and his clothes were stained and torn; there were lines in his face and bags under his eyes that had not been there before that day. But his voice was firm and his body language confirmed the fact that, although he was tired, he was ready to go another round. He was in control.

"Give me fifteen clone troopers and one transport aircraft. Give me all the cover you can, and I'll fly it right onto the mesa. I won't do it directly. Under the cover of your attack, I'll proceed to the off-loading point and then head in this direction"—he gestured at the display—"and fly about a hundred kilometers north, to this point, and then dogleg back in this direction, dogleg again and come in from behind. I'll fly fast and skim just above the ground. I'll land under the cover of your fire, get into the center, and free the remaining hostages. Once that's done and they're safe, let the fleet do the rest." He sat down.

"Let me get this straight," a colonel, Halcyon's operations chief, said. "Sir, you propose attacking with fifteen clones—"

"Actually, seventeen soldiers in one transport aircraft. I'm taking the two guards with me."

"—seventeen, yessir. And with these seventeen you expect to break into the center, find the hostages, and evacuate them?"

"That is correct, Colonel."

"It can be done," Slayke said, smashing a fist forcefully into a palm. "It's brilliant. It'll probably get you killed, but it's brilliant nonetheless." He grinned at Anakin.

"You don't even know where they're keeping the hostages," the operations chief pointed out.

"Yes, I do," Anakin answered.

"How do you know that, sir?"

Anakin smiled. "Trust me, Colonel. I'm a Jedi," was all he said. The colonel's face turned red.

"You'll need someone who knows his way around in the center," Halcyon remarked.

"I know my way around there, sir," Odie interjected. "I've been in the center many times."

The officers all looked at her, and she nervously shifted her feet.

"What were you doing in there?" Erk asked.

"Uh, well . . ." She glanced nervously at all the officers. "I knew someone on the defense force and . . . We had lunch up there and—" She shrugged. "—I got to know how the center was laid out."

"Take her along," Halcyon said.

"Sir," Erk put in, "take two shuttles. You'll need a backup."

"If we had a cleaning droid in here, maybe we could ask it for advice, too," an officer remarked.

"Excuse me, sir, but that's standard procedure, and if you do that, I volunteer to fly the second shuttle," Erk said. "And if you're taking my wingmate here," he added, laying his good hand on Odie's shoulder, "you've got to take me, too. I insist."

"Lieutenants don't insist," Anakin said, "they follow orders."

"I insist, sir. I know you. I know your reputation. Well, I'm a fighter pilot, one of the best, and I'm tired of being stuck here on the ground."

Anakin looked intently at Erk for a moment. Then he nodded.

Erk grinned at him. "Looks like I got my orders."

"But you're wounded, Lieutenant," Halcyon protested.

"I'm better now, sir. Besides, I'm so good I could fly with my feet if I had to."

"I believe him," Anakin said. "I'll take him, the recon trooper—and two shuttle craft."

"Very well." Halcyon shrugged. "If nothing else it'll

get all these hangers-on out of my command post and give me room to breathe in here. When will you leave?"

"As soon as I gear up and we study the layout of the center, sir."

"Very well." Halcyon turned to his officers. "We'll lay everything we've got on those lines again. I want all the infantry to maneuver as if we're attacking with our entire force right up the middle. Soon as we've got the enemy's attention, Anakin goes in. When he's rescued the hostages and we know they're safe, Admiral, you direct everything you've got against that mesa. Slag the place. We can rebuild the communications center later. Commander Skywalker, this plan of yours is very risky—but I think it'll work. That commander up there will never see it coming." He held out his hand. "May the Force be with you, Anakin," he said. Then he shook hands with each of the other four.

"Well," Anakin said, "let's do it."

The two guards slapped palms.

27

Dondo Foth, captain of the picket frigate *Mandian*, was a thoroughgoing professional military man who spent most of his time when he was aboard his vessel on her bridge, alert, tending to the affairs of running a starship. That was one reason his vessel had been picked to patrol the outer rim of the cordon Halcyon had thrown around Praesitlyn. At this time he was 150,000 kilometers from the orbital fleet, a bit farther out than his orders called for. But acting on his own initiative, he took up his patrol course at that distance.

"Just in case," he told Lieutenant Commander Vitwroth, the *Mandian*'s executive officer. "Frankly, I think we should be out a million kilometers, far enough away from the main fleet that we can give them plenty of warning if anyone tries to sneak up on us."

"Well, it's mighty lonely out here, Skipper," Vitwroth replied. "I like bright lights and plenty of company." He grinned.

Foth was from New Agamar, stocky, approaching middle age. He grinned back. "Let's see those promotion packets," he said to the military protocol droid that had been programmed to be his writer. One of the crew, probably with the droid's connivance, had stenciled a first-class yeoman's chevrons on its forehead. The crew's name for the droid was Yeoman Scrapheap.

"They are all ready, perfectly prepared according to naval regulations, Captain," the droid answered. "You are recommending six of the crew for promotion: one to chief, two to first-class ratings—"

"Yeah, yeah, I know their names, too, Yeoman Scrapheap," Captain Foth said. "I just want to make sure you haven't made any mistakes. Last week you transposed two letters in a report to fleet. Tsk, tsk, we'll have to have you scrapped if that happens again."

"That was a mere software glitch, Captain," the droid protested, "and it has been fixed, I assure you."

"You don't assure me of anything, Yeoman Scrapheap—it is I who assures you, and I assure you, it's the Lucky Bag for you." The "Lucky Bag" was a storage compartment on the vessel where useful odds and ends were kept. Captain Foth laughed and took the promotion disks. Even though the droid was a machine, sometimes it was impossible not to think it was sentient, and Foth enjoyed sparring with it like this. He had no intention of relegating Yeoman Scrapheap to the Lucky Bag.

"Captain," the watch officer called, "we've detected an approaching object, twenty-five degrees to starboard, three hundred thousand kilometers out, closing slowly!"

"Sound general quarters," Foth responded in a normal tone of voice. He handed the promotion disks back to Scrapheap. "I'll look at these later. Lieutenant," he said, turning to the watch officer, "get me a visual.

Give me its speed and course. Notify fleet. Blasters, lock on target."

"General quarters, sir," the watch officer responded.

"Visual, sir. I do not see any other objects out there, Captain," the rating operating the *Mandian*'s radar suite responded.

"Message to fleet, sir," the signals officer responded.

"Speed, twenty-one thousand. It's headed directly toward Praesitlyn," the ship's navigator reported.

"Guns locked on target, sir," the gunnery officer announced.

"Twenty-one thousand kilometers an hour? Whatever it is, it's moving slowly. Where are those visuals?" The screens gradually revealed a shapeless black object, almost a cloud. "Give me more definition," Foth ordered. "Blasted thing doesn't look like a vessel."

"That's the best our equipment can do until it gets closer, sir."

"We didn't have time to upgrade our visual observation equipment before we left Coruscant," Vitwroth said.

"I know, I know. Guns, when will it be in range?"

"At that speed, on my mark, two hours, twenty-seven minutes—mark."

"Then we wait, unless fleet orders us to approach closer. Do you think it's a cloaked Separatist ship?" Foth asked Vitwroth.

"We have to assume it is, sir."

"Sir, fleet message received and authenticated: 'Maintain your position, observe and report. Fire only if fired on,' " the signals officer announced.

"So we wait," Foth announced. "Two hours? Two

hours, twenty-seven minutes, no, twenty-six minutes now, and then maybe we'll find out more." The palms of his hands were sweaty, but to the crew on the bridge he appeared icy calm. "Everybody, on your toes. This could be it."

"We're going in fast and we're traveling light," Anakin told his assault force, gathered in a small bunker attached to the command post. The force had grown to include a squad of fully armored clone infantry to go in Erk's ship as security for the transport craft while they were on the ground inside the center. "Erk, we're going to push those transports at top speed and fly them as close to the ground as we can get. Are you up to that?"

"Yessir."

"Getting out of here is going to be a problem. The ships are protected in revetments, but in order to avoid being hit by enemy gunners, we're going to have to make a dash for it, so everyone be prepared for a very hard takeoff. I expect to have hard landings, too, but we'll talk about that later. Everyone look at this graphic of the mesa and memorize as many of the features as you can in the short time we've got. Also, this display." He punched up a floor plan of the main communications building. "Trooper Subu, does any of that look familiar?"

"Yessir. This long corridor leads to the main control room." She used a laser pointer to highlight the area she was talking about. "These side corridors here," she said, pointing to three corridors in quick succession, "lead to various other parts of the complex. Here, this leads to the courtyard where the staff often take their breaks and eat their meals. These rooms are staff quarters. Back here are storage rooms, repair shops. Where are they holding the hostages?"

"In the main control room. If they move them, I'll know. Everyone look at this." Anakin highlighted an area outside the main building. "We are going to land here, among these outbuildings, hopefully screened by them and these trees. We'll go in hard, so everyone be sure to secure yourselves for a rough landing. From there it's a very short sprint." He pointed to a large doorway. "If it's locked, we blow it open. It leads directly down this corridor to the main control room. Hardly any possibility of getting lost on our way to the main control room. It's these side corridors that we should worry about. They offer opportunities for an ambush, so I want to leave one trooper at each intersection to cover them so we can leave our exit route open. Sergeant," he said to the clone trooper, "you pick those troopers now, and deploy them as we go in. You two—" He turned to the guards, Raders and Vick. "I want you in the transport with me. Your job will be to patrol that main corridor and back up the troopers who'll be watching the side corridors. Shoot anything that's made of metal and moves.

"We're traveling light, weapons and equipment only. If we're in there more than ten minutes, we'll be visited. The hostages are heavily guarded. Surprise will be our best weapon. We've got to get in there, take the guards out, and get the hostages to the transports as quickly as possible. If I go down, he will be in charge—" Anakin pointed to the ARC sergeant. "Lieu-

tenant H'Arman, you stay with your transport and the
infantry escort. Trooper Subu, you come into the building with me. Your job will be to get the hostages moving and back to the transports."

Private Vick gave Odie a grin. She smiled back. Erk
noticed the exchange and, despite himself, felt a tiny
twinge of jealousy.

"How many hostages are there?" he asked, taking
his mind off Odie.

"The original staff was fifty technicians and special-
ists. We don't know how many of them may have been
executed. I know none of you saw the clip of Reija
Momen, but she said the Separatist commander threatened to kill one hostage every hour that we didn't give
in to their demands. We think the enemy commander
was bluffing, but, well, he had fifty potential victims—
some could have been executed. We won't know until
we get in there. Remember this: we won't have any
time to search for anyone left behind. The hostages
themselves can tell us if we've gotten everyone out.
We'll just have to rely on that to ensure we don't leave
anyone behind. It's a chance we're going to have to
take."

As Anakin spoke, Odie watched him closely. He was
a handsome young man, maybe only a little older than
she was, but it was clear from the way he spoke and
the way he held himself that he was very much in
charge.

"Everyone take a few minutes and study these charts
until they're burned into your brains. One more thing.
The signal for the fleet to open fire is the common Basic
word *finished*. When that signal is transmitted to Gen-

eral Halcyon, the fleet will open up with its heavy weapons, so we need to be totally clear of that mesa when the signal is given." Anakin leaned forward toward his team. "This operation has to come off with split-second timing. Once the enemy realizes we're in the center, he'll kill the hostages. He knows as well as we do that once the hostages are no longer in his power, his lease on life is up. All right, five minutes until we mount up."

Strapped into the copilot's seat, Odie's heart pounded with excitement; she had never traveled this fast over the ground before. Anakin kept the aircraft no more than fifteen meters above the ground as it roared along at top speed. He controlled the craft expertly, almost effortlessly as far as Odie could tell. His adjustments of his flight pattern were so perfectly in time with his ve-locity, it was as if he could see the terrain before it showed up in front of them.

"Ever fly in one of these?" he asked her conversa-tionally.

"Not up in the cockpit," she answered. A small hill flashed beneath them as Anakin spurred a few meters of altitude out of the transport.

"Ever do any Podracing?"

"Nossir."

"That lieutenant behind us is one fine pilot," Anakin observed. "I understand that you're pretty good on a recon speeder." He keyed his throat mike. "Okay, Erk, we break here. Just follow me. Everyone get ready, check your weapons and equipment. Three minutes to touchdown."

"Yessir, I am pretty good as a recon trooper." Odie was surprised at how level her voice was; she'd been scared before, scared plenty, but this was terrifying. Calmly, hands steady, she undid the flap on her blaster holster, checked the charge and the safety, and slid it back in. Anakin, on the other hand, seemed almost happy to be at the controls of a ship that could crash one second or be blown out of the sky the next. That must be how Erk felt in his fighter during combat, she thought.

Odie's checking her weapon didn't go unnoticed, and Anakin smiled. "You know how to use that thing, don't you?"

Her sunburned face turned even redder. "Yessir."

Anakin realized she thought he was thinking about the incident with Grudo. "What happened with Grudo was an accident," he told her. "I don't hold it against you—put it out of your mind. Think about what's ahead of us and get ready to use that blaster again."

The mesa loomed a few kilometers ahead. It glowed and pulsated with artillery fire, both incoming and outgoing. Halcyon's attack was proceeding.

"Prepare for landing," Anakin announced on his command net. "Erk, set down next to me. All right, everybody, here we go!"

Anakin's landing craft slammed down between two low buildings and stopped in a swirl of dust just in front of a grove of trees. Even before it was stopped, the rear ramp thudded down and the ARC trooper and clone infantry were out and running for the entrance to the main communications building. All around them the air hummed and buzzed and cracked with the blasts

from high-energy weapons; a hundred meters beyond
the trees was a maelstrom of fire as Halcyon's guns
blasted Tonith's positions, but so far no one seemed to
have noticed the landing craft—two now, because
Erk's landed just beside Anakin's and the clone infantry emerged to set up perimeter security. The ARC
trooper blew open the door to the communications
center and, followed closely by Anakin and Odie,
dashed inside.

"It's about forty meters from here to the main control room door," Odie shouted.

"Move fast but keep a sharp lookout," Anakin ordered over the tactical communications net. "Be sure
of your targets before you shoot. No unnecessary fire."

He sprinted down the long corridor, followed by the
rest of his force. The side corridors flashed by, but all
seemed empty just now. As ordered, the clone sergeant
began deploying his troopers. A corridor leading off to
the left of the structure lay ahead, and the doors to the
main control room were just beyond that.

Anakin had his lightsaber out. He was a good three
meters ahead of the fastest clone infantryman when
a battle droid popped around a corner and fired its
weapon. The bolt hit the trooper behind the Jedi. The
trooper gasped and collapsed to the floor in a clatter.
Anakin disposed of the droid with one swift sweep of
his lightsaber, but other battle droids, six or eight of
them, emerged and took up positions directly in front
of the control-room doors and immediately began firing. Odie, the clone troopers, and the two guards hit
the deck and the bolts lanced harmlessly over them,
caroming off the walls and ceiling. None of them could

fire back because Anakin was in the way. To Odie, lying on the floor watching him, he seemed at the center of a cyclone of blue light as his lightsaber whirled and slashed at the droids whose blaster bolts, aimed directly at him at point-blank range, bounced off the high-energy blade and tore into the walls and ceiling. In seconds, the droids were smoking piles of junk. Anakin leapt over the mess, brought his lightsaber down in one swift motion, burst open the doors to the control room, and stepped inside. The whole fight had taken only seconds, and to those behind him watching it seemed he had merely strolled through the droids and pushed open the doors.

Odie and the others lay gasping and coughing on the floor behind him. The corridor was filled with the choking stench of vaporized droid metal and components. Anakin had already disappeared into the control room before she got to her knees and shouted, "Follow him!"

The droids in the main control room had been given strict orders to guard the prisoners, so when Anakin appeared suddenly among them, his lightsaber flashing, it took several fatal seconds for any of them to recognize him as a threat. One fired directly at him, but it was as if Anakin knew the droid's intention even before it moved. With an almost casual sweep of his blade, he deflected the blaster bolt and cut the droid in two. Odie, coming through the ruined doors behind him, was horrified to see Anakin holding off six battle droids. Fortunately for her and the infantry troops who pounded in just behind, the droids' attention was all focused on the Jedi. To Odie, his movements were so fast that by comparison the droids' defense was in slow motion. She knelt and fired at a droid in a far corner of the control room. The sergeant and his troopers took up shooting positions, but Anakin had so quickly dispatched the droids inside the control room that there were no opponents left for them to shoot at.

"Secure the hostages," Anakin ordered. "Quickly! Quickly! A counterattack is on the way."

Pors Tonith, who up to this point had fought a brilliant defensive action, had made one big mistake, and that was moving the hostages into the main control room. He had done it to make guarding them easier, and he had never planned on an attempt to free them. Now he issued a fateful order: "Kill them, kill them all!"

Anakin stood in the center of the control room surrounded by the steaming piles of debris that had been the hostages' guards. To Reija Momen, who only moments before had been sitting dozing against a wall in the corner of the room surrounded by her companions, the Jedi's arrival among them occurred in a burst of sound and fury so astonishing and unexpected that at first she couldn't grasp what was happening. The ARC trooper came up to her, offered her a hand, and said something. She got to her feet. Other clone troopers were helping her companions up and ushering them through the ruined doors. But Reija moved toward the solitary figure standing in the center of the room. The kiss she placed on Anakin's cheek came as a total surprise to him. In his mind he knew the droid counterattack was almost on them, and he knew what direction it was coming from. He had been about to activate his lightsaber again when Reija kissed him.

Without even knowing who was standing beside him, Anakin automatically put his arm around her shoulders and drew her close. She said something and he smiled and looked down at her. What he saw in that brief instant was a profound flash of recognition. In this maelstrom of death and destruction, in this desperate situation with the enemy sweeping down on him and escape a perilous possibility at best, Anakin Skywalker experienced—peace. In that brief instant of the unexpected kiss a profound lassitude had come over him; he wished to lay his head on this woman's shoulder and rest, just rest. Maybe sleep, leave this nasty place and not have to get up the next morning.

What happened next would have consequences yet undreamed of; it was as if Anakin Skywalker were having an epiphany. In a microsecond he saw what was coming and knew where it would lead him, but he was powerless to interfere. He felt like a headstrong and disobedient child being forced to sit still and watch a puppet show. A battle droid stepped into the room from the far side and leveled its blaster at Anakin. Reija Momen stepped in front of him just as the droid fired. The bolt, fired at low power, hit her squarely in the chest and slammed her back into Anakin. She didn't scream, didn't cry out, but her mouth formed a tiny O, and her eyes looked up at him, pleading. He held her under the arms and looked into those eyes and watched the life force drain out of them. Memories of his mother's death flooded him and he felt the rage rise.

The droid stood there, staring at Anakin. It was as if it were waiting politely until Reija Momen was gone before it fired again. The control room was silent for a long moment, broken only by a repeated *click, click, click* as the droid impotently pulled the trigger of its blaster. Anakin was saved by poor maintenance. In that instant he once again became an Avenger.

28

There are so many of them," Lieutenant Commander Vitwroth said softly as he watched the enemy fleet slowly filling the *Mandian*'s screens. He turned to Captain Foth, who sat silently in his chair, fingers drumming softly on one arm, and said, "I've never seen so many ships in one place before."

The main fleet around Praesitlyn had been warned of the approaching danger. *Now what?* everyone on board the *Mandian* wondered. Everyone but Captain Foth.

"Pretty impressive, isn't it?" he commented.

"They were able to mask them until they got within range, sir," Vitwroth said. "I wonder how they did that."

"The same way they blocked communications earlier. They've got the money to pay for research and development," Foth replied. "Now we'll see how well they can fight."

"Enemy ships are within range, Captain," the gunnery officer announced. "We are ready to open fire, sir."

"Belay that. Our job is to see and flee, and we are now going to flee. Helmsman, get us out of here."

The smell of Reija's hair still in his nostrils, Anakin reached deep into the Force. A sense of invincible power came over him, infusing him completely. Even during the desperate battle with the enemy tank droids and the attack on the hill he had not experienced the Force as fully as it now flowed into him. In that instant when he achieved total oneness with the Force he knew he could do anything, and it felt good. All thought of his mission, retreating to the transports, evacuating the hostages, giving the signal to Nejaa that would spell victory, evaporated. "Follow me!" he commanded the clone troopers.

Chaos reigned outside the building. Odie, assisted by Corporal Raders and Private Vick, ushered the hostages into Erk's transport. She could see Erk in the cockpit giving the thumbs-up sign and smiling broadly. The Separatists, however, were now aware of their presence and, despite the continuing bombardment from the artillery, had sent the battle droid infantry against them. The clone troopers were engaging from their defensive perimeter.

Erk's voice crackled in Odie's headset. "Good work. Get on board and let's get out of here."

"We can't. The commander's still inside," Odie shouted back.

"Come on. He can take care of himself," Erk ordered. "Get on board and let's get these people out of here." As if to emphasize Erk's words, a stray blaster bolt skipped between Odie's legs and caromed off into the side of the building.

"What's the holdup?" Raders asked, running up to where Odie stood and looking up at Erk in his cockpit.

"The commander's still inside. We can't just leave him," Odie said.

"Yes, we can," Raders replied. "Come on, mount up. You've done your job."

"No!" She shook Raders's hand from her shoulder and stepped back, just avoiding a blaster bolt that sizzled past her nose. "I'm going back inside!"

"You're crazy!" Raders cursed. "You'll get us all killed standing out here."

Vick ran up. "What's going on here?" he gasped. "They're closing in, our line is collapsing. We've got to get the hostages out of here!"

The trio was on the ground in the shadow of Erk's transport. A clone infantryman ran up. "We can't hold them any longer," he said, his voice as calm as if he were standing on the firing range. "Our line is collapsing. What are your orders?" As he stood there a blaster bolt hit him squarely between the shoulders, propelling him forward as it burned completely through his body armor and exploded out through his chest.

"That's it, you're leaving," Vick shouted.

The deflective armor on Erk's transport had so far saved it from any serious damage. His power system was up and ready. He shook his head sadly and raised the ramp. "Good hunting," he whispered, his voice cracking. His transport slowly began to move forward. "I guess it wasn't meant for us to spend our lives together." In that instant one of the enemy's heavy guns ranged on Anakin's ship, and it exploded in a brilliant cascade of flame. The concussion buffeted the three on the ground and knocked out the walls on the nearby building, but they were unhurt and Erk's ship was away undamaged.

The three looked at one another.

"Thanks, trooper, you've just effectively killed us all," Vick said bitterly.

The clone troopers' fire had ceased, and from where they lay on the ground the three could clearly see enemy battle droids moving toward them. Odie leveled her hand blaster at the nearest droid.

"Not yet." Raders laid a restraining hand on her shoulder. "Let's make a run for the building. Maybe the commander and his clones are still alive in there. Maybe we can get out somehow before they blow this place."

"Oh, we're dead, dead, dead!" Vick groaned.

"Stop whining!" Raders snapped. "What do you think they pay us for? On my command, run like mad for that hole in the wall over there. Ready? *Go!*"

Nejaa Halcyon sat as if transfixed. He knew the disturbance in the Force he was experiencing was a result of Anakin's tapping into it. He knew Anakin was still alive. But there was something troubling—

"General, urgent report from fleet." A staff officer stood at Halcyon's elbow. He hadn't even been aware of the man's approach.

Slayke, who was standing nearby, smiled. He realized the Jedi Master had been absorbed in a reverie, and it amused him that even Jedi sometimes let their minds wander. Yet he also knew that Halcyon's reverie concerned Anakin, and that the Master was worried about him. Despite their former differences, Slayke had come to respect, even like, Halcyon.

Halcyon sat bolt upright when he read the message just handed to him. "Listen up!" He gestured at the officers around him and beckoned at Slayke to come closer. "This campaign is shifting into a new level. A large enemy fleet is approaching."

Slayke betrayed not even a twinge of emotion. "It's the relief fleet. Nejaa, we're now between a rock and a very hard place."

"Yes, we are." Halcyon stroked his chin. What was happening on the mesa? He turned back to the staff officer. "Have the fleet prepare for battle. Captain Slayke, I will join the fleet. You take over here and—"

"General, the hostages are free," a communications officer reported. "The shuttle commander has just reported in." Several officers applauded and broke into smiles.

"Pipe him in so we can all hear his report," Halcyon ordered. "Anakin? Is that you?"

"Nossir, Lieutenant H'Arman here. Commander Skywalker is still in the communications center and his shuttle has been destroyed. I have the hostages aboard and am bringing them in."

"Good work, Lieutenant. Land at the resupply point and wait there for further orders."

"Well, isn't this just great," Slayke said. "You can't fight that fleet and leave this enemy force behind here, Nejaa. I'm sorry, but you have to give the order to destroy the mesa before our ships are fully engaged."

Halcyon turned to Slayke. "No. Not yet. Let's wait a little."

"Whatever you say, sir," Slayke answered, but it was evident he thought Halcyon had just made a fatally wrong decision.

"Just a little while. A few more minutes won't hurt either way."

"Nejaa, I know how you feel about Anakin." Slayke laid a hand on Halcyon's shoulder. "He's a fine young commander. But the success of this entire expedition depends on your decision now. We have to be able to turn our full attention to this new threat. You have to give the order."

"Yes. But not just now."

Anakin moved with the swiftness and brilliance of a burning sun. Droids rushed against him, their weapons firing indiscriminately. His lightsaber flashing in a blinding symphony of light and destruction, he parried the bolts effortlessly, sending some ripping through the walls and roof, others back into the very droids that had fired them.

He wasn't defending now, he was attacking, attacking with such fury and destruction that nothing could stop him. And he knew where he was going—he was headed for the enemy command post.

The droids, unable to give way, unable to surrender even if Anakin would have spared them, flew apart like cheap dolls as the lightsaber cut through them in a broad swath of destruction. The clone troopers following the Jedi had difficulty finding targets, and stumbled over the debris he left in his passage through the complex. They merely followed in his wake, covering his back. Before long he was outside the building and heading with unerring accuracy toward Pors Tonith's bunker. It seemed as if Tonith's entire army was firing at Anakin, but as he ran at full speed over the uneven ground that separated the communications facility from Tonith's command bunker, not a single bolt touched him. The troopers following hugged the ground and crawled painfully onward while their commander stood erect and ran unscathed through the burning trajectories of death.

Tonith's engineer droids had constructed the command bunker with standard internal blast walls to baffle the explosive force of any demolition charge an attacker might use to blow the entrance doors open. Anakin set a thermal detonator at the base of the bunker's massive doors and took cover in a slight depression about twenty meters from them. He counted the seconds, and was ready when the massive detonation erupted. Even before the debris from the blast had settled, he was up and through the gaping hole. The first blast wall inside had been destroyed, but where the entrance tunnel turned sharply to the right the protective permacrete was intact—and three droids waited there, weapons leveled.

Inside the bunker, Pors Tonith stood calmly, a cup of tea poised in front of his purple lips. They'd all felt the concussion of the thermal detonator when it went off, but Tonith and his technicians had been unharmed by the blast. Several of the technicians made as if to flee for cover somewhere.

"Everyone stay at your station," he ordered. "We do

not have the means to resist and we shall not." He could clearly follow the fight in the entrance corridor by the sounds that Anakin's and the droids' weapons made in the closed space. In seconds all had fallen quiet.

He sipped his tea. One of the technicians began to whimper. "Silence!" he snapped.

Anakin stepped into the control room, his clothing smoldering from near hits, his eyes blazing with fury. The technicians gasped and shrank away from the ghastly figure. Tonith, however, merely gazed upon Anakin with a slight smile on his face. The room went deathly silent except for the gentle hum of the Jedi's lightsaber, which he held before him, shifting its blade slightly back and forth as if looking for targets. Nobody moved.

"I surrender," Tonith announced, smirking. "I surrender to you, Jedi Knight." He bowed slightly from the waist, careful not to spill any of the tea in his cup. He sipped the liquid and smacked his lips. "You have won," he continued, "and I congratulate you."

"Give the order for your troops to cease fire," Anakin rasped. His voice, reverberating hollowly throughout the room, sounded as if it had come out of a deep well. "Do it! Do it now!"

Tonith nodded at the technicians, who were more than happy to communicate the cease-fire order to the droid commanders.

"My dear sir," Tonith intoned, "I am now your prisoner and claim for me and my sentient beings here and elsewhere on this position the status of prisoners of war." He lifted his cup and insouciantly, in full confidence that he was now protected, swallowed the remaining tea. He smiled, showing his stained teeth.

Anakin was so fully filled with the Force that he was barely aware of himself. All he knew was the joy of the Force, a greater joy than he'd ever felt before. There was so much power in the Force, and all that power was his—*his!*—to do with as he would. He knew that, and he knew that the Muun before him was the one who led the Separatist army that had attacked and occupied the Intergalactic Communications Center. Tonith was the one who had commanded the forces that had wiped out General Khamar's army, that had killed most of Captain Slayke's Sons and Daughters of Freedom, the one who had brought the fight that killed so many of the clone troopers.

This was the one who had given the order to the droid that had shot down Reija Momen in front of him.

This Pors Tonith deserved to die, and Anakin Skywalker was the one to kill him.

These technicians were traitors to the Republic who had aided Pors Tonith in his murderous operation; they deserved to die, as well. Let this vile, stained-tooth creature watch as his underlings died, so he would know his fate, and fear before he died.

Anakin Skywalker, filled with the Force, the agent of vengeance, raised his lightsaber and advanced toward the nearest technician.

He stopped as a voice came unbidden into his mind.

"You must use the Force for good, Anakin."

Confused, he looked around. The voice sounded like that of Qui-Gon Jinn, Obi-Wan's Jedi Master—the one who had seen the potential in the child Anakin and helped win the boy's freedom from slavery. But Qui-Gon Jinn was dead . . .

"Master Jinn?" Anakin breathed.

"The Force is too strong to use for anything but good, Padawan. Remember that, and you can be the greatest Jedi of all," the voice said.

Anakin stood unable to move for a long moment. Then he shook himself and severed his connection to the Force. He almost staggered from the sudden loss of so much joy and power, but controlled himself so rapidly that he was the only one in the room aware of his momentary disorientation.

Kneeling on the floor in front of him was a cowering form; Anakin realized he had been about to murder the hapless technician and shuddered.

He glanced at the others, then turned to face Pors Tonith.

"You are my prisoners," he choked out. "I will take you back to Coruscant and hand you over to the Republic Senate for assignment to trial." He didn't turn off his lightsaber.

Pors Tonith, captured admiral of the Separatists, rattled a chuckle deep in his throat.

"Please, sir," B'wuf begged in a tiny voice from the corner in which he still sat, "may I get up now?"

29

Private Vick whistled when he led the others into Pors Tonith's control room.

Trooper Odie Subu looked up at the Muun and asked, "Is he the one in charge?"

Anakin, still breathing heavily, kept staring at Tonith and didn't reply. For his part, Tonith was no longer defiant. He'd become afraid of this young Jedi who had captured him; he thought he was unbalanced and unpredictable.

"They've stopped fighting outside," Corporal Raders announced. "The firing stopped just before we reached the bunker, sir, and—oh." He stopped talking when he took in the tableau.

"Sir," the ARC sergeant said in a sergeant's command voice, "your lightsaber."

That got Anakin's attention. "What?"

"Your lightsaber, sir."

"My . . ." Anakin looked at his hand and flinched, as though surprised that his lightsaber was activated. He turned it off and attached it to his belt.

He staggered slightly as he turned toward his troopers. Odie, thinking he was reacting normally for a soldier who'd just come through deadly combat, rushed forward to assist him. She saw his face close up—it was white as a sheet, drained, and he had lines around his mouth like those of an old man.

He waved her away, saying, "Thanks, I'm all right, I'm all right." He smiled weakly. One of the guards, he couldn't remember which one, handed him a canteen of electrolyte fluids and he thankfully drank it dry in one long, thirsty gulp. He handed the empty canteen back. "Thanks, thanks very much," he said, wiping his lips with the back of one hand. He gestured at Tonith and the others. "All of these are our prisoners. Take charge of them, would you, Sergeant? Take them to General Halcyon to be locked up."

B'wuf spoke up. "I was only a hired hand, sir. I was not a part of what this creature did here!" He pointed at Tonith. "He saved my life," he said, pointing a finger at Anakin. "They were going to execute me. I told the admiral that what he was doing was evil and I wasn't going to serve him anymore, and he was going to have me executed. The Jedi saved my life. They were going to kill me—he saved my life!"

The comlink installed on Anakin's wrist bleeped. He vaguely remembered it bleeping regularly as he'd fought his way to the bunker, but he'd ignored it at the time. Now he answered it.

"Anakin?" It was Halcyon. "Is that you? Are you all right? The enemy has just stopped fighting. What's going on?"

"Master Halcyon," Anakin said tiredly, "I'm fine. I'm in the control bunker with my troopers. I captured the Separatist commander and his staff. We're about to bring them to you."

"That's a relief," Halcyon said. "Give your prisoners to the clone commandos to secure. I'm sending a transport to pick you up. The Separatist relief fleet is on the way, and I'm told it's a big one. I'm having our starfighters ferried down here at once. We've got a big fight on our hands, and I need you right away."

Only the technicians looked at Tonith when he gave out an anguished wail—if only he'd been able to hold out for a few more minutes!

"I'll be there as soon as I can," Anakin replied. He turned to the ARC sergeant. "You heard that?" When the sergeant nodded, he ordered, "Take control of these prisoners and secure them."

"There's an enemy fleet coming, sir?" Corporal Raders asked, a troubled expression on his face.

"It sounds like it." Anakin stood erect, oddly feeling better at the prospect of more action.

The Republic fleet commander had not been idle while Halcyon pursued the ground war against the Separatists' forces on Praesitlyn. He had planned carefully for an attack like this. Several scenarios were considered, but it was decided that whatever tactic the enemy might use, the fleet would remain intact in order to concentrate and coordinate its combined firepower. If the enemy attacked by squadrons from different directions, the Republic fleet would take on each squadron in turn; if they attacked with their ships in line ahead, an attempt would be made to use superior speed to cross the enemy's line of advance and rake their ships with every weapon available. Whatever tactic was used, Halcyon's ships would be screened by his fighter fleet.

But every battle plan becomes useless after the first shot is fired. The enemy commander chose to attack in a box formation with his flagship in the center, protected by his ships, and the fighters met in a wild melee between the two armadas. It's not always the number and size of the ships engaged that wins battles, but the way they are used.

For this battle, Nejaa Halcyon chose to give over command of the fleet to Admiral Hupsquoch, while he led the fighter fleet against the enemy.

"A fine ship, sir!" the clone pilot who'd ferried *Azure Angel II* to the surface of Praesitlyn said as he helped Anakin into her cockpit.

Anakin smiled as he strapped himself in. He was in his true element now. "Thanks for bringing her down here," he said. "How'd she handle?" *Azure Angel II* was heavily modified. Even though clone troopers had the natural ability to learn how to handle any aircraft, flying a modified starfighter without knowing what had been done to it could be very tricky. Anakin was both very proud and very jealous of the modifications he'd made to her on his own.

"Just fine, sir. I was very careful to follow the 'shiny switch' rule once I saw you'd made some major aftermarket adjustments to her control panel."

"Very wise. Just a few customized adjustments." He really felt uncomfortable that someone else had flown his starfighter, but that had been necessary to allow the fighter to take off from the surface. He changed the subject. "I see a big scratch along the port side. It wasn't there before." He grinned as he put his helmet on. The pilot just stared at Anakin, uncomprehending. "I'm only joking," Anakin assured him.

"Oh, yessir! I understand," the pilot replied without smiling. He jumped to the ground and saluted solemnly as Anakin sealed the cockpit and gave him the traditional thumbs-up sign.

Anakin adjusted the mouthpiece to his headset and dialed in the frequency for ship-to-ship communications. "General Halcyon?"

"Anakin, won't you ever learn to use proper comm procedure?" Halcyon muttered. "You know the rendezvous point. Let's get there, fast." He glanced over his shoulder at Anakin's starfighter. He could just see the young Jedi through the cockpit. His airfoils were deployed. They'd be useful up to twenty thousand meters. Already Anakin's repulsorlift engines were raising a cloud of dust around *Azure Angel II,* and as Halcyon watched, the machine gradually rose vertically from the ground.

Anakin armed his blasters and proton torpedoes and engaged his IFF system. Gradually he increased his airspeed. At twenty thousand meters he retracted his airfoils and engaged his sublights to attain escape velocity. Now all the horror of the recently concluded ground combat faded away as he settled into the exhilarating world of high-speed, high-tech destruction, where pilots and machines disintegrated instantly in clean blossoms of flame, and pain and terror were endured only for milliseconds.

He passed through the fleet without incident. A thousand kilometers beyond, he got a visual on the fighter fleet. Beyond that, not yet within human eyesight but already registering on his instruments, was the enemy.

"I'm right on your six," Halcyon announced.

"General Halcyon, won't you ever learn to use proper comm procedure?" Anakin laughed.

"Switch to the guard channel," Halcyon ordered. He was serious now, and he was right to be—Anakin's instruments showed hundreds of blips fast approaching, the enemy fighter screen. They were now in among their own fighter fleet ships. The plan agreed upon in advance was that an element of fighters led by Halcyon would head for the heart of the enemy fleet. The rest of the fighter arm would run interference. If the enemy chose to employ the same tactic, then a lot would depend on whose pilots were better. There was no doubt in Halcyon's mind whose were.

"This is Halcyon Six. Follow me!" A hundred other fighters peeled off from the formation and followed him.

The enemy commander chose to use his fighters to engage the Republic craft one-on-one.

Anakin flashed through the fighters, guns blazing. He would save his missiles for the capital ships that lay just ahead. The enemy fighters zooming at him appeared as tiny points of light, which were their blaster cannons firing. As good as he was, Halcyon could barely keep up with the young Jedi pilot, and instead of leading the attack formation, in essence he became Anakin's wingmate.

In seconds they were through the enemy fighter screen

and in among the larger ships. Now it was everyone for him- or herself as each pilot selected a target and attacked. Anakin concentrated on a destroyer looming just off his starboard wing. Its outline seemed blurred and indistinct. He couldn't determine if it really was a destroyer or a frigate, because it was using a cloaking device that distorted its image. He flashed beneath the ship as its ion guns reached deadly fingers out at him, but he was moving too fast—almost three thousand kilometers per hour—for even a warship's target acquisition system to get a bearing and range in time to hit him. He turned and approached the vessel from the stern and, as he started into a huge looping maneuver, fired a proton torpedo into its engines.

The death of the destroyer would have been a beautiful sight to behold if Anakin had stayed around to witness it. First a bright flash as the missile detonated; then the vessel appeared to shudder. Next, fingers of fire flashed forward from her stern, causing the aft part of the ship to blaze in a brilliant blue light. In the airless, soundless depths of space, no ear heard the mighty ship's death knell as her propulsion system detonated in a brilliant flash of intense white light. It lasted only a fraction of a second and then, where the ship had been, were only myriad glowing orange dots of light, like a swarm of luminescent insects in the night, the melting fragments of her structure producing their own oxygen as they floated in space. The display lasted mere seconds, and then there was nothing but dead debris.

Halcyon witnessed Anakin's attack, but then lost

him in the melee. Other pilots had not been so successful, though some had. There were now conspicuous
gaps in the enemy's formation. They had done what
they came for. "This is Halcyon Six, break off the fight.
I repeat, break off."

Anakin heard the command, but now the Force was
upon him again. He knew what he had to do. Ahead
floated a massive vessel. The cloaking device the enemy
was using could not obscure it entirely, and he knew it
had to be the Separatist flagship. He roared straight in
at what he assumed was the ship's bridge but, in the
last fraction of a second before colliding, zoomed past
it at five thousand kilometers per hour. This time the
target was so huge that the extra split second it took
him to pass her gave her gunnery system the opportunity to acquire him as a target. It was fortunate that the
shot that got him was from a blaster cannon. *Azure
Angel II*'s armor deflected most of the destructive force
of the shot, but the damage was severe. "I'm hit," he
announced calmly.

"How bad?" Halcyon asked.

"Get out of here" was all Anakin said in reply.

"Anakin!"

"Get out of here," Anakin repeated.

Halcyon realized that Anakin was about to put another shot up this ship's spout. "Don't do it—you'll go
up with her."

"Say hello to the missus for me." Anakin's voice was
calm, well measured—even, Nejaa thought afterward,
tinged with a slight flavor of wry humor.

"No, Anakin, no!"

The enormous blast from the destruction of the Separatist flagship decisively tilted the odds toward the Republic forces by engulfing many of the enemy's ships unlucky enough to be in the vicinity. It also engulfed Anakin Skywalker.

30

The dust had hardly settled from Halcyon's landing before Zozridor Slayke and the entire army staff were running toward him, before even the maintenance droids had trundled out to service the craft. Halcyon popped the canopy and breathed the hot, dry air of Praesitlyn. He ran a hand across his face, rubbing away dry crystals of salt left behind from his perspiration—and his tears. He felt drained, not so much physically as emotionally.

Slayke and another officer climbed up on the wing and reached helping hands into the cockpit. Halcyon needed the assistance to get out.

"Brilliant! Wonderful. The enemy fleet is in disorder and withdrawing. Your troops are dismantling the droids. A complete victory. Sir, I never thought I'd live to see such a stunning success." Slayke pounded Halcyon on the back with one hand as he steadied him with the other. Dozens of officers and soldiers clustered around, all offering their hands and words of congratulation. Where scarcely minutes earlier the fate of the entire campaign had hung precariously in the balance, now it had been decided in their favor, and before them stood the man responsible for it.

"Not me, it was Anakin," Halcyon croaked. He was surprised at the sound of his voice, surprised that he was able to speak at all. He held up a hand to silence the crowd. "Commander Skywalker, at the cost of his own life, destroyed the enemy flagship and turned the tide for us. And it was Anakin who captured the brains behind the droid army." He paused and shook his head. "You and me, Captain, compared to him, we're just a couple of old, used-up dishrags in this business of war."

The crowd had gone still. "I knew the lad had it in him," Slayke said, breaking the silence.

The maintenance droids arrived, humming and clanking, hesitating to approach the fighter while all the living beings were standing in the vicinity.

"Someone shut those things down," Slayke growled. "They're always getting in a man's way." He put an arm around Halcyon's shoulders and gently led him through the crowd that closed in behind them as they walked slowly back toward the command post. "How would you like *Plooriod Bodkin* back, *General*?" Slayke asked.

Halcyon stopped and pretended to think for a moment. "No, Captain, you earned her—maybe not square, but fair. She's in good hands now." He put his own arm around Slayke's shoulders. They continued toward the bunker.

"Could you tell us what happened?" Slayke asked.

Halcyon stopped. "Gather 'round," he told the crowd. He had regained his composure now. "What that young Jedi did shall live in the annals of the Jedi forever." His voice was normal again. He thought, *I'll seek out Padmé and tell her how her husband died.* He'd have time to prepare himself for that. It was then that he noticed Odie standing with Erk and the two guards. Her cheeks, too, were tear-stained. "You, come closer," he said, gesturing to the quartet who'd been standing at the back of the crowd.

Raders pointed to himself. "Me?"

Halcyon smiled and nodded. "Yes, you four. They were with him, up there," he informed the officers and nodded at the mesa where Tonith's forces had made their last stand. "You tell us about that"—he gestured at the officers standing around—"and I'll tell what happened."

"Sir," Odie began, "he was a one-man army." The news of Anakin's death had hit her hard. It was difficult not to cry while she related her part of the tale.

"I've never seen anything like it, sir," Vick volunteered. He filled them in as best he could. "He really laid them low. Nothing could touch him. Just like you, sir, on the *Ranger,* only—only—he wasted a lot more droids!" He grinned apologetically at Halcyon.

"What's your name, son?" Slayke asked.

"I'm Private Slane Vick, sir, and this here is my corporal, Ram Raders."

"Well," Halcyon began, "let's get under cover now. We've got a lot of cleaning up to do." He was feeling more himself again. The hurt deep inside his heart still throbbed painfully, but his duty was paramount, and the emotional scars of war would heal in their own time. They resumed walking back to the bunker.

"Someone's coming in for a landing," someone announced. He looked toward the horizon, shading his eyes with a hand. "An aircraft is coming in, sir," he reported. "It looks like a Delta-Seven Aethersprite."

They all looked up at the sky. "Yes, it's a Delta-Seven," Halcyon said. As it got bigger and bigger coming in for a landing, he stiffened. It couldn't be! "Do you recognize that starfighter?" He turned to Slayke.

Slayke shrugged. "Looks pretty beat up to me. One of yours from the fleet, I suppose."

Halcyon's fatigue had vanished. He began to run toward where the fighter was preparing to land. The others stared after him in amazement and then slowly, first by ones and twos, and then as a crowd, followed him. As soon as the group had moved away from Halcyon's fighter, the droids trundled in and began servicing the craft.

The incoming Delta-7 hovered in its vertical mode and gradually settled down, raising a thick cloud of dust that billowed out to engulf the bystanders. The canopy was pitted and scorched so they couldn't see the pilot; the fuselage was blackened, and most of the paint so badly scored it was hard to determine the original colors. The two blaster cannons on the starboard side of the craft were missing entirely.

"It's him," Halcyon whispered, gripping Slayke by an arm. "It's him!" He pointed at the partially destroyed Podracer symbol just aft of the cockpit. "It's Anakin! How could this be!" He broke into laughter and began thumping Slayke on the back.

Slayke looked at Halcyon as if he'd lost his mind. "But—you told us—"

"No, no! I was wrong. This is Anakin's *Azure*

Angel II. I'd know it anywhere." He let go of Slayke's arm, rushed forward, and climbed onto the ship's airfoil. He banged mightily on the cockpit canopy. "Anakin! Anakin!" he shouted. Faintly, the officers standing nearby could hear someone pounding from inside the craft. "Get a service droid up here right away," Halcyon shouted. "The canopy is fused shut. Come on, get one of those things up here!" He gestured helplessly at Slayke, who grinned and stepped forward to lend a hand.

A maintenance droid dutifully rolled up, but it was only programmed to work on undercarriages and armaments. "Someone in maintenance has got to tell them to work on the canopy first, otherwise they're programmed to service these things in a certain order," Halcyon said. "Does anybody have a prybar?"

Frustrated, he drew his lightsaber. "Lean as far forward as you can," he shouted at the pilot, and began cutting away the canopy. When they could see the pilot's head through the gap, Slayke put a pair of gloves, waved Halcyon away, and straddled the canopy.

"I knew sooner or later I could do something useful around here," he said. He made a show of spitting into his palms, grinned fiercely at Halcyon, grasped the canopy with both hands, and began to pull. At first nothing happened. Slayke's muscles bulged visibly beneath his tunic and his face turned a deep red; veins stood out in his neck and a low growl emerged from deep inside his chest. A droid with an extensible body rolled up, raised itself to the level of the cockpit, and said, "May I be of service, sir?"

"Get lost," Slayke grunted, and the next instant the canopy popped off.

The pilot removed his helmet and grinned up at the two commanders looming over him. "Hi, Master Halcyon, Captain Slayke," Anakin said, extending a hand. "Give me a lift out of here, would you?"

"Would you mind telling us how you did that?" Halcyon asked.

They sat in the command post, Anakin with his legs spread out before him and a huge, almost empty container of water at one elbow. He ran a grimy hand through his hair. "Well, you know I always tinker with machines. I rigged *Azure Angel II* to give her a hyperspace capability—just something I cooked up." He shrugged. "At the last instant, just before the missile detonated, I engaged the drive and jumped free." He snapped his fingers. "Piece of cake."

"Sir," an officer asked, "just how did you know when to disengage?"

Anakin stood up, drained the last of the water, and wiped the drops from his lips with the back of his hand. "The same way I always knew what the ground was like before I could see it when I was Podracing." He shrugged. "It must be the Force."

"Sir?" Erk stepped out of the circle surrounding Anakin. Odie came up to stand beside him. "We'd like to ask you for a favor, sir."

"I'll grant you two any wish I have it in my power to grant," Anakin replied. "You name it!"

"Well, sir, I need a wingmate. I need someone I can

rely on. You know how it is, zooming through the combats of life. A man can do just so much by himself and he needs someone to watch his six. You see—"

"Commander Skywalker," Odie interrupted, "would you marry us?"

EPILOGUE

"... and thus by the power invested in me as an officer of the Grand Army of the Republic, I now pronounce you husband and wife." Anakin leaned forward and kissed Odie lightly on the cheek. The aroma of her freshly washed hair brought back memories—*Padmé*—and his heart raced with joy. Soon he would be reunited with his own wife. Already, the horrors of the Praesitlyn campaign and his role in them were receding. "I wish you both long lives and much happiness," he told the couple. His smile was huge and genuine. "Every cloud has its silver lining," he told them, "and today that's you two."

Halcyon stepped forward and offered his best wishes. Anakin exchanged glances with him and smiled again. How ironic that he, who had married secretly and against the rules of the Jedi Order, had been called upon to perform a legitimate public marriage rite. Halcyon smiled back and nodded. And Halcyon, also clandestinely wed, and with a child by that marriage, as well!

"Commander," Slayke said, offering his hand, "I don't think I've ever met anyone quite like you. First you win a war single-handed, and then you perform a marriage ceremony."

"Well, I had help, Captain—with the battles, that is."

"Commander Skywalker, I think you're someone who's going to change a lot of things in this galaxy, mark my words. I'm going to keep an eye on you, son." They shook warmly.

"Ah, Captain Slayke, I was just doing my duty." But Anakin wondered what assignment the Jedi Council would give him next and found himself looking forward to it.

"We shall invest him with his Jedi Knighthood when he returns," Mace Windu said.

Yoda nodded. "From Praesitlyn very satisfying the initial reports are; Jedi Knighthood he has earned." He blinked his huge eyes. "In the Force great disturbances there were. Sensed them, did you, my old friend?"

"I did. Evidently Anakin called upon it more than once, but the fighting was desperate. We were right to send these two to command the expedition."

Yoda nodded again but said nothing. There was—something—he was missing in all of this, like the uninvited guest at a wedding feast, mysterious and just beyond his grasp. He would have to think about it. But for now, young Anakin was a sharp new tool in the service of the Jedi Order. Yoda was looking forward to his investiture.

Count Dooku's Master, Darth Sidious, considered. His minions on Praesitlyn had been defeated, as he'd expected they would be, and the losses had been tremendous. But he had gained something much more valuable than military victory. He, too, had sensed the disturbance in the Force that was troubling Yoda—it was not the first time recently either.

He had watched young Skywalker for some time and was now convinced he had been right about the boy. He would become *very* useful in the future.

Darth Sidious folded his hands in contentment and smiled grimly.

A Star Wars mystery revealed at last!
Turn the page for a preview
of the long-awaited

Star Wars: Outbound Flight
by Timothy Zahn

Available from Del Rey Books
October 25, 2005

The room was compactly furnished, containing a three-tier bunk bed against one wall and a fold-down table and bench seats on the other. Beside the bunk bed were three large drawers built into the wall, while to the right was a door leading into what seemed to be a compact refresher station.

"What do you think he's going to do with us?" Maris murmured, looking around.

"He'll let us go," Qennto assured her, glancing into the refresher station and then sitting down on the lowest bed, hunching forward to keep from bumping his head on the one above it. "The real question is whether we'll be taking the firegems with us."

Car'das cleared his throat. "Uh . . . should we be talking about this?" he asked, looking significantly around the room.

"Oh, relax," Qennto growled. "They don't speak a word of Basic." His eyes narrowed. "And as long as we're on the subject of speaking, why the frizz did you tell him we knew Progga?"

"There was something in his eyes and voice just then," Car'das said. "Something that said he already knew all about it, and that we'd better not get caught lying to him."

Qennto snorted. "That's ridiculous."

"Unless there were survivors from Progga's crew," Maris pointed out.

"Not a chance," Qennto said firmly. "You saw what the ship looked like. The thing'd been peeled open like a ration bar."

"I don't know how he knew," Car'das insisted. "All I know is that he *did* know."

"And you shouldn't lie to an honorable man anyway," Maris murmured.

"Who, Mitth'raw'nuruodo?" Qennto scoffed. "Honorable? Don't you believe it. Military men are all alike. And in my experience, the smooth ones are the worst of the lot."

"*I've* known quite a few honorable soldiers," Maris said stiffly. "Besides, I've always had a good feel for people. I think this Mitth'raw—whatever. I think he can be trusted." She lifted her eyebrows. "I don't think trying to con him will be a good idea, either."

"It's only a bad idea if you get caught," Qennto said. "You get what you bargain for in this universe, Maris. Nothing more, nothing less."

She shook her head. "Your problem is that you don't have enough faith in people, Rak."

"I got all the faith I need, kiddo," Qennto said calmly. "I just happen to know a little more about human nature than you do. Human *and* nonhuman nature."

"I still think we need to play completely straight with him."

Qennto snorted. "Playing straight is the last thing you want to do. Ever. It gives the other guy all the advantages." He nodded toward the closed door. "And this guy in particular sounds like the sort who'll ask questions until we die of old age if we let him."

"Still, it might not be a bad idea to hang around here for at least a little while," Car'das suggested. "Progga's people are going to be pretty mad when he doesn't come back."

Qennto shook his head. "They'll never pin it on us. Not a chance."

"Yes, but—"

"Look, kid, let me do the thinking, okay?" Qennto said, cutting him off. Swiveling his legs up onto the bunk, he lay back with his arms folded behind his head. "Now everyone be quiet for a while. I've got to figure out how to play this."

Maris caught Car'das's eye, gave a little shrug, then turned and climbed up onto the bunk above Qennto. Stretching out, she folded her arms across her chest and gazed meditatively at the underside of the bunk above her.

Crossing to the other side of the room, Car'das folded down the table and one of the bench seats and sat down, wedging himself more or less comfortably between the table and wall. Putting his elbow on the table and propping his head up on his hand, he closed his eyes and tried to relax.

He didn't realize he'd dozed off until a sudden buzz startled him awake. He jumped up as the door opened to reveal a single black-clad Chiss. "Commander Mitth'raw'nuruodo's respects," the alien said, the Sy Bisti words coming out thickly accented. "He requests your presence in Forward Visual One."

"Wonderful," Qennto said, swinging his legs onto the floor and standing up. His tone and expression were the false cheerfulness Car'das had heard him use time and again in bargaining sessions.

"Not you," the Chiss said. He gestured to Car'das. "This one only."

Qennto came to an abrupt halt. "What?"

"A refreshment is being prepared," the Chiss said. "Until it is ready, this one only will come."

"Now, wait a second," Qennto said, taking a step forward. "We stick together or—"

"It's okay," Car'das interrupted. The Chiss standing in the doorway had made no move, but he'd caught a subtle shift in lighting and shadow outside that indicated there were others outside the humans' line of sight. "I'll be fine."

"Car'das—"

"It's okay," Car'das repeated, stepping to the doorway. The Chiss moved back, and he walked out into the corridor.

There were indeed more Chiss waiting by the door, two of them on either side. "Follow," the messenger said as the door closed.

They trooped down the curved corridor, passing three cross corridors and several other doorways along the way. Two of the doors were open, and Car'das couldn't resist a furtive glance inside each as they passed. All he could see, though, was unrecognizable equipment and more black-clad Chiss.

He had expected Forward Visual to be just another

crowded high-tech room. To his surprise, the door opened into something that looked like a compact version of a starliner's observation gallery. A long, curved couch sat in front of a convex floor-to-ceiling viewport currently giving a spectacular view of the glowing hyperspace sky as it flowed past the ship. The room's own lights were dimmed, making the display that much more impressive.

"Welcome, Jorj Car'das."

Car'das looked around. Mitth'raw'nuruodo was seated alone at the far end of the couch, silhouetted against the hyperspace sky. "Commander Mitth'raw'nuruodo," he greeted the other, glancing a question at his guide. The other nodded, stepping back and closing the door on himself and the rest of the escort. Feeling more than a little uneasy, Car'das stepped around the near end of the couch and made his way across the curve.

"Beautiful, isn't it?" Mitth'raw'nuruodo commented as Car'das arrived at his side. "Please, be seated."

"Thank you," Car'das said, easing himself onto the couch a cautious meter away from the other. "May I ask why I'm here?"

"To share this view with me, of course," Mitth'raw'nuruodo said dryly. "And to answer a few questions."

Car'das felt his stomach tighten. So it was to be an interrogation. Down deep he'd known it would be, but had hoped against hope that Maris's naïvely idealistic assessment of their captor might actually be right. "A very nice view it is, too," he commented, not knowing what else to say. "I'm a little surprised to find such a room aboard a warship."

"Oh, it's quite functional," Mitth'raw'nuruodo assured him. "Its full name is Forward Visual Triangulation Site Number One. We place spotters here during combat to track enemy vessels and other possible threats, and to coordinate some of our line-of-sight weaponry."

"Don't you have sensors to handle that?" Car'das asked, frowning.

"Of course," Mitth'raw'nuruodo said. "And usually they're quite adequate. But I'm sure you know there are ways of misleading or blinding electronic eyes. Sometimes the eyes of a Chiss are more reliable."

"I suppose," Car'das said, gazing at his host's own glowing eyes. In the dim light, they were even more intimidating. "Isn't it hard to get the information to the gunners fast enough?"

"There are ways," Mitth'raw'nuruodo said. "What exactly is your business, Jorj Car'das?"

"Captain Qennto's already told you that," Car'das said, feeling sweat breaking out on his forehead. "We're merchants and traders."

Mitth'raw'nuruodo shook his head. "Unfortunately for your captain's assertions, I'm familiar with the economics of star travel. Your vessel is far too small for any standard cargo to cover even normal operating expenses, let alone emergency repair work. I therefore conclude that you have a sideline occupation. You haven't the weaponry to be pirates or privateers, so you must be smugglers."

Car'das hesitated. What exactly was he supposed to say? "I don't suppose it would do any good to point out that our economics and yours might not scale the same?" he said, stalling.

"*Is* that what you claim?"

Car'das hesitated, but Mitth'raw'nuruodo had that knowing look about him again. "No," he conceded. "We *are* mostly just traders, as Captain Qennto said. But we do sometimes do a little smuggling on the side."

"I see," Mitth'raw'nuruodo said. "I appreciate your honesty, Jorj Car'das."

"You can just call me Car'das," Car'das said. "In our culture, the first name is reserved for use by friends."

Mitth'raw'nuruodo lifted his eyebrows. "You don't consider me a friend?"

"Do you consider *me* one?" Car'das countered.

The instant the words were out of his mouth he wished he could call them back. Sarcasm was never the option of choice in a confrontation like this. Particularly not when the other side held the power of life and death.

But Mitth'raw'nuruodo lifted an eyebrow. "Not yet," he agreed calmly. "Perhaps someday. You intrigue me, Car'das. Here you sit, captured by unfamiliar beings a long way from home. Yet instead of wrapping yourself within a blanket of fear or anger, you instead stretch outside yourself with curiosity."

Car'das frowned. "Curiosity?"

"You studied my warriors as you were brought aboard," Mitth'raw'nuruodo said. "I could see it in your eyes and face as you observed and thought and evaluated. You did the same as you were taken to your quarters, and again as you were brought here just now."

"I was just looking around," Car'das assured him, feeling his heart beating a little faster. Did spies rank above or below smugglers on Mitth'raw'nuruodo's list? "I didn't mean anything by it."

"Calm yourself," Mitth'raw'nuruodo said, a distinct touch of amusement in his voice. "I'm not accusing you of spying. I, too, have the gift of curiosity, and therefore prize it in others. Tell me, who is to receive the hidden gemstones?"

Car'das jerked. "You found—? I mean . . . in that case, why did you ask me about it?"

"As I said, I appreciate honesty," Mitth'raw'nuruodo said. "Who is the intended recipient?"

"A group of Hutts operating out of the Comra system," Car'das told him, giving up. "Rivals to the ones you—the ones who were attacking us." He hesitated. "You *did* know they weren't just random pirates, didn't you? That they were hunting us specifically?"

"We monitored your transmissions before we were in position to intervene," Mitth'raw'nuruodo said. "Though the conversation was of course unintelligible to us, I remembered hearing the phonemes *Dubrak Qennto* in the Hutt's speech when Captain Qennto later identified himself to me. The conclusion was obvious."

A shiver ran up Car'das's back. A conversation in an alien language, and yet Mitth'raw'nuruodo had been able to memorize enough of it to extract Qennto's name from the gibberish. What kind of creatures *were* these Chiss, anyway?

"Is the possession of these gems illegal, then?"

"No, but the customs fees are ridiculously high,"

Car'das said, forcing his mind back to the interrogation. "Smugglers are often used to avoid having to pay them." He hesitated. "Actually, considering the people we got this batch from, they may also have been stolen. But don't tell Maris that."

"Oh?"

Car'das winced. There he was again, talking without thinking. If Mitth'raw'nuruodo didn't kill him before this was over, Qennto probably would. "Maris is something of an idealist," he said reluctantly. "She thinks this whole smuggling thing is just a way of making a statement against the greedy and stupid Republic bureaucracy."

"Captain Qennto hasn't seen fit to enlighten her?"

"Captain Qennto likes her company," Car'das said. "I doubt she'd stay with him if she knew the whole truth."

"He claims to care about her, yet lies to her?"

"I don't know what he claims," Car'das said. "Though I suppose you could say that idealists like Maris do a lot of lying to themselves. The truth is there in front of her if she wanted to see it." He took another look at those glowing red eyes. "Though of course that doesn't excuse our part in it," he added.

"No, it doesn't," Mitth'raw'nuruodo said. "What would be the consequences if you didn't deliver the gemstones?"

Car'das felt his throat tighten. So much for the honorable Commander Mitth'raw'nuruodo. Firegems must be valuable out here, too. "They'd kill us," he said. "Probably in some hugely entertaining way, like watching us get eaten by some combination of large animals."

"And if the delivery was merely late?"

Car'das frowned, trying to read the other's expression in the flickering hyperspace glow. "What exactly do you want from me, Commander Mitth'raw'nuruodo?"

"Nothing too burdensome," Mitth'raw'nuruodo said. "I merely wish your company for a time."

"Why?"

"Partly to learn about your people," Mitth'raw'nuruodo said. "But primarily so that you may teach me your language."

Car'das blinked. "Our *language*? You mean Basic?"

"That *is* the chief language of your Republic, is it not?"

"Yes, but . . ." Car'das hesitated, wondering if there was a delicate way to ask a question like this.

Mitth'raw'nuruodo might have been reading his mind. Or, more likely, his eyes and face. "I don't plan an invasion, if that's what concerns you," he said, smiling faintly. "Chiss don't invade the territories of others. We don't even make war against potential enemies unless we're attacked first."

"Well, you certainly don't have to worry about any attacks from *us*," Car'das said quickly. "We've got enough internal troubles of our own right now."

"Then we have nothing to fear from each other," Mitth'raw'nuruodo said. "It would be merely an indulgence of my curiosity."

"I see," Car'das said cautiously. Qennto, he knew, would be into full-bore bargaining mode at this point, pushing and prodding and squeezing to get everything he could out of the deal. Maybe that was why Mitth'raw'nuruodo was making this pitch to the clearly less experienced Car'das instead.

Still, he could try. "And what would we get out of it?" he asked.

"For you, there would be an equal satisfaction of your own curiosity." Mitth'raw'nuruodo lifted his eyebrows. "You *do* wish to know more about my people, don't you?"

"Very much," Car'das said. "But I can't see that appealing very much to Captain Qennto."

"Perhaps a few extra gemstones added to his collection, then," Mitth'raw'nuruodo suggested. "That might also help mollify your clients."

"Yes, they'll definitely need some mollifying," Car'das agreed grimly. "A little extra loot would go a long ways toward that."

"Then it's agreed," Mitth'raw'nuruodo said, standing up.

"One more thing," Car'das said, scrambling to his feet. "I'll be happy to teach you Basic, but I'd also like some language lessons myself. Would you be willing in turn to teach me the Chiss language, or to have one of your people do so?"

"I can teach you to understand Cheunh," Mitth'raw'nuruodo said, his eyes narrowing thoughtfully. "But I doubt you'll ever be able to properly speak it. I've noticed you don't even pronounce my name very well."

Car'das felt his face warm. "I'm sorry."

"No apology needed," Mitth'raw'nuruodo assured him. "Your vocal mechanism is close to ours, but there are clearly some differences. However, I believe I *could* teach you to speak Minnisiat. It's a trade language widely used in the border regions around our space."

"That would be wonderful," Car'das said, nodding. "Thank you, Commander Mitth—uh . . . Commander."

"Yes," Mitth'raw'nuruodo said dryly. "And as long as we're going to be spending time together, perhaps I can make it easier on you and the others. You may call me by my core name, Thrawn."

**The *Star Wars* adventure doesn't end here!
Read *Star Wars: The New Jedi Order*.**

THE COMPLETE NJO SERIES

VECTOR PRIME by R. A. Salvatore

DARK TIDE I: ONSLAUGHT by Michael Stackpole
DARK TIDE II: RUIN by Michael Stackpole

AGENTS OF CHAOS I: HERO'S TRIAL by James Luceno
AGENTS OF CHAOS II: JEDI ECLIPSE by James Luceno

BALANCE POINT by Kathy Tyers

RECOVERY by Troy Denning (eBook)

EDGE OF VICTORY I: CONQUEST by Greg Keyes
EDGE OF VICTORY II: REBIRTH by Greg Keyes

STAR BY STAR by Troy Denning

DARK JOURNEY by Elaine Cunningham

ENEMY LINES 1: REBEL DREAM by Aaron Allston
ENEMY LINES 2: REBEL STAND by Aaron Allston

TRAITOR by Matthew Stover

DESTINY'S WAY by Walter Jon Williams
YLESIA by Walter Jon Williams (eBook)

FORCE HERETIC I: REMNANT by Sean Williams & Shane Dix
FORCE HERETIC 2: REFUGEE by Sean Williams & Shane Dix
FORCE HERETIC 3: REUNION by Sean Williams & Shane Dix

THE FINAL PROPHECY by Greg Keyes

THE UNIFYING FORCE by James Luceno

WWW.READSTARWARS.COM
Published by Del Rey/LucasBooks • Available wherever books are sold